Dear Liz,
   So glad you enjoyed
'The Wrong Envelope'!!
Hope you enjoy this
   sequel.
with best wishes, Liz x

The Wrong Direction

Liz Treacher

Liz Treacher

Dornoch 2019

First published 2018 by Liz Treacher
Tollich, Skelbo, Dornoch, IV25 3QQ.

ISBN: 978-0-9955877-6-2

Cover design and typesetting by Raspberry Creative Type

Contents

Autumn 1920

Maiden Voyage

The circle was divided into two halves. Pale blue sky at the top; dark blue sea at the bottom. Cassie squinted through her home-made telescope. It wasn't a perfect circle – the telescope was made from a rolled-up magazine, so the right side buckled slightly where the pages were stapled together. But Cassie liked looking at the view through it. Without the telescope, the horizon was overwhelming: mile after mile of sea and sky, stretching both to the left and right, as far as the eye could see.

Cassie swung round and pointed her telescope back towards land. Dover was disappearing fast and the houses that clustered round the harbour were getting smaller and smaller, shrinking first into dolls' houses, then matchboxes and finally dots, as if everything was slipping away and out of sight.

Once the harbour was no longer visible, she turned back to the open Channel. A breeze had picked up, a refreshing breeze that lifted the ends of her brown bob and played with her silk scarf, teasing it away from her neck, unfurling it like a flag. Cassie lowered her telescope and shut her eyes, feeling the warmth of the afternoon sun on her face.

It was hard to believe it was autumn. The weather had been unusually mild. Day after day, warm sunshine had bathed the south of England in a golden haze. An Indian summer, her father had called it. And Cassie felt confident that the weather could only improve as she travelled south. She smiled – everything would improve as she headed south.

The magazine, now lying in her lap, was bent from being rolled up, and the cover was creased, but she could still read the headlines. WHAT TO EAT WHEN COOK'S ON HOLIDAY; HOW TO DRESS FOR A GROUSE SHOOT; LONDON ARTIST TO MARRY DEVONSHIRE SWEETHEART.

There was a boom, like the sound of a cannon. Cassie gave a start and grabbed the guard rail. The magazine slipped off her lap and onto the wooden deck. Another boom followed, this time accompanied by a spray of water. The sun took fright and disappeared behind a cloud. A wall of waves loomed ahead and a strong wind started blowing; not hard enough to worry a sailor, but enough to trouble a tourist. As the ferry listed to the left, Cassie gripped the guard rail tighter.

'Keep your eyes on the horizon!' the strident voice of the guide cried above the waves. 'Remember the Channel is as narrow as it is choppy! We will soon be back on dry land!'

Sure enough, the low outline of France was already visible. How long would it take to get there? Two hours? Three? Cassie pulled her coat around her and rested her forehead on the rail.

'Are you all right, Miss Richardson?' called the guide.

Cassie didn't answer.

'You know you are more exposed sitting on your own, there's safety in numbers, you should stick with the group.'

But Cassie had no intention of sticking with the group. She didn't know any of her travelling companions and she didn't think she wanted to. Five young, unmarried ladies like herself, putting up with a ferry crossing, followed by a train journey through France, all to see the wonders of Italy. Still, it would be away from London – far away. She kept her head down.

The wind lifted the magazine and flung it at the guard rail. The pages fluttered noisily, like birds against the side of a cage. Cassie stamped on them with the heel of her lace-up boots and the pages lay still. She looked down at the cover. DEVONSHIRE SWEETHEART. She gave the magazine a swift kick. It flew under the guard rail and flapped chaotically towards the water – a gull with a broken wing. It floated for a second on the surface, then vanished.

Cassie sighed and sat up again. The waves were getting rougher and the coast of France was now appearing then disappearing in a rather alarming manner. She quickly shut her eyes.

'Are you feeling unwell, Cassandra?' The guide had struggled along the deck to check on her. A stocky lady, dressed head to toe in tweeds, the guide had a large, leathery face, which looked rather yellow.

'I am not feeling sea-sick,' Cassie said, defiantly.

'Then you are the only one.'

'I am *not* feeling sick,' repeated Cassie and she glared at the older lady until she retreated down the deck, staggering back towards the others.

No, she didn't feel sick, or at least no sicker than she had felt in London, just before she left. The city had grown terribly oppressive in recent days and Cassie knew that if she didn't get away for a bit, she would burst. Besides, England was so dull; Italy was bound to be exciting – in Italy, she could blossom. She glanced at the gaggle of girls. There would be no one to cramp her style in Italy.

London Artist to Marry Devonshire Sweetheart

Friday 22 October

This week in our Court and Social column, we bring you sensational news. Bernard Cavalier, the fashionable London artist, and the man we thought would never settle down, is finally engaged! He will tie the knot with Miss Evie Brunton, a hard-working post lady! But how did it happen? Country Lives has investigated and discovered it was the magic of Devon! From what we understand, Bernard went there to prepare for his recent exhibition and became enchanted. With all those leafy lanes and herring-bone skies, what is a man to do but fall in love with the first siren that passes. And if she happens to be a post lady – tant mieux! We are modern now – flexible and fluid! Aristocrats are marrying their maids, heiresses their butlers, and artists are eschewing their models and proposing to post ladies.

Besides, Miss Brunton is quite a catch. She is blonde and blue-eyed, sweet and pretty. And she has had a career! Up until very recently, she toiled as hard as the next chap. Any bachelor reading this column should note that girls in employment are really rather interesting (although it is hard to meet them if they are out working). Granted a working girl does not come with an enormous dowry, but if your best friend is a chocolate baron like Toby Whittington-Smyth, the wedding will take care of itself! We enclose a picture of the happy couple and wish the artist and his future bride every possible happiness.

By Miss Edna Michaels

An Engagement Party

It had taken a few days, but he had finally found the perfect spot. Bernard sat down on the bench under the apple tree and lit his pipe. Smoking, Mrs Brunton had explained, was not allowed in the house. She had looked very embarrassed when she said it, and Bernard assumed that the rule had been thought up, not by her, but by Mr Brunton. Well, he was a guest. He would play along with their rules. Besides, it was a lovely evening.

He sat back and inhaled, drawing the tobacco smoke into his lungs and then expelling it again, puffing it out in rings which floated up and over a flower bed of autumn crocuses back towards North Lodge.

It was a delightful house from the outside. A flint and brick cottage, with small paned windows and a slate roof. Inside it was less delightful. The hall was dark and dingy, the dining room was poky, and there was hardly enough room to swing a cat in the parlour. As for the furniture! Dear, dear. Hideous flowery armchairs which showed up a faded sofa. Funny how he hadn't noticed them when he had perched on the sofa a few weeks earlier and begged Mr Brunton to let him marry his daughter. But now the nasty colours really got to him. It wasn't a question of snobbishness; it was aesthetics. Once an artist, always an artist! Twilight was falling and a cloud of midges danced in the air above his head. Bernard took a few more puffs of his pipe, then he stood up. He'd better get back, after all he was the life and soul of the party! He grinned and walked up the narrow garden path, through the front door, then turned left into the parlour.

Evie pushed past him in the doorway, holding an empty decanter.

'Stop shirking your duty!' she scolded, but she was smiling.

'Where are you going?'

'Refill,' she held up the decanter, 'there's more sherry somewhere.'

'Can I help?'

'You can go and make polite conversation,' she gestured into the room behind her.

'But I want to help you.'

He slipped his arm around her waist and pulled her towards him. Close up, her skin was rosier than usual, her face slightly flushed from the sherry. Lovely.

'Bernard! Someone might see you!'

'I don't care.'

'Well, I do,' and she disappeared into the kitchen.

Bernard sighed and ambled into the parlour.

'So, how are you enjoying Devon, Mr Cavalier?' asked Mr Gosling. A short man, with thick round glasses, Mr Gosling was one of Mr Brunton's few but loyal friends and also doubled up as his dentist.

'Marvellous, marvellous!' Bernard smiled, 'I'm eating like a hog and sleeping like a log!'

'Oh!' said Mrs Brunton, who was passing around sausage rolls. She gave a little giggle.

'And where *are* you sleeping?' asked Mrs Gosling, 'I think this house only has two bedrooms—'

'In the piano room,' said Evie, who had reappeared, 'we have an occasional bed in there. Would you like a top-up of sherry?'

Mrs Gosling glanced at her half-empty glass. 'No thank you, it's a bit sweet for me, dear.'

'Dreadful stuff, hey, Mr Gosling!' and Bernard slapped the dentist on the back.

The dentist cringed.

Mr Brunton, who had just come in from showing Dr Wilson his vegetable patch, arrived in time for Bernard's joke.

'Well, you've drunk quite a lot of the dreadful stuff,' he observed dryly.

Bernard opened his mouth, then shut it again. Instead he beamed at the assembled company.

'Charming, charming,' he said, as if he was judging a flower show.

And they were all charming in a way. Dr Wilson, with his lined but inquiring face; Mr Gosling, small and bespectacled, beside his dark-haired wife. Mrs Brunton, with her soft face and greying bun, from which hair was always escaping. She would have been blonde once, like Evie. He tried to imagine her young, but it was hard; perhaps she had always been plump and homely. Then there was Mr Brunton…no, there was nothing charming about Mr Brunton. He was tall and stooped and dry as a stick. They had got off on the wrong foot and Bernard wasn't sure they would ever find the right one. Besides, he had always found lawyers tricky. But he had to be grateful to Evie's father for his slim figure and regular features, both of which he had passed on to his daughter.

'And will the marriage take place in Colyton?' asked Mrs Gosling.

'London,' said Mr Brunton. 'It appears that Devon is not fashionable enough.'

'Mayfair!' exclaimed Mrs Brunton. If she had noticed her husband's irony, she chose to ignore it.

'Mayfair? But won't that be rather expensive…' began Mrs Gosling.

'I have a friend,' said Bernard. 'Toby,' he added, as if that explained everything.

'Whittington-Smyth,' said Mr Brunton. 'The chocolate that keeps you in business, Mr Gosling, by ruining people's teeth, is also paying for my daughter's nuptials.'

'Oh,' said Mr Gosling. A pause. 'Well, here's to Toby.' He raised his sherry glass but didn't drink from it.

'And to the happy couple!' smiled Dr Wilson.

'Hear, hear!' said Mrs Gosling. 'And will you live in London?'

'We're renting a mews flat in Pimlico,' said Evie.

'Without a garden,' said Mr Brunton.

'It has a patio,' said Evie.

'Exactly,' retorted her father.

'Funny, *mews* always makes me think of cats!' exclaimed Bernard.

'Do you have one?' enquired Mrs Gosling.

'It was a joke!' said Bernard. No one laughed. He glanced over at Evie. Her blue eyes flashed – so many shades within the one blue, and they changed constantly, like the sea.

'Is Pimlico nice?' asked Mr Gosling.

'Oh yes. And it's near the Tate,' Bernard said, keen to sound cultured and make up for his joke. *Should he mention his picture? After all, he had a painting hanging in the Tate. Not only that, it was a portrait of Evie.* 'I have—' he began.

But Dr Wilson was looking at his watch. 'Heavens, is that the time? I hate to break up a party, but I should get going.'

'Really?' cried Mrs Brunton. 'So soon? I've just put the kettle on.'

'It's been nice to meet Mr Cavalier, but now I must leave you all in peace. Thank you, dear Mrs Brunton, for allowing us to celebrate your *good news.*' He gave Mrs Brunton a peck on the cheek and Evie a peck on both cheeks, shook hands with the gentlemen and left.

'And we must be on our way too,' said Mr Gosling.

'I'll see you all out,' smiled Mr Brunton. He looked rather relieved the party was over.

'Well, I think that went quite well,' said Mrs Brunton doubtfully, as she collected up the plates and glasses, 'I find parties rather tricky.'

11

'Especially without drinks,' laughed Bernard, 'well, real drinks, anyway.'

'Bernard!' hissed Evie, and then to her mother, 'It was very kind of you to throw a little do for us.'

'We wanted to show you off to our friends,' said Mrs Brunton and she blushed.

'Mrs Brunton!' exclaimed Bernard. He grabbed her hand and kissed it gallantly.

'Shall we help wash up?' asked Evie.

'I'm rather tired tonight, let's leave it for the morning. I think I'll retire.' Mrs Brunton gave a little bow and toddled upstairs.

'An early night is good for the brain,' said Mr Brunton, who had returned from the garden. He looked pointedly at Bernard.

'Then I need lots more of them,' Bernard chortled.

Ignoring the joke, Mr Brunton went upstairs, leaving Evie and Bernard alone.

'At last!' he cried, dragging her into the parlour and pushing the door to, 'I thought those old codgers would never leave!'

'They're not that old. Still, you behaved quite well, considering...'

'What do you mean, *considering*?'

'Considering you always play the fool.'

'The fool?'

'You know, saying things just to tease.'

'Oh.' He looked quite wounded. 'So you don't love me?'

She laughed, 'Of course I do!'

'Then show it!' He pulled her close, running his hands through her hair, searching for her mouth through closed eyelids.

'My father will be listening.'

'Who cares.'

They stood in the parlour, locked in a tight embrace.

'I can't wait,' he whispered.

'It's only a week now,' she whispered back.

'But that's forever!' he moaned.

'Evie, are you coming up?' called Mr Brunton from the upstairs landing.

'On my way!' She broke away from her fiancé and opened the parlour door. 'Goodnight, Bernard,' she said, more loudly than necessary.

'I can't wait,' he whispered again.

'See you in the morning, Bernard.'

He lurched away from her, stomped into the hall, then the piano room and shut the door.

Alone in the parlour, Evie looked around at the brightly coloured armchairs, sagging sofa and standard lamp. How cramped it had felt tonight, full of her parents' friends, yet it was still her home and she loved it. She had lived here all her life. Twenty-two years in the quiet town of Colyton and now London beckoned. But would she like her new life or would she miss Devon?

She wandered over to the fireplace and fingered the different ornaments spread out over the wooden mantlepiece. A silver vase, a green enamel pot, a photograph of Aunt Maud. She had always lived with these things, played with them as a child. And soon she would have her own possessions. It seemed very grown-up, acquiring things. She tried to imagine herself at an auction, bidding for furniture, raising a gloved hand to secure an antique. Or choosing a tea set in Heals. What did they say on wedding days: something old, something new…The word *wedding* filled her with terror. It was the thought of a London church – probably big, and all those friends of Bernard's – probably bohemians. She glanced in the mirror above the mantlepiece. At least her hair was growing, curling down just below her shoulders, recovering from a drastic cut in the summer. It would look all right, on the day. Besides the wedding would whizz past in a flash, and then it would just be her and Bernard. Upstairs, her father was starting to snore. Evie turned off the light and walked down the hall towards the staircase.

As she passed the piano room, the door suddenly and silently opened. A large arm shot out and a huge hand grabbed hers. She jumped with surprise. The arm pulled urgently. Evie tried to loosen the grip of the enormous hand but it clung to her like a limpet to a rock. She glanced upstairs. All was quiet, apart from her father's snores. She allowed the hand to reel her into the piano room. The door shut quietly behind her, like a flower closing for the night.

Second Thoughts

On second thoughts, it might have been nicer in Colyton. Mrs Brunton shifted uneasily in her seat. Her fuchsia dress was slipping slightly on the shiny wooden pew and she had to keep digging her shoulders into the back rest to stop herself sliding right off. St Andrew's was a cosier church, with a friendlier feel, and the honey-coloured stone would have glowed in what was turning out to be yet another sunny day. But perhaps it was raining in Devon? Rain would never do. Not for a wedding.

And another advantage with Devon was that there would have been more people there, from their side at any rate. In Devon, she could have asked her friends and neighbours, and there would have been a crowd of people in the churchyard afterwards, clapping and cheering, throwing confetti. Instead, the bride's side of the church was almost empty. Some cousins of Mr Brunton's from Blackburn, Aunt Maud from Torquay, Evie's old boss, Mr Thornber, from the sorting office. And that was it. They were a quiet group, bunched up together near the front, taking up no more than two and a half pews, studying their hymn sheets.

On the other side of the aisle, things were noisier. Bernard seemed to have a thousand friends, all dressed in rather 'interesting' clothes for a wedding. There were pre-Raphaelite sirens, wafting through the church in floaty ensembles; dishevelled-looking older men with beards and enormous bow

15

ties; younger, more tortured souls in corduroy suits; all talking and laughing raucously, as if they had just arrived at the theatre. The pews on the groom's side were filling up fast and the church was looking more and more lopsided. If it was a ship, Mrs Brunton decided, it would have capsized by now. She looked around, furtively caught the eye of an usher and, very discreetly, beckoned him over.

'Do feel free…' she began, gesturing vaguely to the motley mob across the aisle.

The usher pushed a floppy fringe out of his eyes and gave her a flash of perfect, white teeth. 'Thank you!' he beamed. 'You must be Mrs Brunton? I'm Toby, Toby Whittington-Smyth.'

'How do you do, Toby. I'm sorry, I thought you were an usher.'

'Best man!' Toby grinned.

'We have so much to thank you for—' Mrs Brunton began.

'Not at all,' said Toby, waving away all possible gratitude. 'Could you really bear to sit with this rabble?' He glanced at the group opposite.

'Of course. Besides, they seem to be running out of room.' Mrs Brunton felt suddenly desperate that some of these sophisticated London types should join their prim pews, liven them up somehow.

'How considerate!' he beamed again.

Toby crossed over from the quiet side of the church to the noisier and ushered the unacceptably attired towards the respectably dressed. Soon she could hear scuffling in the rows behind and a murmur of voices: an animated hum, punctuated by the odd raucous roar, quickly stifled, as if they understood that this was the sedate side of the church.

Mrs Brunton could feel herself warming to Bernard's friends. She could imagine Evie getting on with them, and that was just as well; she knew almost no one in the capital. What a pity about Cassie. What on earth could have happened between her and Evie? They had been such good friends as children, and now Evie was moving to London, they would be living close to each other again. Yet Evie had been adamant that she didn't want Cassie at the wedding.

'But why, darling? After all these years…'

They had been in the tea room at Liberty's, a brief reprieve between dress fittings, and Evie had looked out of the window, studying the traffic through the leaded panes of glass.

'Did you have a fall-out?'

'Not a fall-out, exactly. A realisation.'

'Of what?'

Evie took a swallow of tea, 'I think she might be jealous.'

'Jealous?'

'Just a bit jealous. It's so difficult for girls nowadays. I mean, after the war and everything. Few men and fewer jobs…'

'I don't think Cassie needs to work, dear.'

'I know, it's just I think women are feeling…I don't know what I mean. Let's just say that I don't think Cassie is pleased for me. You know, Bernard and all that.'

Mrs Brunton did know. It was what she had always wanted for Evie: a nice husband and the chance of children. And it had seemed so unlikely. First the war, with almost every young man in Colyton flying away to the Front. Then Armistice and the slow trek home – the young men older and sadder; many wounded, many dead; some still missing, even now. All that time, Mrs Brunton had dreamt of *Bernard and all that*. So, if the dream coming true meant that Cassie was not invited to the wedding, well, it was a small price to pay.

There was a cheer from the back of the church. Mrs Brunton turned round to see Bernard coming in. Silver morning suit, paisley handkerchief and tie and, in his lapel, an enormous lily bobbing around in a very artistic manner. She was always surprised to see him: he was rather startling to look at. Bernard was a big man, tall and broad with bright red hair. He had a large face and everything in it was large – even his piercing blue eyes and tombstone teeth. On top of this, he exuded a confidence and charisma that made him take up more space than other people. He could fill a room, she'd noticed; he certainly filled her parlour. Even in a spacious London church, he could hold his own, competing with the stained glass and gargoyles for people's attention. Now he trotted down the aisle, slightly out of balance, like a creature on two legs instead of four, stopping at the end of every pew to shake hands with the men and kiss the ladies. He certainly knew a lot of ladies.

Luckily for Mrs Brunton, by the time he got close to the front Bernard had lost interest in shaking hands and kissing and had taken to waving at his audience, like a conductor at an orchestra. Then he and Toby put their arms around each other and clapped each other so vigorously on the back that those in the stalls broke out in a spontaneous round of applause. It felt quite wrong in church and Mrs Brunton was very relieved that Mr Brunton wasn't there to see it.

A vicar appeared – a sobering apparition in a long black robe, and the clapping stopped. Then an organ wheezed into life and the church was filled with the buzzing sound of *Jesu, Joy of Man's Desiring*. Bernard and Toby talked to the vicar with their backs to the congregation; Bernard occasionally glancing behind him, down the aisle towards the door.

Mrs Brunton stared resolutely ahead. Even when the organ started playing *Here Comes the Bride*, she managed to keep her eyes facing the front. But then the church door swung open, filling the aisle with light, and everyone turned. And there she was, leaning on her father's right arm: Evie. Mrs Brunton stifled a sob. She looked so lovely. And the dress worked. Mrs Brunton had been worried about the plainness of the long white skirt and the simple bodice, which relied on the shine of raw silk, rather than bows and frills. Sometimes at their Liberty dress-fittings, Evie had looked a bit like a ghost in it – not that Mrs Brunton had said anything. But today, she looked like an angel. And the white roses crowning her head seemed to light up her fair hair.

There was a ripple of approbation from the crowd as father and daughter started to walk down the aisle. And it became quickly obvious that there was a difference in pace between the two. Evie kept her head down in a charming manner, but her satin-shoed feet stepped forward briskly, as if she was starting a post round; and Mr Brunton trailed ever so slightly, as if he was trying to delay the moment when they would reach the altar. And so the two of them made their way towards Bernard, the father dragging his feet; the daughter racing towards her future. And Bernard stood watching, head nodding, lily bobbing, beaming with joy.

Over the Threshold

'Crikey! I didn't realise you were so heavy!'

Bernard had managed to carry his wife through the elegant front door of their mews flat and half-way up the stairs to the inner door, now he was struggling. He grabbed hold of the bannister to steady himself; Evie clung tighter to his neck.

'Don't drop me!' she laughed.

'I won't,' he wheezed.

'A mews flat was your idea!'

'Well, there are too many stairs,' he panted. 'I won't be doing this again. Right, here we go. Hold on!'

He set off again, staggering up the remaining steps and reached the inner door.

'Where's the key?' he gasped.

'I don't know. In your pocket?'

'For goodness' sake!' He held onto her with his right hand and rummaged in his pockets with his left. 'Got it!' He fumbled with the lock, opened the door and almost fell into the flat; she tumbled out of his arms and onto the carpet.

'Made it! Are you all right, Evie?'

'Fine, luckily!' She jumped up and looked around. 'Gosh, it's bigger than I remembered. And, it's lovely!'

She ran like a child from room to room, inspecting the drawing room, two bedrooms and a bathroom. Bernard stood grinning in the hall, leaning on the wall to get his breath back. She came dashing past him and into the kitchen.

'Oh no!'

He followed her through.

'What's all this?' She pointed to five or six packing cases on the kitchen floor beside a shiny black range.

'Our wedding presents, remember.'

'But is it all cooking stuff?'

'Not all of it. But there's a coffee set from Carruthers, a silver service from Toby, saucepans from his mother...'

Evie looked suddenly disheartened.

'What's wrong, don't you like cooking?'

'I don't know yet. I've never really done any.'

'Oh.' A pause. 'Anyway, you can unpack tomorrow.'

'Can't you help?'

'Well, I should get back to the studio. And Carruthers wants to see me at the gallery. There are loads of commissions waiting, lots of portraits to paint.'

'But we haven't even had a honeymoon. Can't you take a few days off?'

'We had two nights at the Ritz—'

'Paid for by Toby! When are you going to put your hand in your pocket?' She was laughing but he looked stricken.

'The thing is, Evie, before I met you I was rather hard-up.' He coughed nervously, 'My last exhibition went surprisingly well, and now I need to capitalise on the interest in my work – interest created by your portrait.' He reached out to touch her hair. 'I have to keep going so we can enjoy London and—' he gestured round the flat, 'so we can live here.' He paused. 'Nothing's cheap in the capital,' he added, lamely.

'I know. And at least we're together now.' She glanced down at the packing cases, 'I'm sure I can learn to cook.'

'Darling!' He opened his arms to her, 'I like most things, although I'm not wild about cabbage.'

'You're not wild about cabbage!' she laughed. 'Now it's all coming out. What else haven't you told me?'

He threw his head back and roared.

'Come on, confess!'

'Well,' he pulled her close, stroking her hair, 'Sometimes, I cut my toenails in the bath…'

'You what?'

'It's ok, I find most of them again…'

'But that's disgusting. What else?'

'Otherwise, I'm perfect!'

'Apart from the time you took a train to Devon,' she teased.

'What train?'

'You know very well, Mr Cavalier.'

'You mean the one with the mole on it?'

'Exactly.'

'But it was irresistible…'

'No excuse.'

'Besides, I was punished.'

'Quite rightly.'

'Put off at Crewkerne.'

'It was unforgivable behaviour. You deserved worse.'

'But I'd fallen in love.'

'What, with the mole?'

'With you!'

He let go of her and sped out of the kitchen, down the corridor and into the drawing room. He ran to one of the wide Georgian windows and yanked it open. Then he stuck his head out.

'I'm in love!' he cried, to the street below.

'Bernard, what are you doing!' she raced into the drawing room and tried to drag him away from the window.

'I'm in love!' he shouted again, the sound of his voice, booming down the street.

'It's all right for some!' laughed an old man, strolling past with his dog. He smiled up at them. 'Where d'yer find such a beautiful girl?'

'On a train.'

'Bernard!'

Evie peered out. Apart from the old man, the pavement was empty.

It was a typical London street: terraces of houses, a mix of Georgian and Edwardian, some scruffier than others. A line of front doors, stretching into the distance, painted every possible colour and all with brass letterboxes. She wondered what it would be like to deliver the post here. A long walk for someone.

'We're just married!' Bernard called down, triumphantly.

'Congratulations!' smiled the man. 'Well then, I mustn't keep you,' and he raised his hat.

Housekeeping

She was flying. At least that's what it felt like. Her bicycle was going so fast it hardly touched the ground. Evie sped down Colyton hill, her hair streaming out behind her. Fields raced past: some ploughed into a sea of furrows, others stubbly like an unshaven face. She flew over bridges, hearing a split second of babbling water and then just the tick-tick of her bicycle wheels and the whoosh of wind in her ears again.

She turned a corner too quickly and a gust caught her bicycle. She swerved slightly and a letter escaped from the top of her postbag. It flew high above the fields – a single piece of confetti, twirling in the air. Then, as if a door had opened, the other letters followed suit, shooting out of the bag like pigeons from a dovecot. They flapped off into the wind, intent on finding their own way home. She squealed to a halt and, throwing her bicycle on the ground, chased after them into the fields, stretching her arms out. The letters danced high above her, and she spun round and round in the stubble, laughing and laughing.

'Wake up, Evie!'

She opened her eyes. Bernard's face was close up, his smile out of focus.

'Where am I?' She knew of course; she was playing for time, giving herself a moment to switch roles, switch lives.

'You're in heaven!' he laughed. 'In your new bed, in your new home, with your new husband. And you look so beautiful today!'

24

She lay and let him admire her. He would be gone soon, back to the studio, but for now he was hers.

'Here's your tea.'

He held out a cup and she propped herself up in bed to take it, enjoying the hot steam hitting her face.

'What are your plans for today?'

His question caught her off guard and she hesitated. 'I don't know, I suppose I should unpack.'

'Marvellous idea! What a wife! I say, any chance of breakfast?'

'Of course.' Evie smiled and got out of bed. Breakfast would be easy. Toast and marmalade. Then, she would deal with the packing cases.

A few hours later, and Evie was not much further forward. She had opened the box from Toby's mother and found about a dozen saucepans. What were they all for? She was aware that different pans did different things. She just wasn't sure what those different things were, or how they did them. But of course, the pans didn't do anything on their own; they needed a cook. She would begin at the beginning. Eggs: boiled, fried, poached and scrambled. How hard could it be?

Evie found the book that Aunt Maud had given her, *Mrs Beeton's Book of Household Management by Mrs Isabella Mary Beeton*. She smiled at the title, enjoying the confidence of an authoress who included her middle name on the cover of a book. Then she opened it and read the first line of Chapter One. *As with the commander of an army or the leader of any enterprise, so is it with the mistress of a house.* A promising start. Well, she no longer had a job, so perhaps being a housewife could replace the satisfaction work had given her. Evie read on.

Mrs Beeton was full of suggestions: early rising was an advantage; cleanliness was essential; frugality and economy were advised. That was lucky, they had very little money. The choice of acquaintances, Mrs Beeton suggested, was important, and hospitality was an excellent virtue. Well, then they would have someone for dinner – two someones, Toby, and his girlfriend. What was she called? Daisy. They would have Toby and Daisy. Perhaps on Friday? But only if she had unpacked. And only when she had found something to cook. Evie moved onto the chapters on food: *General Observations on Quadrupeds*. Heavens, what were they? She turned the pages. *Boiled Artichokes...Very Good Puff-Paste...* Where was the recipe for shepherd's pie? And why on earth had she never watched her mother making it?

Evie spent the rest of the day perusing Mrs Beeton, but by four o'clock, she was bored. Too late to start on the packing cases now; Bernard would be home any minute. Besides, if she hadn't unpacked the kitchen stuff, they would have to go out for supper. One supper wouldn't hurt. She could cook tomorrow. Evie wandered into the drawing room and looked out of the window. Which way would he come? She gazed down the street in both directions, imagining him in her mind's eye, charging along the pavement, rushing home to her. She felt a butterfly, just a small one, dancing in her stomach.

She hopped over to the mirror, smoothed down her hair and gave her cheeks a pinch. Then she went back to the window. The street was empty. She swung round; the clock on the mantlepiece said ten past four. What had he told her? *I'll be home about four.* And what did *about* mean? She craned her neck. No one coming round the corner, either from the right or left. This wouldn't do – what if he caught her looking? She went back into the kitchen, spotted the packing cases, turned on her heels and walked back to the drawing room again. She sat down on the sofa, put her head back and gazed up at the ceiling. Another butterfly had joined the first, a bigger one and it seemed to be bumping into her ribcage. Or perhaps it was a moth, one that buzzed and hummed and crashed into things. Evie jumped up again and returned to the window.

And there he was, strolling along the street, arms swinging by his sides, head down as if he was counting the cracks in the pavement. He walked with a lumber and yet there was a skip in his step that turned the lumber into a lollop. He crossed the road and she got a view of the top of his head. She'd never seen him from above before and she noticed the way his copper hair sprung out of his crown, straight upwards, shooting towards the sky. He was on her side of the pavement now and he glanced up at the flat, first at the other window, then hers.

'Evie!' she couldn't hear him through the glass, but she saw his lips moving. He grinned up at her and raised his right arm in an enormous wave and then suddenly he was running. She heard the thudding of large feet on the stone steps leading up to the flat and she raced to open the door.

Bernard tumbled in, almost on top of her. He smelled of turps and oil paints.

'Evie!' He kissed her until she could hardly breathe, 'It's just so wonderful!'

'What is?'

'Having you here. Knowing that you're in London, that you're not in Devon.'

He kissed her again.

'I'm afraid I haven't got far with the unpacking.'

'That's all right. We'll go out for supper. There's a pub on the corner and they do lovely pies.'

'Not a restaurant then?'

'We're poor, Evie, poor but happy!'

'I could get a job...'

'But you have a job! Two, actually. Wife and housewife.' He glanced into the kitchen, where the unopened packing cases lurked, 'Do you want a hand with those?'

'No, I mean yes, but not now. I'll get it done, eventually. Then I thought we could ask Toby and Daisy for supper.'

'What, you'll cook for them! For my friends! Evie, you're a marvel!' Bernard beamed at her, 'I say, your eyes look more turquoise today.'

'Really?'

'Yes, today they are the Aegean. Yesterday they were the Mediterranean.'

Evie laughed, 'How do you know?'

'Well, the Aegean is greener.'

'Have you been there?'

'No. But I've seen it in paintings.'

'Let's travel, Bernard. Let's see the real thing.'

She looked at him, at his wide face, slightly pock-marked in places, at his large nose and his thin lips, usually dry. His eyes were always the same colour: a cornflower blue. But she wouldn't tell him that. Well, not yet. She hardly knew him.

'Don't you want to travel?' she asked instead.

'Yes, yes of course. But not now. For now, I want to stay in London and paint. Make a name for myself. I want to make you proud, Evie. Very proud. But right at this moment, I want a cup of tea and then a bath, preferably with you.'

'I've never had a bath with anyone before!'

'Haven't you?'

'Of course not! Why, have you?'

'Um, well no, I don't suppose I have. I mean I haven't been married before!' he laughed uneasily. 'But tea first, I'm dying of thirst...' And Bernard took his wife's arm and ushered her into the kitchen.

They took their tea cups into the bathroom. Bernard balanced them precariously on the rim of the tub while he turned on the taps. Soon the room was full of steam. He threw off his clothes and, leaving them where they landed on the floor, jumped into the bath. She was more cautious, removing her garments one by one and placing them carefully over a chair.

'Don't be shy!' he called.

But she was. This was new territory, undressing in front of a man in broad daylight and then getting into a bath with him. Did her parents do this? It was hard to imagine. Perhaps it was just artists and bohemians. Well, she had married someone who was both of those – she would just have to get on with it. She gingerly lowered herself into the water. There wasn't much room, what with Bernard's long legs, but she found a space for her back between the taps, one hot, the other cold, burning and freezing her in turn, and slipped her legs under his.

'Lovely!' he smiled. 'Now where's the soap?'

He grappled around in the bathtub and finally located it. It jumped about like a fish, but he caught it eventually.

'I want to wash you.'

'I can wash myself.'

'Come here.'

He pulled her towards him, scooped her hair away from her neck with his huge hands, and started soaping her all over, from her face right down to her feet. He was gentle, very gentle; he washed her like a mother might wash a child, and with great concentration as if he was studying her as he washed. He was so tender that Evie felt her eyes fill with tears. She picked up her tea and took a big gulp.

When he had finished washing her, Bernard leaned out of the bath and caught hold of her stockings, hanging on the back of the chair.

'What are you doing?'

He held them up to his face, eyes twinkling, and wrinkled his nose.

'I'll do them, Bernard,' she stretched her hand out.

'No.' He held them out of her reach and searched for the soap again. Then he lathered the silky material, humming quietly to himself, carefully rubbing the stockings together so as not to snag them.

'I can't believe you're washing my stockings,' she could hear her voice beginning to break.

'But I love them.'

He plunged the stockings under the water, wriggled them about, lifted them back out and gave them a gentle squeeze, then he wrapped them both around his neck like a scarf.

'There, how do I look?'

She threw her head back and laughed.

'Daft! Really daft!'

'How rude!' He gave her a splash, just a small one.

'That's not fair!' She splashed him back.

'Oi!' He splashed harder and a tidal wave of water leapt out onto the floor.

She retaliated and so did he. Soon everything was soaking – her clothes, lying on the chair; his lying on the floor.

'So sorry,' he said.

'No you're not!'

He grinned at her, revealing his large creamy teeth, 'Well, not very!'

She pulled out the bath plug, then they climbed out and he wrapped her in an enormous towel.

She held onto him and they stood for ages on the sopping floor, hugging each other, listening to the gurgling of bathwater and the dripping taps.

Shepherd's Pie

It took Evie two days to unpack, and two phone calls home to get the shepherd's pie ingredients right. During the first call, Evie had written ¼ lb of mince, instead of 1¼ lb and so she had come back from the butchers with a minute amount of meat which wouldn't have fed a cat. It wasn't the butcher's fault. He had said, 'Are you sure, Ma'am?' a few times, before handing over the tiny packet. And she had said, 'Yes,' and slipped the parcel in her basket and left the shop as quickly as she could. It was all so embarrassing – no one had ever called her *Ma'am* before. In Colyton, everyone called her *Evie*. She had telephoned her mother again and her mother had reread her the recipe and Evie had sought out a different butcher, which meant another trek in the rain and the traffic was dreadful.

On top of this, the mince didn't really behave properly when she braised it. It seemed to take an age to brown, so she went off to dust the drawing room. Then, as soon as her back was turned, it burnt slightly and halved in size. You needed more than one cook, she could see that now. If only Bernard was there to help. But he was busy in the studio, promising to return at six o'clock, just before Toby and Daisy were due.

Evie decided to prepare extra mash, to disguise the fact most of the mince was missing. The whole thing was exhausting and she had only just got the shepherd's pie in the oven when the doorbell rang.

'Good evening!' Daisy came in looking gorgeous, with Toby on her arm. 'Evie, how lovely to meet you properly. The wedding was so busy and you were in great demand…' She held out a manicured hand and Evie offered her own, hoping it was free of potato.

Daisy looked divine, in a gold crossover tunic, with a plunging neckline. Evie was wearing her best dress, a light blue cotton shift, with tiny mauve dots. Next to Daisy, with her green eyes and dark bob, she felt as if she was fading away. Toby looked dapper as always, in a suit and tie – and all for shepherd's pie. Evie gulped nervously.

There was the sound of the front door banging and someone running upstairs – Bernard.

'Sorry, I'm late,' he gasped. He smiled apologetically at his wife and turned to his guests, 'Welcome to our humble home!'

'Not so humble!' cried Toby. 'I mean, what a place!'

'You'll love it,' Bernard beamed, as he ushered them into the drawing room.

'Delightful,' Daisy said, catching Evie's eye. They smiled at each other.

'Thank you. And now I must check on supper.'

'My wife is an amazing cook!' Bernard boasted.

As Evie made her way along to the kitchen, Toby stuck his head out of the drawing room.

'I say, Evie, just to let you know, I can't take crustaceans.'

'Sorry?'

'I mean, I'm allergic to any sort of crevette, crab or lobster…'

'We're having shepherd's pie.'

'Perfect,' smiled Toby. 'My favourite,' he added.

Evie doubted it somehow and her doubts grew when she took the pie out of the oven. The mince had mostly evaporated, leaving a mound of mash with a few traces of gravy showing through, like muddy cart tracks through snow.

She hurriedly put it back in the oven and went to set the table. Perhaps if she used the very best of their wedding presents, it would make up for the food.

Ten minutes later, the table was groaning with Wedgewood plates and crystal glasses and Evie could put off the moment no longer.

She poked her head into the drawing room where Bernard was pouring wine.

'Ready,' she said weakly.

The extra ten minutes had not helped the shepherd's pie. She decided to serve it in the kitchen, dishing out four helpings of what looked like the least appetising meal she had ever seen.

If the guests felt the same, they kept their counsel. In fact, they said nothing at all. Even Bernard seemed lost for words.

'Do start,' smiled Evie bravely.

'*Bon appétit*,' Bernard said, finally finding his tongue, but it sounded like *good luck*.

They tackled the shepherd's pie bravely: four archaeologists on a dig, looking for crumbs of mince beneath a rubble of potato.

After a couple of minutes, Evie put her knife and fork down. The others immediately followed suit.

'I'm afraid it's inedible,' she said. She didn't know whether to laugh or cry.

There was an awkward silence.

'I'm so sorry.'

'Nonsense!' cried Daisy. 'I can't cook for toffee.'

'But what will we eat?' asked Bernard.

'Let's go to the Embassy,' suggested Daisy.

'Yes please!' Bernard looked delighted.

'My treat,' offered Toby.

'But,' Daisy glanced at Evie's dress, 'the Embassy's ridiculously formal. I'm afraid you'll have to change.'

Change into what? She didn't have anything else. Evie nodded, got up from the table and disappeared into the bedroom. What a disaster. Monstrous mince and now nothing to wear. She paced up and down, quite distracted, then she noticed her pearls hanging on the dressing-table mirror. At least they would cheer up her dress. She snatched them up and fastened them round her neck.

When she went back through to the dining room, looking exactly the same except for the necklace, a look of mortification flashed across Daisy's face.

'There, you look lovely!' she exclaimed. 'And what gorgeous pearls!' She jumped up from the table and gave Evie a tight squeeze. Evie knew it was a hug of apology. 'What a looker you are,' Daisy started to gabble, taking her by the arm and leading her out of the dining room. 'I mean, Toby told me you were. *She's a beauty,* he said, but I didn't believe it till I saw you at your wedding—'she broke off, mid-sentence and glanced round at the men, knocking back their drinks before getting up from the table, '—I say, are you chaps coming or not?'

'On our way.'

'Well, you'd better hurry, because if we get to the Embassy before you, Evie will be swamped by admirers.'

It was such a ridiculous image, Evie started to giggle.

'What fun you are!' cried Daisy. 'I think we will be friends, you and me,' and she gave Evie's arm another squeeze.

Babes in the Wood

The next day, despite a late night and several glasses of champagne, Bernard woke his wife early.

'Time to get up, Evie! It's a beautiful day. We're going on a crawl.'

'A what? Oh no, not a pub crawl!'

'No, a park crawl.'

'Don't you have to work?'

'It's Saturday, silly. We're going to explore lots of parks. Hyde Park, Green Park, St James's Park.'

'Why?'

'Because the trees will look spectacular. London trees are magnificent in the autumn and right now they'll all be turning gold.'

He pulled back the bed covers and threw open the curtains. Sure enough, the sky was a deep blue and the sun was shining.

'But first we're going out for breakfast.'

'Ooh, lovely.' Evie jumped out of bed. She waited for her head to pound as she hit the floor, but it didn't. That was the joy of expensive wine. She winced, imagining the bill at the Embassy. Good old Toby.

Soon they were outside, walking in the fresh air. The pavements were covered with leaves of all shapes and sizes, a jigsaw that was almost finished, just a few grey gaps of concrete in the tangle of colours.

'There's a nice café near the Tate.' He glanced at her, 'You've got to see it sometime.'

Evie winced again.

The café was right opposite the gallery. They had tomatoes on toast and numerous cups of tea. As soon as the clock struck ten, Bernard jumped up to pay the bill, then he took her hand and led her firmly across the road.

'If we go in now, it'll be quiet.'

Sure enough there was almost no one there. They wandered through the galleries, past the Richard Dadds and the William Blakes, and suddenly there it was: *The Wrong Envelope* by Bernard Cavalier, 1920. And there she was, sitting on a faded sofa, reading a letter. Her golden hair was cropped quite short, revealing a large mole, nestling at the nape of her neck, enjoying the limelight.

Evie looked at the painting with her hands half over her eyes. 'I can't bear it!' she groaned. 'Still, at least you can't see my face.' She had another quick peep, 'And you can't read the letter.'

Bernard blanched. 'No, I want to forget that letter.'

'I remember every word.'

'You don't!'

'Oh, but I do.'

She leaned against the wall beside the portrait and faced Bernard – a strange effect: the same girl but two heads; one looking away, one looking towards the room; one made of flesh and bones, the other of canvas and oil paints.

'Dearest, you really are the sweetest creature and I admire you enormously—'

'Stop!' moaned Bernard. He put his hands over his ears. 'It was meant for Phoebe, not you.'

But Evie didn't stop. 'The thing is, I have recently met someone else and we have become very friendly and I am beginning to realise I am in love with her.' She was smiling, but there was a flash of anger in her eyes.

'Evie, stop!' Bernard tried to put his hand over her mouth.

'Get off me!' She shoved him away and *The Wrong Envelope* swung slightly to the left.

An attendant came running over. 'I must point out that this a valuable painting. If you are going to have a row, please do it elsewhere.'

'But I'm the...' Bernard started, then changed tack, 'the one to blame,' he finished. 'I'm sorry, we were just leaving.' He pulled Evie away from the wall, tucked his hand forcefully under her arm and marched her out of the gallery.

Outside in the long corridor they broke into a run, charging past a room full of Turners, and another full of Rembrandts, rushing out into the fresh air, two children escaping from trouble. They burst outside, breathless and laughing. He grabbed her arms and pinned her against a lamp post.

'Please forgive me!'

She squirmed away from him, 'Only if you don't take me to see that dreadful picture ever again.'

'It pays our rent.'

'I don't care what it pays. I never want to see it again.'

He let go of her arms. 'All right, I promise. Am I forgiven now?'

She took his hand, considered it for a moment, then she slipped her own inside. They walked away from the Tate, heading for Green Park, leaning into each other, talking, laughing, kicking up the yellow leaves so they flew high into the air.

Green Park was stunning. Every tree illuminated by the morning sun, each one a different light with a different lampshade. A forest of Tiffany lamps. They wandered down a path between the trees and found a quiet bench. He sat down, pulled a rough bit of paper and some coloured crayons out of his coat pocket and started sketching. She lay with her legs stretched out along the bench and her head in his lap so she could look up into the branches. She kept closing her eyes, then opening them again, and each time there was a different kaleidoscope of colours above her.

They were so still that a magpie landed on the ground beside them. Bernard gently lifted her head, jumped up and shooed the bird away.

'One for sorrow,' he said.

'You don't believe that superstitious clap-trap!' she scoffed.

'No.' He looked caught out. 'I just don't like them. And now we've scared off the big boy, we've got smaller friends.' He pointed to two long-tailed tits and a great tit, which had landed beside them.

'Tit – such a silly name for such pretty birds,' Evie said. She stood up, 'I'm going for a walk.'

'I'll wait for you here.' He returned to his drawing.

Evie wandered down the different avenues that slanted across the park, each one lined with different trees. Branches from both sides leaned across the path, almost touching each other, creating an arch of leaves above her head. *Oranges and lemons,* she thought, remembering the children's game. She turned onto a different path and was almost blinded by the sun. It shone through the trees, splintering into rays and landing on the path as shards of light.

She reached Hyde Park Corner and crossed the busy intersection of roads into Hyde Park. Suddenly there was space, so much space it swallowed her up. It was like being on the beach in Devon; she was just a dot in an empty landscape. She felt dizzy with the freedom it gave her: no traffic, no houses, just grass and sky. She stretched her arms wide and twirled round and round like a sycamore seed, flying across the park, feeling the wind whoosh past her, wanting to take off.

Bernard scrabbled around in his pocket for a brown coloured crayon and started shading in his sketch. Evie had been gone a few minutes, but he could still feel the warmth from where her head had rested in his lap. And if he shut his eyes, he could still see her: straight nose, tiny mouth, strands of blonde hair falling over her left cheek, large eyes that were a cobalt blue today, like the sky. None of her features were perfect, but they worked perfectly in unison. There was a force behind her face that seemed to glue everything together, and with a fluidity that meant that everything in her face moved as one, responding to whatever was happening around her. Emotion. That was it. She was full of emotion; but not emotional – she was too strong for that. So many girls would have hung around, simpering and clawing as he sketched, but not Evie. He loved the way she had quickly got bored and wandered off. She shared his restlessness: a need to do something new, a desire to move on to the next thing. It was charming. And it made it easier for him, knowing she was independent, that she could look after herself.

He chose a red and an orange pencil and returned to his drawing, but after a few moments, he lifted his eyes and peered down the path she had taken. No sign of her yet. Well, she would be back soon. He folded the sketch and thrust it in his coat pocket, then he lay back on the bench, wanting to see for himself what she'd been looking up at. The branches bounced up and down, in and out of focus, as if they were trying to escape the grip of the wind and shake themselves free. It was rather unnerving and Bernard sat up again and looked around. What had she said? *I'm going for a walk.* But that was twenty minutes ago. And the park wasn't that big. He stood up and walked a few paces from the bench to where several paths intersected. Still no sign. He examined each path again and again, turning to check each one in turn, faster and faster, until he was whirling around like a windmill. Where on earth was she?

When Evie got back to Green Park, she met Bernard, marching down an avenue looking anxious, his coat open and streaming out behind him.

'I was worried, Evie, I thought I'd lost you.'

'How silly you are.'

'I felt so alone all of a sudden, as if you'd left me.'

'Left you! We've only been married a few days!'

'Where've you been?'

'I went into Hyde Park. It's wonderful, all that space.'

He grabbed her, hugging her to him, as if they'd been separated for years. 'I love you so much, Evie. Please don't leave me.' His voice came out shaky.

'I'm not going anywhere. And now I've seen Hyde Park, there's just one more to go!'

She took his hand and they crossed Pall Mall into St James's Park. It was busy with couples strolling arm in arm and mothers with perambulators. A little boy ran past with a hoop, then a young man, his pockets full of birdseed, pigeons hopping hopefully after him. They rounded a corner to find a pavement artist hard at work. He was kneeling on a mat, drawing flowers in coloured chalk, a duster on the ground beside him.

And then she remembered, 'Can you show me your sketch?'

Bernard pulled the paper out of his pocket. A network of branches criss-crossed the drawing; some covered with burning leaves, others already bare. And beneath the branches was a girl, staring skywards, lost in her own world.

The Fish

The weekend flew by. After the shepherd's pie, Evie kept out of the kitchen. On Saturday night, Bernard took her back to his local for another ale and pie. And on Sunday they had supper with Bernard's father, Benedict. Evie still wasn't sure about Benedict – a man with the same exuberance as Bernard, but with much more sophistication, which made him quite scary to talk to. But he had a butler called Jones and Jones made the most delicious *coq au vin,* which meant another night off.

Evie woke on the Monday, determined to get to grips with the art of cooking. At breakfast she rashly promised Bernard trout. He looked delighted and went off to work with more than a spring in his step. So now she had to deliver. She picked up her basket and walked to the fishmongers.

'I'd like some trout, please,' she said authoritatively.

'For two, ma'am?'

'For two,' she smiled gracefully. There – it was easy.

The fishmonger handed over a newspaper package and Evie put it in her basket and carried it home again, feeling as triumphant as if she'd caught the fish herself.

But when she opened it up on her kitchen table, she got a terrible shock. It had the most unattractive face. Or perhaps it was just because she wasn't expecting to see it. When she'd asked for trout, she'd meant a faceless one. Headless, tail-less, fin-less. She'd wanted an anonymous fish. This one had a personality and a heritage. This trout was clearly very proud of its past, but very glum about its future. Instead of a sleek, silver body – all ready to pop into the range, she'd unveiled a monster. So now what? She'd never had to deal with a whole fish before. There was nothing for it: she would have to telephone her mother.

'Mummy, is that you?'

'Evie, what on earth is the matter, you sound upset.'

'I bought trout!'

'And? I don't understand.'

'It's got,' Evie glanced at the dead fish and then put her hand half over the receiver, so it couldn't hear her, 'it's still got a head on it,' she whispered.

'How much did that cost you?' wailed Mrs Brunton. 'Didn't you ask for fillets? Always ask for fillets!'

Evie gritted her teeth, 'Just tell me what to do with it.'

'Does it still have guts?'

'I don't know.'

'Well, have a look. Is the body slit?'

Evie lifted the newspaper slightly. 'Yes.'

'Good. Now, you will need a bread board and, let's think – I know, the meat cleaver our butcher gave you.'

'I don't think I can.'

'Of course you can. It's just a matter of chopping off the head, oh, and the tail.'

'I can't,' said Evie, in a wobbly voice.

'Don't be silly.'

Silence.

'Evie! Are you there, Evie?'

But Evie was sitting at the kitchen table, her head in her hands.

A few streets away, in his Pimlico studio, Bernard was excitedly daubing paint onto his canvas, a pipe bouncing at the corner of his mouth. He had got Cynthia just right: from her long black hair, which fell in waves over her pale alabaster body, right down to her sweet silver shoes. The shoes were a playful touch, contrasting with her bare flesh and picking up the sparkle in her tiara, transforming her into a naked princess. The dreamy afternoon light had somehow permeated the canvas, giving a warm glow to Cynthia's skin. Bernard gazed proudly at the way he'd portrayed her silver slippers: slim and shiny, like two little fish. And then he remembered – at this very moment, his wife, his wonderful, wonderful wife, was cooking trout. His stomach rumbled. Smiling at his model, he surreptitiously extracted a watch from his trouser pocket. Five o'clock.

'Heavens, is that the time!' he exclaimed. 'I'm afraid we'll have to call it a day. I must get home, you see my wife is cooking trout tonight.' With a wave of his hand he dismissed the gorgeous nude, splayed sleepily over his chaise longue.

'Well, I mustn't delay you then.' Cynthia got up and slowly started to dress, bending over to put on her stockings.

Bernard meanwhile buzzed around the studio like a demented bee, flinging brushes into jam jars, screwing the lids back on tubes of oil paints, throwing off his painting smock and pulling on his jacket. He glanced over at his model, but she was still drooped over her stockings.

'Hurry up!' he muttered under his breath. He closed the shutters with a slam, plunging the room into darkness.

'All right, all right,' muttered Cynthia. She slid into her dress, picked up her shawl and shoes and stumbled across the studio, groping for the entrance.

'Same time tomorrow?' smiled Bernard, ushering her through the door.

'You was more fun before—' began Cynthia.

But Bernard had taken off across the road, winging his way along the pavement, flying home to Evie. He was dying to see her and he could almost smell the baked trout she'd promised. He dashed across another street, narrowly avoiding a man with a barrow-load of flowers.

'Oi, look out! Where d'yer think yer going!'

43

'Home to my beautiful wife!' cried Bernard, diving across another road in front of a cab and a bicycle. Two more streets and there was their tiny mews. Bernard raced across the cobbles, through the large front door, up the stone steps and into the flat.

'Evie! I'm home!' he cried. He was a knight returned from battle, proud and triumphant. She was the maiden, trapped in the tower, waiting to be rescued.

'Evie?' He galloped into the kitchen.

She was sitting at the table, blowing her nose.

'I've thrown it away,' she said gloomily.

He felt full of joy at the sight of her. 'Thrown what away?' he beamed.

'The trout. I couldn't stand its face.' She burst into tears.

'Oh Evie!' He picked her up in his arms, kissing her on her cheeks, her chin, her forehead and on her cheeks again. 'Darling, you're so lovely.'

'Put me down, Bernard.'

'I can't.' He carried her into the sitting room and sat down on the sofa, still holding her tight. 'I miss you so much at work, I can't tell you—'

'But we've nothing for dinner.'

'Really?' He loosened his grip and sat back to look at her. 'Nothing at all? Can't you cook something else?'

'What?'

Bernard made expansive gestures with his hands, 'I don't know, rustle something up.'

'But what?'

'There must be something in the cupboard.'

'Only green beans and potatoes.'

Bernard considered the revised menu for a few moments, then he gently slid Evie off his lap. 'That's all right, darling. Don't worry at all. I'll manage.' He stood up and readjusted his neckerchief in the mirror above the fireplace.

'Where are you going?'

Bernard looked contrite. 'I have to go to the theatre,' he confessed. 'It's those annoying Murphys at the Shaftsbury.

They've promised me a commission to paint their leading lady, but they want me to see her in a show, just so I get a feeling for her performance.'

'But you haven't eaten.'

'Don't worry about me. You go ahead and have supper.'

'What, on my own? Don't you like green beans?'

'To be honest, Evie, I'm not wild about beans.'

'You didn't tell me.'

'You didn't ask.' A petulant pause and then he recovered himself. 'I'll see you later,' he smiled. He gave a cheery wave, blew her a kiss and then lolloped out of the sitting room. The front door, which just five minutes earlier, had burst wildly open, swung slowly shut again.

Letter Home

3, Warwick Mews, Pimlico, London, SW.
Tuesday 16 November 1920

Dear Mummy,

I'm so sorry about making such a fuss about the fish. I'm perfectly fine again today. It's amazing what a good night's sleep can do. I'm afraid it's going to take me a little while to learn how to cook. The trouble is, I don't feel very excited about Eton Mess, Beef Wellington or any of the dishes that women are supposed to be able to whip up to delight their other halves. You really spoiled me, doing all the cooking when I lived at home. I'm so glad you did! I can see that marriage is a bit of a life sentence as far as meals go. They seem to stretch into the distance, as far as the eye can see, all those stocks and gravies… I feel very grateful that I didn't spend my single years in the kitchen. I'd rather be a bewildered novice than an experienced but worn-out chef!

I've made a few friends here. Daisy, Toby's girlfriend, is lovely, although she has no idea about cooking. And Daisy has a friend, Lavinia, who sounds good fun, although I'm not sure she's really my type. There must be plenty of girls in London who are, but I haven't met them yet.

I hope Daddy is well. I expect he's busy pruning, before the frost starts. It makes me homesick to think of him pottering around the garden in the early morning mist. I do miss you both. London is full of people, but it can feel a bit lonely sometimes. Of course, Bernard is sweet and kind and everything, it's just I thought marriage might be a bit more companionable. I mean, you and Daddy seem so cosy. Bernard and I have great fun and his friends are hilarious, but I'm on my own quite a lot. I suppose it's the nature of his job, he has to work long hours in the studio and sometimes evenings as well. He has to be 'out there' and wives aren't always invited. Anyway, I'm going to nip down to the market now with the aim of cooking a more successful supper!

Do write soon and I promise to buy trout fillets in future!

Your loving daughter,

Evie xxxx

PS Any news from the sorting office?

Mr Brunton folded the letter into its envelope, slid it back between the sofa cushions, where he'd found it, and then sat, with a grim expression on his face, waiting for his wife to wheel in the tea trolley. He might have known. Such an unsuitable suitor was bound to make a hopeless husband. So, Bernard was already back to his bachelor ways: gadding around London, and not long after their wedding. Marrying the cavalier was almost certainly the most stupid thing his clever daughter had ever done. All those years as a solicitor had taught him it only took one mistake to ruin someone's life; and his retirement, as a gardener, had taught him something else. If a plant was repotted at the wrong time and in the wrong way, it would never flourish in its new home. Great care was needed to help a transplanted seedling to blossom. And was Bernard tending to Evie? Probably not. Certainly not as much as she needed.

Mrs Brunton appeared pushing the tea trolley. It seemed overflowing with goodies today: fruit cake, ginger biscuits and his favourite – scones. She hadn't baked scones for a long time now. His legal mind smelt, if not a rat, at least a ruse. She was up to something.

'You haven't changed your gardening trousers.' Mrs Brunton nodded at his grass-stained tweeds. It was a gentle accusation, but an accusation all the same.

'Which is why I'm sitting on the old sofa, rather than your newly covered armchairs.'

Mr Brunton had offered a strong line of defence and she appeared to accept it, smiling dutifully and passing him a plate and a napkin.

'Well, this is cosy!' he said, before he could stop himself.

Mrs Brunton gave a little start and the scones she was passing him slid momentarily sideways. One slipped right off the plate onto the hearth rug.

Mr Brunton immediately regretted his glib little joke. Now she would know he had read the letter.

'I think I might pop up to London,' she ventured, picking up the dropped scone and putting it onto her plate.

'Are you going to teach her to cook?'

'Just a few tips.' She smiled weakly.

'Someone will have to – he'll be hard enough to hold on to.'

'I don't know what you mean.' Mrs Brunton put the untouched scone back on the trolley.

'Aren't you having one?'

'I've no appetite today.'

Mr Brunton could tell that his wife was, to all intents and purposes, already on the train: watching the fields rush past the windows; pushing wisps of grey hair behind her ears; her suitcase on the seat beside her because she was too small to reach the luggage rack.

'I think you should go next week,' he pronounced.

She turned to look at him and her worried expression suddenly transformed into a pretty little smile.

Recipe for Disaster

'Evie, are you paying attention?' It was only the second day of the cookery course, but already Evie seemed to have lost interest. Her hands were obediently rubbing the butter into the flour, but her eyes were looking absent-mindedly out of the window. Mrs Brunton followed her gaze. In the street below, a postman was striding along the pavement, stopping at almost every house, rummaging in his postbag, taking out a letter and slotting it through a letter box before striding on a few paces to the next one, whistling as he went. The regular stops and starts, together with the whistling, transformed the delivery into a sort of dance – a postman's hornpipe.

'There are four posts a day here,' said Evie, dreamily. 'In Colyton, there are only three.'

Mrs Brunton glanced down at the mixture. 'I think it's time to stop rubbing in the butter, dear, or it'll get too heavy.'

'And this postman doesn't need a bicycle,' continued Evie, 'because the houses are too close together.' A pause. 'I can't imagine delivering the post on foot.'

'Where's the sugar?'

'The sugar? Oh help, I forgot to buy any.'

Mrs Brunton gave a little sigh. 'We'll need sugar dear, or the scones won't be nice.'

'I'll nip out and get some.' Evie wiped her doughy hands on her apron, whisked it off and threw it on the table. 'Back soon,' she smiled, picking up her velvet purse and flying out of the kitchen.

Suddenly at a loss, Mrs Brunton wandered into the tiny garden, if you could call it a garden: a small patio bordered with dark leafy shrubs, a couple of wrought-iron chairs and a table. But it was south facing and the low afternoon sun created a feeling of warmth that was very welcome in November. Mrs Brunton sat on one of the chairs and put her face up to the light. Once the sun disappeared behind the chimney pots, she knew white frost would come creeping over the patio, but for now the flagstones looked rosy. She pulled her cardigan around her, closed her eyes and imagined Mr Brunton carrying his geraniums into the greenhouse.

She sensed a shadow in front of her face and opened her eyes again. Bernard was standing between her and the sun, its pale rays lighting up his head and shoulders.

'Good afternoon!' he said warmly. 'So glad you're enjoying the garden!'

'Evie's nipped out for sugar.' Mrs Brunton wished he'd found her ironing, not sitting about.

'Yes, I bumped into her on my way home. She won't be long.' He plonked himself down on the low table and whipped off his shoes and socks. 'A fine pair of feet!' he exclaimed appreciatively. 'But dear, oh dear.' He shook his head, took a small pair of scissors out of his pocket and started trimming the toenails of his left foot. Mrs Brunton watched in amazement as the clippings pinged merrily around the patio. 'It's extraordinary, how quickly they grow! Your husband grows vegetables, I grow toenails!' he laughed.

The silver scissors flashed and another fleck of toenail bounced onto the patio. Mrs Brunton squirmed.

'I need to tend to them every couple of days,' he confessed, as he changed feet. Another ping as another nail flew over the flagstones, narrowly missing Mrs Brunton's chair. 'And it's quite an art.' Ping. 'Does your husband have the same problem?'

'No, I mean I don't know. He keeps his toilet private.' Mrs Brunton's pointed remark flew over his head as more clippings shot past her. Ping, ping, ping.

'There!' Bernard smiled, admiring his handiwork. 'Yes, I cut mine in the toilet as well!' He beamed at her. 'And I thought Mr Brunton and I had nothing in common!'

That night Mrs Brunton lay in the guest room, turning the day's events over in her mind: Evie's flat, tasteless scones; Bernard's fast-growing toenails. And there was more. Evie obviously missed working and Bernard couldn't seem to stop. He was out all hours, in the studio or socialising with clients, popping home only for meals. Was it a recipe for disaster? Surely not – they were young and in love. Surely that was all that mattered.

An Old Friend

'Why Cassie, it's lovely!' Daisy held the paper-weight up to the light. The glass dome was a deep sea-blue and inside it tiny shards of coloured glass glowed like coral.

'I'm so glad you like it. I wanted to bring you a little memento from my travels.'

Cassie readjusted the skirt of her salmon pink jersey dress. It was a sophisticated design with tiny silver scallops around the sleeves and neck. The warm pink suited her, softening features that would have been rather hard otherwise.

'Well, thank you for thinking of me,' smiled Daisy.

'It was nothing. Venice was full of them.' A pause. 'But this was the nicest one I could find.'

There was an uneasy silence, during which Daisy's maid came in with a fresh pot of tea.

'And how is Evie Brunton doing?' asked Cassie, as Daisy topped up her cup.

'Cavalier,' said Daisy quickly. 'I didn't think you knew her.'

Cassie coloured slightly, 'Oh, it was years ago. When I lived in Devon. I didn't want to let on before now. I knew you would be meeting her eventually and I didn't want to colour any opinion you might form of her yourself.'

'What do you mean? Evie's lovely.'

'Is that the impression she's given you?' Cassie tossed her short, brown bob and smirked. 'Well, lovely is not the first word that comes to mind. I would say impetuous and hot-headed.'

'Heavens!' said Daisy. Her green eyes narrowed as she considered her visitor thoughtfully. 'You weren't at her wedding.'

'We lost contact when I moved up to London.'

'Will you be calling on her?'

'Perhaps. Eventually. I'm in no rush.'

'Well, don't wait too long. She knows almost no one in town. Oh, and do you know if she plays tennis?'

'Evie? Definitely not.'

Another Old Friend

Evie and Bernard were lying on the sofa together. They had just put Mrs Brunton on the train back to Devon, and now they were enjoying being on their own again. Bernard had one arm round his wife and, with the other, he was attempting to fill his pipe in a one-handed fashion.

The phone rang.

'Can you get it?' mumbled Evie, turning onto her front and burying her head in a cushion.

Bernard put down his pipe, got up and picked up the telephone.

'Hello. Why – hello…Fine, thank you, we're both fine… Yes, I did get it. I was going to reply, but, well things have been a bit hectic.'

Evie lifted her head and caught his eye. 'Who is it?' she mouthed.

'Phoebe!' he mouthed back.

Evie sat bolt upright. Phoebe Carson! Her stomach turned over.

'Of course…That would be lovely…No, you must have it with us…Not at all. See you then.'

Bernard placed the telephone back on its stand.

'What did she want?'

'She's coming to see us. Only don't worry, she's bringing her beau with her. She's far too happy to be cross with me anymore.'

'I don't suppose you can uninvite her now. When's she coming?'

He grinned sheepishly, 'Tomorrow.'

'Tomorrow!' Evie jumped up and started wringing her hands, like Lady Macbeth. 'I don't want her to come!' she wailed.

'But she's met a Mr Hazlitt. She wants us both to meet him, so she must be all right about everything. I'm sure the two of you will get on famously.'

Great clouds of apprehension loomed in Evie's mind and, in the clouds, flashes of static sparked on and off, making her head hurt.

'Any plans for lunch, tomorrow?' Bernard enquired.

'Lunch! You invited her for lunch!'

'Them. Phoebe and her chap.' A pause. 'Could you perhaps make something nice?'

Evie was furious, 'You don't want me to let you down in the cooking department – you want to make it obvious you made the right choice, is that it?'

'Don't worry, Phoebe is no oil painting.'

'You monster! Is that all that matters – looks and lunch?'

'And what is for lunch?' he enquired again.

'Fish soup and plum duff, both made by my mother, just before she left. I'll struggle to ruin them.'

'Excellent, excellent! You and Phoebe have so much in common – and not just me! I can hardly believe you've never met.'

But they had met, it was just that Bernard didn't know they had. Evie hadn't quite got round to telling him about her trip to Saffron Walden. She could still remember Phoebe's gloomy vicarage, the fire burning in the parlour and the clock ticking 'Trai-tor, trai-tor' while Phoebe crashed around making tea.

'Do you know Mr Cavalier?' Phoebe had asked.

'No, he isn't on my round,' she had replied.

And now Phoebe was coming to lunch. She could hardly bear it.

Past Lives and Plum Stones

By the time Miss Carson and Mr Hazlitt rang the doorbell the next day, Evie was so nervous she nearly dropped the soup tureen. Bernard rushed to the door but she stayed in the kitchen, leaning breathlessly against the dresser.

A muddle of voices and laughter, one laugh much louder than the others, and then a man said: 'What an enchanting flat, don't you think Phoebe? Enchanting.' Evie heard the laugh again, warm and friendly. It coaxed her out of the kitchen.

Miss Phoebe Carson stood in the drawing room, nodding at the furniture, smiling at Bernard. Then she spotted Evie.

'Mrs Cavalier!' She rushed over to Evie and grabbed her hand in a firm handshake. 'So lovely to meet you, so lovely,' she beamed. 'For the first time,' she added, pumping Evie's hand up and down.

Evie swallowed her relief. Either Phoebe hadn't recognised her, or she had immediately forgiven her.

'Please call me Evie,' she said weakly.

'Thank you!' smiled Miss Carson. 'And please call me Phoebe. Anyway, I feel as if I already know you,' she continued mischievously, bright eyes dancing behind her spectacles. 'From a past life perhaps? What do you think Robert?'

So she'd forgiven and forgotten. Evie wanted to hug her.

'Oh yes, a past life! Why not!' Mr Hazlitt laughed again. It was more of a horsey laugh this time, a sort of bray which ended in a sniffing snort or was it a snorting sniff. Evie couldn't decide, but it was infectious and she almost laughed along with it. He was a delightful looking fellow, a slight man, with a round, friendly face, and he seemed a bit older than Phoebe.

'How wonderful to meet you, Mrs Cavalier,' he said, as Bernard handed him a glass overflowing with champagne.

'Please call me Evie.'

'And please call me Robert, unless you'd rather call me Reverend!'

'So, you're a man of the cloth!' exclaimed Bernard. 'Do you have a parish?'

Robert ran a hand through his thinning hair. 'I shall be inheriting Phoebe's father's parish eventually. When he retires, I shall be Vicar of Saffron Walden.' He smiled awkwardly at his girlfriend.

'Well, chin, chin to that!' said Bernard, raising his glass and gulping down his champagne.

'Chin, chin,' echoed Robert. He took a sip of his drink and turned back to his hostess. 'And what do you think of London, so far?'

'Confusing.'

'Not really. You just have to divide it into quarters: north and south, east and west. The Thames divides north from south and it flows west to east. In the west they're rich as lords and in the east, poor as church mice.'

'I think that's a bit simplistic,' began Bernard.

'And never the twain shall meet,' continued Robert, 'except in Hyde Park on a Sunday.'

'Hyde Park?'

'Speakers' Corner. There you will find every sort of 'ist. Marxists, Communists, Trade Unionists...there's lots to see, Evie, once you get accustomed to the city.'

'I suppose you're right.'

'It takes time.' Robert looked at her warmly and then grinned at Bernard. 'You have a beautiful wife. I think you made the right choice.'

There was a gasp from both ladies.

'What I mean is, thank you so much for *not* choosing Phoebe!' As he spoke, Robert's left arm shot out and grabbed Phoebe's small gloved hand, squeezing it tight. Phoebe blushed but smiled. They looked at each other briefly, a look full of tenderness. Then a mischievous thought crossed the Reverend's face: 'Besides, I don't think I'm Evie's type!'

He threw his head back and laughed heartily at his own joke, his guffaw splashing out like a wave, spittling the side of his champagne glass before funnelling around the drawing room. Phoebe and Evie laughed along with him, bobbing up and down: small boats in a sea of merriment.

Bernard clung to the mantelpiece, like a barnacle to a rock, as if he was terrified of being swept away. But after a few moments, he let go and nervously stretched his hands out – a prophet trying to calm choppy waters. The gesture seemed to work. Robert produced an enormous handkerchief, wiped his eyes, then put it away again. Evie and Phoebe's laughs turned to titters.

'Perhaps we could eat?' Bernard asked, looking anxiously at his wife.

Mrs Brunton always made a good fish soup and today was no exception, but she would have been disappointed to know that her daughter had burnt the plum duff while heating it up.

'I'm so sorry,' Evie said, as she showed them the blackened pudding, avoiding Bernard's eyes.

'Oh, don't worry,' said Phoebe. 'Just take the top off it and we'll eat the plums.'

Evie smiled gratefully. She delicately removed the cremated topping and spooned out the sticky fruit beneath. Soon they were all negotiating the glutinous stew.

'Delicious,' smiled Robert, 'and we can play the *Career Game*.'

'The what?' asked Bernard. He looked nervous again.

In answer, Robert extracted a plum stone from his mouth and placed it on the rim of his pudding bowl. 'Tinker!' he cried triumphantly.

'Oh that game!' Bernard giggled, like a naughty school boy keen to join in a prank.

'Do we all have to play?' asked Phoebe, doubtfully. 'I've quite enough to do at the Vicarage without another occupation.'

'Well, I will,' laughed Evie. 'I need a job!'

'Tailor!' cried Robert, pulling out another stone and placing it carefully beside the first.

'Soldier!' boomed Bernard, showing off three stones, delighted to be in the lead.

After that the stones came thick and fast. Bernard was a sailor; Phoebe was a rich man; Evie was a poor man, which was not the result she'd been hoping for; Robert was still going strong.

'Beggar man!' he finally roared. He stared in mock anguish at his line of stones, then suddenly slumped down and half-disappeared under the table, taking some of the tablecloth with him.

'I say!' shrieked Bernard, enjoying the spectacle of the cloth creasing up dangerously so the pudding bowls rocked.

Soon only Robert's head was showing, balanced on the table top like Charles the First.

'Beggar man!' he bellowed again, crossing his eyes.

They were all crying with laughter. Phoebe's nose started running; the braying head noticed and discreetly passed her a handkerchief.

What a sweet man. Evie silently thanked him. His jokes had worked. He'd used humour generously, slapping it on like wallpaper, sealing up the cracks between past and present so they couldn't see the join between *now* and *then*. And thanks to the irreverent Reverend, she and Phoebe could be friends.

'They make a lovely couple!' After huge thanks and hugs and promises of a prompt reunion, Phoebe and Robert had left to catch the afternoon train back to Saffron Walden. Their host and hostess were clearing the table.

'Yes,' agreed Bernard. 'It was altogether a lovely lunch.' A pause. 'And now I must get ready.'

'Ready for what?'

Bernard looked evasive. 'Didn't I mention it earlier? I've agreed to umpire a tennis match at four o'clock.'

'No, you didn't mention it. It's Sunday, Bernard, the only day when we can spend some time together.'

'And we will next week.'

Evie piled up the pudding bowls and marched with them out to the kitchen. Bernard followed her out with the wine glasses.

'Evie, don't get cross. It's a one-off.'

'A one-off!' She clanged the bowls down on the kitchen table and set off back to the dining room. 'There are so many one-offs, Bernard. Too many. Who's playing anyway?'

'It's a Ladies' doubles.'

Evie, poised to stack the side plates, glared at him. 'Which ladies?'

Bernard scratched his head. 'Let's think,' he mumbled. Was he playing for time? She wasn't sure. 'Daisy, Lavinia, Maureen—'

'Don't know Maureen,' interrupted Evie, 'and who's the fourth?'

Bernard hesitated. 'Cassie.'

'Cassie Richardson?'

He busied himself with the napkins.

'So you're spending your Sunday afternoon with Cassie Richardson, a girl who once went out of her way to be horrid to me.'

'Daisy asked me to umpire. It's her game.'

'And did you tell her I played tennis?'

'Do you?'

'Not well, but that's not the point.'

'Why don't you come along then?'

Evie banged the side plates back down on the table so hard that one of them cracked. 'I don't want to *come along* as an extra, as the umpire's appendage. I don't want to stand on the sidelines.' She left the plates where they were and stormed back to the kitchen.

'You mean the tramlines,' he corrected, following her through with the napkins.

'I don't mean the tramlines!' She was yelling now. 'I mean the sidelines! The sidelines of your life!'

A red mist descended on Evie. She picked up the nearest thing she could find and hurled it at her husband. The weapon she'd seized was a sieve and so the physical damage was minimal, but Bernard clearly felt mortally wounded inside. He gave her a very hurt look, both sad and disappointed, then stormed out of the house. She watched him from the kitchen window, trotting along the street, racing away from her.

The Custard Club

'Good evening Carruthers!'

The bar of the Embassy was crowded with people jostling to buy a drink and Carruthers had to swing round to see who had grabbed his arm.

'Bernard, what are you doing here?'

'Getting blotto.'

'And Evie?'

'She's at home, resting.'

'It must be tiring, being married to you.'

'Exhausting!' Bernard chuckled as he got out a cigarette. 'Would you like a *Lucky Strike*?' He peered at the label: 'Protects the voice and eliminates coughing.'

'I thought you only smoked a pipe?'

'Oh, I'll smoke anything. But I only smoke cigarettes socially. So, don't tell Evie.'

'How's the painting going?'

Bernard rolled his eyes. 'Trust me to meet my agent on a night off. And I thought you would just buy me a drink!'

Cavalier, the young, red-headed artist, and Carruthers, the suave but grey-haired agent, stood at the bar, like a contrasting pair of bookends, clutching their drinks and gazing at the dance floor, where energetic couples danced the 'Shimmy' to a lively jazz band. Curls of smoke crept everywhere. They caught the light from the chandeliers and turned into translucent snakes that opened their mouths to mist the mirrored wall and smother the dancers in a thick golden fog.

'So how's it all going in the studio? Are you still painting nudes?'

'I've got a lot of commissions,' said Bernard, testily. 'You know that.'

'Yes, yes, but I'm hoping you'll be ready for another exhibition sometime next year.'

'We'll see.' Bernard knocked back his whisky. 'My round?'

'Shouldn't you be getting home?'

'Normally yes, but tonight I thought I might pop over to Bloomsbury. The Custard Club is having another initiation ceremony. I wasn't going to go, but, well now I am.'

'Who's the victim this time?'

'Some playwright – Donald Someone. You know the play that's on at the Empire? Well, he wrote it. It's doing very well so the Custard Club thought he deserved a baptism.'

'Rather him than me,' grimaced Carruthers. 'When will you all grow up?'

The two men parted company and Bernard traipsed across town to Bloomsbury Square. It was quite a walk but it was worth it. He loved coming here, to the wild house on the corner belonging to Gloria and Gordon Lee. Gordon had been in manufacturing, in the north, but a shrewd business sense had allowed him to retire early and live a more bohemian life in the south. Gloria and Gordon weren't artists, but they were 'arty' and they were founding members of the club. At least once a month, a 'newbie' was invited to be immersed in a cold bath of custard in return for lifelong membership. It was a feather in an artist's cap to be invited to join, and it was a passport to an underworld of eccentricity – all in the best possible taste. Bernard was already beaming with anticipation when he rang the doorbell.

Gloria opened the door in a purple silk kaftan and a Liberty patterned turban. Enormous hooped earrings dangled from her ears and, on the hoops, tiny silver dogs.

'Bernard! Where's your wife?'

'Resting.'

'You are a naughty boy! You should have brought her. Anyway, come in, come in.'

The house was already bursting at the seams. There were people everywhere, filling the hallway, sitting on the stairs. Bernard pushed through into the drawing room: a crush of intellectuals, writers, painters, actors, musicians, all squashed together as if they were on a crowded tube train. Everyone was smoking something; Bernard felt in his pocket for his *Lucky Strikes*.

The walls looked different. Gone was the usual stripy wallpaper; instead the drawing room was covered with newspapers – papers from every country, juxtaposed brilliantly, side by side, the black and white newsprint stained brown and glazed with a shiny varnish.

Gordon Lee approached with a glass of champagne.

'You've been decorating!' cried Bernard. 'And it looks marvellous! You are an original, Gordy!'

'Trying, trying!'

'Have I missed the initiation?'

'Afraid so. Poor Donald almost drowned. He's drying off in the kitchen.' He laughed, a funny *he-he* laugh, like a yelping dog.

'How's Bertie?' asked Bernard, remembering their Maltese terrier.

'Top notch again today, but he nearly killed himself yesterday – tried to swallow a ball of wool with a knitting needle in it and what a bother we had getting it out again. Have you eaten? We've got a buffet next door – Turkish tonight. You have to wear a fez while you're eating and if it falls off there's a forfeit.'

'Lovely!' smiled Bernard.

Donald Grayling, the playwright, came staggering in, flecks of custard still on his suit and in his hair. His shoes were squelching with it. Everyone roared, hurrahed and lifted their glasses.

Bernard stretched out his hand in greeting, 'Welcome to the Custard club. You'll love us, we're all mad.'

'Thank you. You must be Bernard Cavalier?'

'Yes, that's right and you're Donald—?'

'Grayling. I say, I don't suppose you've seen my play?'

'Not sure, what's it called?'

'*Down with the Ship.*'

'Not yet.' Bernard looked evasive.

Donald looked a tad disappointed, 'So, what are the benefits of the Custard Club?'

Bernard took a swig of champagne. 'Well, the main advantage is that you only have to do it once – the custard bit I mean. After that, you can enjoy watching hundreds of others suffer the same sticky fate. And the champagne's marvellous.' Bernard slapped the playwright on the back. 'Now, if you'll excuse me, Donald,' a pause, 'Grayling,' Bernard smiled triumphantly at his superb memory, 'I'm going to grab a plate of grub.'

Bernard squeezed back through the rush-hour of party goers and out into the hall. And there was Cynthia, leaning against an enormous pot plant, looking rather the worse for wear. She smiled when she saw him: a beatific smile, the smile of a martyr just before death. Then she started to crash down towards the tiled floor of the hallway. Bernard caught her just in time.

'Watch out Cynthia!' He propped her back against the wall but kept one hand on her, just in case. Even plastered, Cynthia was the most attractive girl at the party. So much dark hair and such a tiny heart-shaped face.

'Yer still married?' she drawled.

'Yes, just!'

'She with you tonight?'

'Not tonight.'

'Well then?'

'No.' He said it quietly. There was a silence. 'I must get some food,' he smiled. He lifted his finger and pointed towards the dining room, like a man explaining something to a foreign tourist.

Cynthia nodded, closed her eyes and slid down the wall so she was sitting on the floor. Bernard turned to tiptoe away.

Cynthia opened her mouth and let out a terrible howl. 'He won't marry me!'

It stopped Bernard in his tracks. 'Who won't?'

'Billy won't.'

'Don't be silly, of course he will, this Billy, whoever he is.' He took her hands in his and squeezed them tight. 'Don't be a silly over Billy!' he laughed.

She started to sob, great racking sobs. Bernard slid down the wall and joined her. Then he gently cupped her face in his hands, lifted her tiny chin and kissed her on both cheeks.

'Kiss me here,' she wept, pouting her lips at him.

He gave her one tiny kiss on the mouth, taking his lips quickly, but not immediately, away. Then he fled, rushing into the buffet.

The spread was sumptuous: everything from köfte to tzatziki. But half way through dessert, Bernard's fez fell off. Not that his head was too big, just that the fez was much too small and it suddenly slid onto the carpet. Gloria noticed, rushed over, grabbed his hand and held it up into the air, as if he'd just won a race.

'Bernard has a forfeit!' she cried. 'Now he'll have to sing for us!'

'Oh, no!' said Bernard with great modesty.

The other diners looked around, ambiguously. They seemed less enthusiastic than Gloria, but perhaps that was just the low light in the buffet room.

'Put down your plate!' commanded Gloria.

Bernard obeyed, suddenly looking forward to showing off. It was a while since he'd composed a song on the spot, but that wouldn't be a problem. He was versatile and spontaneous – a real artiste, fluent in the two glittering spheres of art and music, bi-lingual, in fact. Gloria led him out of the buffet and back through the hall. He peered anxiously around the pot plant.

'I've put Cynthia in a taxi and sent her home,' said Gloria.

'Oh good.' There, everything was working out beautifully.

Gloria burst into the drawing room with her hostage. 'Bernard dropped his fez! I've insisted on a song for his forfeit.'

'Just one, I hope!' said a writer near the piano.

Ignoring those who were jealous of his talents, Bernard nipped nimbly over to the Bechstein. 'I have a little song about Bertie,' he smiled.

'That's one too many!' scoffed a man by the door.

'Just because you're a *real* composer,' said Bernard, stressing the *real* with one hundred per cent irony. He settled himself at the keyboard and gave an important cough.

'Silence!' yelled Gloria. An expectant hush fell over the room. Bernard hesitated, still thinking up the words.

'Get on with it!' yelled a voice at the back. Bernard put his hands on the keys and started playing the opening bars of *Daisy, Daisy*.

'Not that one again!' cried a lady. Everyone started laughing, but in a good way. He already had them in the palm of his hand. He opened his mouth and started to croon.

Bertie, Bertie,
You're a dog with no need for a muzzle,
Yet when you swallowed a needle,
It gave your parents a puzzle.
They managed to pull it out,
So now you can bark and shout—

'Dreadful!' moaned someone.

'Rubbish!' shouted someone else. Bernard tossed his head and carried on regardless.

And you look sweet,
On your four little feet,
Yes, you look swell,
For now you're well—

'Get him off!' snarled the *real* composer.

Bernard took the opportunity to stop. It was perfect timing because he'd run out of words. He stood up and gave his concert pianist bow. Everyone cheered, either with appreciation or relief, it was hard to tell. But Bernard didn't care. Singing the song had reminded him of the last time he'd sung it: cycling in a Devon lane with Evie. A hot summer's day, the hedgerows humming with life. Evie had worn a lovely white blouse and a cream skirt and her hair had streamed out behind her. *Evie.* He should get home to her.

'And now I really need to go,' Bernard beamed at his hostess.

'Just one more time!' cried Gloria. 'I'll fetch Bertie to hear it.'

'It's long past Bertie's bedtime,' said Gordy, coming up to shake Bernard's hand. 'Well done, sir. Lovely song. And thanks so much for gracing our little soiree with your presence.' He skilfully guided Bernard towards the threshold of his artistic home and over the other side of it.

Bernard smiled and waved. Then, once the door was shut, he walked quickly home. Evie would be asleep by now. Well, he wouldn't disturb her; he'd crash out in the drawing room and tomorrow it would all be lovely again. He crossed street after street, road after alley, trotting across town. And all the while she was like a star, shining in the sky, guiding him safely home – back into the harbour of Warwick Mews.

Tea for Two

'It was only a sieve!' wailed Evie and blew her nose loudly on her linen napkin.

Daisy could hardly believe the sudden transformation in her tea companion. When Evie had floated into Fortnum's tea room just a few minutes earlier, she'd looked like an angel. Her golden hair glittered in the sunlight flickering in through the windows; her blue eyes shone and her skin positively glowed. An out-of-date dress could not conceal her slim, sporty figure which was now 'all the rage'. Almost every man in the room had noticed and silently admired. Now, only one cup of tea into their afternoon session, she'd turned into a monster from the deep: bug-eyed from crying, skin blotchy, nose all red and swollen.

But it hadn't put the gentlemen off. Like wasps at an afternoon picnic, two waiters hovered round their table. One refilled Evie's teacup, the other added milk and enquired about sugar. In the far corner, a mournful Spanish guitarist craned his neck towards them and his haunting melodies seemed to be directed only at Evie. Daisy wished Bernard was there to see it.

'What do you mean, it was only a sieve?'

'It didn't hurt him at all, but he made such a fuss.' Evie paused to blow her nose again. 'I wish I'd thrown something harder.'

Daisy considered her friend thoughtfully. How had Cassie described her? *Impetuous and hot-headed.* She was obviously right. Heavens, had she made friends with a hysteric?

'And why did he merit a sieve – or worse?'

'Well, it all started when I made lunch for his old girlfriend.' Evie started sawing into her cucumber sandwich with a force that shook the table legs. 'I tried my best, I burned the duff—'

'Duff?'

'Plum. And then, as soon as they were gone, even though it was a Sunday, and that's the only day he's free, Bernard took off and played tennis with,' a pause to take in the horror of it all, 'Cassie Richardson, of all people!'

'Umpired,' said Daisy. A bright red blush spread over her face, all the way from her long pale neck, right up to her neatly trimmed fringe. 'Bernard only umpired. And it's my fault. I asked him to. Only I thought you didn't play tennis?'

'Not well.'

'But you do play? I'm so sorry, it's just I thought, well I was under the impression you didn't.'

Evie shrugged, 'Bernard still doesn't know much about me.'

But it wasn't Bernard who had said Evie didn't play. Daisy reconsidered her friend. She suddenly didn't seem quite so hot-headed.

'So what's wrong with Cassie Richardson?'

Evie waved her knife helplessly in the air, 'Oh there's nothing wrong with her,' she sighed. 'She tried to put a spoke in the wheel of my romance with Bernard, that's all. We were good friends before that.'

'I see.' Daisy took a dainty bite out of an éclair. Tea with Evie was turning out to be delicious. She shooed the waiters away and whispered, 'Was she jealous of you and Bernard?'

'Not of Bernard exactly, just of me having any sort of interest from a man. She tried to put me off him, saying he was caddish.' Evie stopped to consider this. 'Which may in fact be true,' she added.

This was an accurate assessment. Daisy revisited Cassie's appraisal of Evie with some concern.

71

'And then, when things between me and Bernard went sour for a bit, she gloated.'

'Gloated?' Daisy was shocked. 'Friends don't do that.'

There, she thought, sitting back in her chair: the jury of one had decided. Evie was innocent, whereas Cassie...

'My dear, I can't sit listening to you blowing your nose without offering you a handkerchief.'

Daisy came out of her reverie to find Benedict Cavalier bending over Evie with some concern. He gently wrestled the soiled napkin from her and passed it to a waiter, who carried it respectfully away, as if it were a holy relic. Then he extracted an enormous spotted handkerchief from the pocket of his jacket and handed it to his daughter-in-law. 'It will be kinder on the nose,' he smiled.

Evie nodded gratefully, but she looked embarrassed.

'Good afternoon, Benedict,' smiled Daisy. She was always tickled by Bernard's father, and what tickled her was that he was so different from his son: small instead of tall, dark eyed instead of blue, yet the same charm around ladies. 'Won't you join us?'

'That's sweet of you darling, but I'm waiting for Penelope.'

'Of course. I do hope you're both coming to the *St Dunstan's Ball*? Lavinia and I are organising it this year. No theme this time, but we're having a car treasure hunt, all over London!'

'St Dunstan's?'

'The blind soldier's charity.'

'Then we'll be there. Are you and Bernard going, Evie?'

'They are,' said Daisy, 'almost certainly going.'

'I hope you're knocking that husband of yours into shape?' said Benedict to his daughter-in-law.

'I am,' smiled Evie ruefully.

'Good, good. And have you visited him when he's working in his studio?'

'No. I wouldn't want to intrude.'

'Not at all, he'd love it. You should pop in one day, unannounced. Artists love surprises. It would really get his creative juices flowing.'

Evie stood up; she looked desperate to get away. 'I've got some errands to run, before the shops shut.' She looked apologetically at Daisy.

'Of course,' said Daisy, but Evie was off, making her way across the tea room, head down, intent on something.

'Do keep the hanky!' cried Benedict.

'Was that really a good idea? asked Daisy, after Evie had disappeared.

'I think so,' said Benedict. 'He needs a shot across the bows.'

Studio

Having walked purposefully out of Fortnum's, Evie stood on the pavement completely at a loss. Why had she cut short her tea with Daisy? Had Benedict frightened her away? He'd certainly unnerved her with his ironic comments. Did he offer his hanky just to show he'd noticed her snivelling? He must have guessed she was crying about Bernard, and yet he thought she should visit his studio. Was he hoping to make things better or worse for her? To add to her confusion, a wintry fog was forming in the air, stealing out of the gutters, cloaking the street in an air of mystery.

She wandered along Piccadilly, towards the Circus. The road was almost completely snarled up: buses and trams; taxis and vans; cars and bicycles. On the islands, in the middle of the traffic, flower girls perched, in crocheted shawls and straw hats. Evie stood and watched their knowing smiles when passing gents stopped for a buttonhole; the confident way they took the money and flung it into the deep pockets of their long skirts.

'Cut flowers, Miss?'

Evie hurried on, feeling exposed: an outsider caught staring. She continued down Regent Street, through St James's Park and into Victoria Street. She wasn't far from his studio now. On the corner of Rochester Row, she saw a middle-aged woman collecting coins as her husband played the concertina. The man wore a suit that was too big for him and his hands

74

shot in and out of the baggy sleeves as his concertina bellowed up and down. His wife wore a smart but threadbare coat and held out a wooden collection box. It was a sign. She should support Bernard in his work.

But she was nervous. She hadn't seen him since she'd thrown the sieve at him yesterday. He'd come back late last night, slept on the sofa and left for work before she was awake. She turned into St George's Drive, found the studio, took a deep breath and knocked on the door. She heard footsteps inside, then the door was flung open. There stood Bernard, in his painting clothes, squinting out into the fog.

'Evie!' He seemed pleased to see her, as if their row had never happened. 'Come in, come in. This is perfect timing. The light was going so we finished early.'

'Is there someone here?'

'No, no. Cynthia's gone. Come in.'

He seemed quieter than usual, as if she'd disturbed an actor in his dressing room, enjoying a break between two different plays. The first play starred Bernard the artist, exuberantly eccentric; the second, Bernard the husband, enthusiastically affectionate. And then there was this Bernard, neither artist nor husband; an in-between Bernard, pottering around his studio before walking home in the fog.

She followed him in. She'd only been here once before and she'd forgotten how small it was: just one room, with a wide Georgian window and, under the window, a chaise longue. Leaning against the walls was a stack of canvases. On the floor, books were piled into rickety towers, and bills and letters were scattered between them, like stepping stones. In the middle of the room, surrounded by a sea of brushes and paints, was an easel and, on the easel, a nude. Evie went up to take a closer look.

'That's Cynthia. She's a popular model.'

'Popular with whom?' How snooty she sounded.

'Popular with my clients. This is a commission.'

Cynthia gazed at Evie with a voluptuous smile, a self-satisfied smile that Evie didn't like at all. 'It's lovely you're here,' said Bernard, sensing her unease, 'although it wouldn't do if I was actually working,' he added. 'So let's enjoy our time together.'

'Can't I model for you?'

'Evie, you're my wife, not a sitter.'

'So I'm not your muse.'

'It's not that, I just don't want to mix you up with my job. I wouldn't want to paint you nude, the thought of other men leering over you—' he shuddered.

'Is that what men do?'

'Look, Evie, this is my career. I'm a professional artist, I need to keep my work and home life separate.'

'So who is your muse?'

'You are.'

'Paint me clothed then.' Hearing the urgency in her own voice made Evie want to cry. She turned away from him and looked out of the darkening window.

'Evie, look at me. When I'm in the studio I miss you constantly. I think about you all the time. You are the lifeblood of my pictures, your heart beats in every brush stroke.'

But she still didn't look at him.

He gently turned her face towards him and she immediately closed her eyes, screwing them tightly shut.

'You have to believe me, Evie. You are the reason I can paint.'

A sound of music started in the street outside. She opened her eyes.

'It's the troubadour,' he smiled, 'same time every night.'

He picked up his coat and led her back to the door. Underneath the gas lamp stood an old man in a large overcoat and bowler hat. Beside him was a wind-up gramophone, balanced precariously on top of a baby's perambulator. Strains of Tchaikovsky's *Nutcracker* came rattling out of the gramophone's battered horn. Evie stood and listened as Bernard locked the studio.

'Early night, sir?' The man spoke with a foreign accent.

'Ivan, this is my wife.'

'That's what you always say,' he winked at Evie.

'You rascal. You deserve nothing tonight!' laughed Bernard, rooting in his pocket for a bit of change and placing it delicately on the mouldy cover of the perambulator.

'Much obliged, sir.'

'Who was he?' asked Evie as soon as they were out of earshot.

'White Russian? Red Russian? I don't know, the ones who had to flee. There's dozens of them in the East End. Oh, hold on—'

He nipped across the road to where a blue-coated bootblack was waiting, shoe brush poised mid-air. Bernard obediently put one shoe and then the other up on the bootblack's box, glancing back at Evie, then leaning in to chat, the two of them laughing at some joke. So this was his routine; it was charming. She felt warmth for him come seeping back, making her arms and legs tingle. When he crossed the road again, she slipped her hand into his and he squeezed it hard.

'Let's walk down to the water, it'll look marvellous in the fog.'

'Where does it come from?'

'All those coal fires – and the damp river.'

They wandered down to the Thames. Dusk was falling and the barges moored at Vauxhall Bridge looked eerie in the dark mist as if they'd sailed straight out of *Great Expectations*.

'So romantic,' said Bernard, 'like a Turner, except now there are hundreds of lights on the other side of the river. That's progress, Evie. Electricity. We live in a modern world.'

'Let's live in Devon.'

'I can't. I earn my living here.'

'Then tell me I'm your favourite muse.'

'You're my only muse.'

He turned her face towards him and kissed her. She clung to his overcoat. They stood, blotted against each other for a long time. Then they walked home, arms entwined; she with her hands in his pockets. The storm was over. And she felt closer to him now. Surely arguments were normal between newly-weds? But life in London made everything so much harder.

Daisy Makes Two Calls

'Hello darling, how are things with Bernard?'

'Much better.'

'So you're coming to the ball?'

'I've nothing to wear.'

'You may not have noticed, Evie, but there are quite a few shops in London.'

'We can't afford tickets *and* a dress. Bernard's still waiting to be paid for his last commission.'

'Will you come if I lend you something?'

'Maybe.'

'So that's a yes?'

'I suppose so.'

'Evie, I need to know. I've reserved you the last two tickets. Please say yes.'

'Yes.'

'You sound subdued. What's wrong?'

'*Country Lives* are doing another article on Bernard.'

'But that's marvellous!'

'Is it?'

'Why yes. I mean your engagement was in and everyone will want to know how you're getting on.'

'Perhaps I don't want them to know.'

'Nonsense. And, would you believe it, they're doing a piece on my car!'

'Your car?'

'Yes, my car! We can be in it together!'

As soon as Daisy had finished her call to Evie, she asked the operator for Kensington 638.

'Cassie, is that you? I'm afraid I've got bad news darling. All the tickets have gone.'

A silence, then, 'But Lavinia told me there were loads, yesterday.'

'That was yesterday. There's been a run on them today. So sorry.'

A Cold Climate

London seemed suddenly colder. From her dressing table, cluttered with shell encrusted brushes from Naples, glass bottles from Venice and gold bangles from Florence, Cassie looked out over Fairholme Road. Dead leaves skittered along the pavement, rattling against the railings that separated the large houses. Some blew up steps to the wide front doors and nestled under porticos of white icing; others flew away in the breeze, down the road and out of sight. So, no ball for her. No canapés, no *pintade farcie*, no gossip. No new dress. How strange. Just yesterday there were plenty of tickets. Now they were all gone. Suddenly. Just like that. And was Evie going?

Cassie ran a hairbrush idly through her bob. One of the little shells fell off onto the glass table top with a ping. She picked it up with a finger, the sharp edge of shell pressing into her skin, and examined the intricate markings. Life was about patterns: patterns on shells, patterns in friendships. Before Evie Brunton came to London, there was Cassie, Daisy and Lavinia, meeting every week at Fortnum's. Now Evie was here, that particular pattern seemed to have faded. There were other girls of course; Daisy and Lavinia weren't the only choices. She could design her social life differently. And the advantage of not seeing as much of Daisy was that she could avoid Evie too. Evie would be embarrassing to be with socially, a real country bumpkin. And the gulf between them would be more obvious now *she* had been to Italy.

But London was her preserve and it was irritating knowing that Evie was in town. Besides, Evie would hate the city: the traffic, the noise, the pea-soupers. She was a country girl; she needed peace and quiet. And she would miss the sea. Well, she'd made her bed, she had to lie in it. Cassie shuddered. Bernard Cavalier. No thank you. She didn't envy Evie having to cope with him. But it was infuriating that Evie had married before her. Pipped her to the post. It was as if she'd treated marriage like a silly race and, desperate to win, had chosen the most unsuitable man in the country, the one no one else wanted. Cassie bent down and flicked the tiny shell into the wastepaper basket. Gone. How she would love to just flick Evie away.

Country Lives

'And what would you say were your main influences?'

The question was posed just as Evie opened the door of the drawing room. She listened with interest as she carefully carried the tea tray over to the fireplace where Bernard was deep in conversation with the journalist from *Country Lives*. Miss Michaels was scribbling in a notebook with a gold pen that matched the gold threads in her Egyptian-style geometric dress. The photographer, a young man in a dark suit, stood leaning against the windowsill, looking out of the window.

'My influences? Well, the Post-Impressionists, the Pre-Raphaelites, Expressionism, Cubism,' Bernard hesitated, 'oh and the Bloomsbury group,' he added quickly. 'I embrace everything and everyone,' he declared grandly. Then, noticing Evie, 'But my wife is my muse!' Miss Michaels glanced round at the approaching tea tray.

'Do muses usually live in the kitchen?' laughed Evie, voicing what she was sure Miss Michaels was thinking.

If she got the joke, Miss Michaels didn't laugh. Instead she crossed and uncrossed her long slender legs, shimmering in their silky stockings, and peered at her from under her bright red fringe.

'It's sweet of you to make scones, but I'm afraid I don't touch them.' Miss Michaels snapped her notebook shut and gave Evie a little smile. 'So, what's it like being married to such a popular artist?'

Evie opened her mouth to reply, but Miss Michaels had turned away and was addressing the photographer.

'We will of course want to photograph *the muse* in her kitchen. But what shall we do with her hair? It's too short to go up and too long to be—'

'Modern?' interrupted Evie, rather tartly.

'Our readers are very discerning,' explained the journalist. 'Perhaps a hat?'

'I don't look good in them; anyway, surely I wouldn't be cooking in a hat?'

'We could photograph Mrs Cavalier cutting up vegetables,' suggested the photographer. 'Mr Cavalier could be at her side, his hand loosely around her neck. That would hide the length of her hair and emphasise his interest in all things domestic.'

'Yes,' Miss Michaels smiled as she opened her cigarette case and extracted a cigarette. 'I think our readers would like that.'

'Even if it isn't true?' asked Evie, testily.

Bernard shot his wife a look and jumped up to light the journalist's cigarette. 'Ah, *De Reszke!*' he beamed. 'Such a classy make.'

Evie could feel her blood starting to boil. 'You asked me a question, Miss Michaels, and I don't think I answered it. You asked me how it felt to be married to Bernard. Well—' she spoke quickly, before they could interrupt, 'well, it's very different to being a post lady.'

A flicker of interest crossed the interviewer's face. 'That's right, you used to work. I remember now. And are you still a post lady?'

The Wrong Direction

She would go to Mount Pleasant. It was the biggest sorting office in the world. There was bound to be a job for her there. She was after all a very experienced post lady. As she changed out of the short dress Daisy had persuaded her to wear for *County Lives* and found her long black and white tweed skirt, Evie went over all her experience in her head, so she could trot it out quickly and easily. *Four years delivering the post for a small but busy sorting office in Devon. Some experience with telegrams. Mentoring younger employees.* What else? She racked her brains. They all mucked in together at Colyton Sorting Office. *Good at getting on with people. Good at prioritising tasks. Good at taking her turn making the tea.* No, she wouldn't say that, it was asking for trouble. Anyway, her real job was delivering the mail, heaving a bulging postbag up over her shoulders, negotiating the narrow lanes of East Devon whatever the weather; being able to steady her top-heavy bicycle in a gale, managing to read addresses when the rain had smeared the handwriting. It was a physical job and it had changed her. Four years of carrying the postbag and pushing her bicycle up hills had left their mark. She had muscular arms, especially the right arm, and strong legs.

She bent to polish her dark lace-up shoes. In the drawing room, Bernard was still drawling on about how marvellous he was and Miss Michaels was still smoking, judging by the smell. Evie grabbed her coat and hat and set off. She felt optimistic, like a butterfly collector setting out with a net into a garden full of flowers. Somewhere in that enormous sorting office, a job was waiting. She just had to find it, creep on it unawares, seize it and take it home, still fluttering, to show Bernard and that infuriating journalist.

It took ages to get there. She walked up to Green Park and took the Piccadilly line, negotiating the hieroglyphic tube map. The underground was quiet, but she wondered what it would be like trying to get to work in the mornings, imagining the crush of people crammed onto the platform. She walked cautiously to the edge and peered onto the track. A rat was running along the bottom, heading off into the tunnel. Then she felt a strange warm wind in her face as the tube train approached. Well, she was used to wind, she could cope with a daily commute. She got off at Russell Square and opted for the stairs rather than the crowded lift. Back in the fresh air, she consulted her guide book of London and worked her way along the busy streets to the sorting office.

Mount Pleasant was hugely impressive: a red-bricked building, with chimneys shooting up from the roof. Evie walked through the gate, across the yard, where both vans and carts were parked, and into the entrance hall.

'I'm looking for a job,' she told the man on the door, suddenly realising her mouth was dry. He gestured to a corridor on the left and Evie went down it. A sign on a door: VACANT POSITIONS – TEMPORARY AND PERMANENT. She knocked.

'Come in!' A clerk was bending over a ledger, his face up close to his scribbled calculations, peering at them through thick pebble glasses. He glanced up, registered Evie's skirt and looked down at his ledger again. 'I'm afraid we're no longer employing women.'

This was not the greeting she'd been expecting. Evie felt completely wrong footed by the man's dismissive tone.

'But I have a lot of experience.'

'Like I said, we're not employing women.'

'You used to.'

'The war's over, Miss.'

'I'm looking for a job, not a history lesson.'

The clerk gave a start. He closed his ledger, took off his spectacles and squinted at her. 'We used to employ a lot of girls like you. But now, well now we can't.'

'Can't?'

'It's policy. We have to prioritise returning soldiers, then married men, then single men. And we've run out of jobs long before the turn of the single men. Are you married?'

'Yes.'

'Then you're right at the back of the queue, behind single women.'

'But there are plenty of women who work in London.'

'I doubt if they're married.' He paused. 'Would you like to have a look around anyway?'

'Yes, please.'

The clerk got slowly up off his seat and limped over to the door.

Evie flushed when she noticed his mangled leg. 'What I said, about the history lesson—'

Waving her apology away, he led her further down the corridor to another door bearing the sign: AUTHORISED STAFF ONLY. He pushed it open and suddenly she was standing on the edge of a huge room as large as an aircraft hangar. It was arranged as if in horizontal layers: sacks of mail, then two rows of post workers with a pile of parcels in between them, then lines of baskets on wheels; then sacks of mail, two more rows of workers before a pile of letters and a final line of baskets. The rows stretched back as far as the eye could see.

There was a great noise, like wind in treetops, a sound of rustling and trundling and the murmuring of men, a sea of them – not a woman in sight. The air was full of hard work and excitement, every letter, every parcel on its own adventure, guided on its flight by hundreds of navigators. Supervisors walked up and down, scolding and encouraging, egging the workers on. This was the post; time was precious. Speed and efficiency – it was exhilarating. Evie stood for a few minutes watching, then the clerk tapped her on the shoulder.

He pulled the door open for her and they walked back through to the quiet corridor. A trip to Wonderland. But now it was over.

Evie looked down at the floor and inspected her polished lace-up shoes. 'I'm headed in the wrong direction,' she said, keeping her tone light and ironic. 'Finding a job, I mean. I'm in the wrong place, at the wrong time, and I'm the wrong sex.'

He hesitated, 'Perhaps you could start a family.'

'Thank you,' said Evie, her tone just ironic this time. She recovered herself and smiled at him. 'Thank you for showing me what goes on here.'

'It's the largest sorting office in the world.'

'That's why I tried.'

Evie decided to walk back to Warwick Mews. It would kill time and ensure that Miss Michaels had finished smoking and simpering and jotting down whatever nonsense came into her husband's head. When she reached the Strand, a flock of sheep was being herded down the middle of the road. They ran along, bleating miserably, herded by a man and a boy with omnibuses bringing up the rear. Poor things, they looked so out of place.

She wandered up Charing Cross Road to the bookshops that lined one side of the street. Dusk was falling and the gas lamps were already lit. Light spilled over the pavements crammed full of stands of books, covering them with a golden glow. People had stopped to look and Evie joined them, enjoying being able to browse without a shopkeeper peering over her shoulder.

She picked up a big book on Paris, handling it as carefully as possible, leaning it on the windowsill as she turned the pages. Then a tome on Florence caught her eye. The bricks and tiles of the ancient city looked so warm and inviting, viewed on a grey London street. There were books on almost every subject: botanical books full of spindly plants; philosophy books by Bertrand Russell; political books by Karl Marx. But there were no books about married women who didn't know what to do with themselves. She glanced around – in fact, no books about women at all.

Speechless

'These are absolutely delicious!' said Phoebe. Evie could have hugged her. The scones, rejected by *Country Lives*, were now two days old, but she had dared to reheat them for her friends, and she'd obviously got away with it.

'It's nice to use them up,' smiled Bernard modestly, as if he'd made them himself.

'Well, in that case,' laughed Robert, and he took two more scones off the tea tray and stuffed one in each pocket of his waistcoat. 'For the train,' he grinned.

'Oh,' said Bernard.

'Robert, you are the only man I know who renders Bernard speechless!' laughed Evie.

'Not at all,' said Bernard, quickly. 'I'm quite unshockable.' He took a swallow of tea. 'It's very nice you dropping in on us like this, but what brings you to London?'

'We've just been to a meeting of the Society for the Protection of Ancient Buildings,' said Robert. 'There's been a ludicrous proposal to knock down twelve churches in the city. I mean, it's preposterous. Some of them were designed by Christopher Wren.'

'Is that so bad?' asked Bernard. 'We've far too many churches and we'll never be able to go up the way, if we don't start flattening things.'

'But why go up the way?' replied Robert.

'To be like New York—'

'We have some news for you both,' interrupted Phoebe.

'News?'

'Oh yes!' Robert put down his plate and, standing up, put his arm around Phoebe's shoulder, 'Reader, I married her!'

'Wonderful!' squealed Evie. 'Congratulations!'

'But you didn't invite us!' exclaimed Bernard.

'We didn't invite anyone, except my father,' said Phoebe. 'We just wanted to get on with it.'

'Are you up the duff?' asked Bernard.

Evie winced. Phoebe blushed the colour of the raspberry jam.

'Of course not,' said Robert. 'But we do want to get started on a family. You see it might be more difficult for me. I'm older than my wife. And then, the war you know, all that gas. I must have endured every possible chemical attack—'

'Not to mention the cigarettes,' added Phoebe.

'And the cigarettes,' agreed Robert. 'So there was no point in waiting, when we were both so sure.' He smiled warmly at his wife.

'A baby, already? You're both quite mad!' cried Bernard, nervously. 'You won't catch me wheeling a perambulator around for years!'

'That's not what you said before you married me,' said Evie.

'Well, that was *before* we married. Babies? No thank you. Not for a long time.'

Mrs Bernard Cavalier

When *Country Lives* was published, a few days later, Evie opened it with trepidation, nervously flicking through the articles. Menus for shooting parties; fashion secrets for an elegant Christmas; the best hotels in Cannes...no, no no. Then, on pages 37 and 38, she found it: a large colour plate of *Mrs Bernard Cavalier and her husband.*

She was smiling awkwardly at the camera, one hand holding the arm her husband had draped around her neck, the other clutching a carrot. Behind her gleamed a black kitchen range. It would have been the picture of domestic bliss except the photograph had been placed over the join between the two pages and, as the pages didn't quite match up, Evie's smile was lopsided and one of Bernard's eyes was bigger than the other, giving him a sinister air. She skimmed through the article that followed it. A few lines jumped out at her: '*My wife is my muse these days...I don't envisage having children for years...Devon was charming, but rather sleepy. London is the place for me.*'

Nothing there that she didn't know already. Evie sighed and quickly turned the page and there was Daisy, grinning out at the camera, smartly dressed in a fur coat and hat beside her new six-cylinder Bentley.

Our readers are no doubt aware that the coal heiress, Miss Daisy Pritchard, has been seen around town with Toby Whittington-Smyth. Here we see the dazzling Daisy beside her new motor. The car has all the usual luxuries: foot-warmers, electric cigarette lighters and a tea basket. But it doesn't have a chauffeur; for Daisy is a modern woman – she drives herself!

Daisy was as kind as she was modern. When she dispatched the promised ball dress to Warwick Mews, she included new shoes and a bag, all in their own boxes. And she didn't deliver it herself. She sent it round in a van, so when Evie opened the door to receive it the evening before the ball, it felt not so much like a handout from a friend as a delivery from a very expensive shop. Marvellous. But would the dress fit?

Evie rushed into the bedroom to try it on. She opened the largest box and a grey gown came tumbling out: a sequined bodice and a long silk skirt. Lovely. She felt like Cinderella as she carefully pulled it over her head.

The mirror in the bedroom was far too small. She could see either the silk skirt by standing on a chair, or the sequined top by kneeling on the floor. The effect was either a bottomless bodice, or a headless dress. She floated through to the drawing room to ask her husband's opinion.

'What do you think?'

Lying stretched out on the sofa, Bernard looked up sleepily. 'Lovely, lovely,' he beamed at her.

'What do you mean, lovely? I know it's lovely material, but do I look all right in it?'

Bernard tried again, 'It's a lovely skirt and you look lovely in it.'

'It's not a skirt, it's a dress. Don't you know the difference?'

'Yes, yes,' he said vaguely, glancing down to fill his pipe, feeling in his pocket for matches. 'I know that's a dress.'

'Only now I've told you. And does it actually fit?'

'I think so.' He looked suddenly doubtful. 'I mean, it's tight at the top and loose at the bottom. Is that how you want it?'

'But is it too tight? Or too loose?'

'No, no.'

'Are you sure?'

'Fairly.'

'That's not helpful, Bernard.'

'Look Evie, I told you it's a lovely skirt—'

'Dress.'

'Dress. It's a lovely dress.'

'Well, it will have to do. It's all I've got.'

Clues

'A marvellous ball, what?'

The old gentleman peered at Evie through his monocle.

'Yes.' Evie glanced around.

The Embassy was packed with people. Half the club had been turned into a dance floor where couples were fox-trotting and tangoing – the women shimmering in long, silky dresses and dancing with what looked like dozens of penguins, dressed in black DJs and white bow ties. In the other half, waiters were rushing to and fro, carrying complicated looking dishes towards a buffet already groaning with food. She looked for Bernard, but he wasn't in sight. Having introduced her to Sir Maypole, or Maple, or whatever he was called, he had disappeared.

'Are you on the committee?' the Lord enquired.

'No.'

'Oh.' Sir Maypole knocked back the rest of his champagne. 'So how do you spend your time?'

'Well...I used to be a post lady.'

'A post lady!'

'Yes.'

'Good for you, doing your bit for the war. Jolly, jolly good.'

'I had to earn my living somehow.'

'Sorry?'

'I needed the money.'

'I see. Well, if you'll excuse me...' The old man looked at his empty champagne glass and wandered off.

'You're scaring the gents away!' laughed Daisy, coming up to hug her. 'But you look absolutely beautiful!'

'It's your outfit.'

'Well, hold on to it. It never looked like that on me.'

Daisy was looking 'to die for' in a long black dress with a very low back and made of thousands of lacy petals, sewn together, promising everything, revealing nothing; a combination of modesty and daring.

'A couple of swells!' laughed Bernard, running up, putting his arms round them both and swinging them round so they could see their reflections in the mirrored wall of The Embassy.

They looked so different. Daisy, pale and dark, with her green eyes, bobbed hair and black petal dress; Evie, blue eyed and blonde, in grey silk.

'Sun and moon!' he laughed, 'night and day.' And he was gone, racing to the bar, slapping his chums on the back.

'You look gorgeous,' said a husky voice by her elbow.

Evie turned to see Penelope Armstrong. Penelope was a bit older than Evie and there was a wild beauty to her. She was like a big cat who could either lick you or bat you away with an enormous clawed paw. But tonight she was a snake, gliding along in a silver scaly gown which spread along the floor behind her and lifted up at the front, revealing slim legs. Her short, thick hair shimmered in the light and silver hoops worked their way up her long neck.

'Thank you, so do you. Where's Benedict?'

'Oh, he never bothers with me at these events,' hissed Penelope sweetly. 'He's too busy trying to act half his age with the bright young things.' She looked lazily around. 'But he always makes up for it with some bauble or other the next day.' She smiled at Evie, 'Lovely to see you,' and she slithered off, towards the bar.

'Nice dress, Evie,' said Lavinia, bounding up to her. 'Daisy, didn't you have something a bit like that, last season?'

Daisy frowned, 'I very much doubt it, grey's not my colour.'

'Anyway, you look great, Evie,' smiled Lavinia.

'So do you.'

'What, this old thing!'

The three girls howled with laughter, remembering the hours they'd spent in *Harrods* while Lavinia agonised over her outfit.

'Evie, will you be on our team, for the Treasure Hunt?' asked Daisy. 'We've got Maureen as well, so that'll make four.'

'But I thought Maureen wrote the clues,' said Lavinia.

'No, she passed the job on to someone else. She wanted to take part.'

Half an hour later, Evie, Lavinia and Maureen were squashed inside Daisy's small but perfectly formed Bentley and zooming off round London, having been given clue number one at the starting line. They were the first car away.

'Hurry up and open it, Maureen!' cried Daisy as she roared down Bond Street.

Maureen tore open the envelope.

It was a great battle between two fierce foes,
But now we're all at peace, don't you know.
No more fighting and no more crying,
The lamb can finally lie down with the_ _ _ _

What a dreadful verse,' muttered Evie. 'Who made these up?'

'Oh, but it's too easy!' laughed Maureen. 'It's the Cenotaph. A great battle means the Great War. Let's drive to Whitehall.'

'No,' said Evie. 'The last word should be lion and there are no lions on the Cenotaph. Where are there lions? I know, Trafalgar Square! Yes, that makes sense – the battle of Trafalgar.'

'Evie you're a star!' Daisy turned the car and flew down Piccadilly.

'Come on everyone!' she cried as she squealed to a halt by the fountain.

'But it's so cosy in the car!' moaned Maureen.

'I agree,' said Lavinia. 'I'll get the next one.'

Evie and Daisy jumped out and hunted in the lions' mouths for the second clue. Sure enough, there was a note in the third lion. Daisy waved it triumphantly at the others.

'Bring it back to the car!' called Lavinia.

'No!' Daisy shouted back. 'You were too lazy to look for it. Now we'll have all the fun solving the riddle.' She unfolded the paper and peered at the verse in the moonlight. '*He is an artist who's really in vogue*. In vogue suggests French. What do you think – Picasso?'

'Could be,' agreed Evie, 'Read the next bit.'

'*He's had lots of models and they never say no*. Goodness, that's a bit *risqué*. Definitely Picasso, or Matisse.'

'Picasso,' said Evie.

'All right, now the third line: *He paints naked ladies and rolls in the hay*. Cézanne painted nudes and also hay stacks. What do you think? Is there a Cézanne at the National Gallery? If there is, it's just over there.' Daisy was starting to gabble.

'What's the last line?'

'I'm so sorry, Evie.'

'What do you mean?' Evie looked over Daisy's shoulder, anxiously scanning the clue, '*His first name is Bernard his last _ _ _ _ _ _ _ _*.'

'We'll have to put it back,' wailed Daisy, 'otherwise the Treasure Hunt will come to a grinding halt.'

'Yes,' said Evie, desperately willing the clue to fly out of Daisy's hands and away over London.

'Leave it to me,' said Daisy. She stuffed the clue back in the lion's mouth and the two girls marched back to the car with fixed smiles on their faces.

'The light was poor so it was hard to read, but we think the clue points to Bernard's studio,' said Daisy, vaguely.

'Evie's Bernard?'

'It's just a hunch,' said Evie.

Daisy started the car again and accelerated away, narrowly missing a yellow convertible full of laughing men, on their way to the lions. Evie sat back in her seat and closed her eyes.

'Are you feeling car sick?' asked Daisy, looking at her anxiously in the mirror.

'A little.'

When they reached the narrow lane leading to Bernard's studio, Lavinia jumped out and rushed down it. She emerged again a couple of minutes later, brandishing a bit of paper.

'Spot on! I found this pinned to the door.' She unfolded the clue:

So, you've reached Bernard's door,
Have you come back for more?
I'm afraid you're too late,
Because he's now at the _ _ _ _

Evie closed her eyes again. This was a nightmare, but it would end, eventually.

'What rhymes with late?' mused Lavinia. 'Tate! Of course, I think the Tate bought one of Bernard's paintings, isn't that right, Evie? That one of you with short hair.'

'Yes,' said Evie, 'that's right.'

'But the Tate's just around the corner from here!' exclaimed Maureen.

'Easy, peasey clues!' laughed Lavinia. 'I wonder who made them up?'

'Cassie Richardson,' said Evie.

'You're right!' gasped Maureen. 'I asked Cassie to write them. But how did you know?'

'Another hunch.'

While Lavinia raced back to pin the clue on the studio door again, Daisy turned around and peered at Evie. 'Darling, you look green around the gills, it's my terrible driving I'm afraid. I think we should take you home.'

'But a detour will add to our time,' said Maureen.

'Too bad,' said Daisy, 'we can't be seen to win anyway.'

She turned the car and headed up to Evie's mews, driving slowly and carefully now, giving her friend sympathetic glances in the mirror. But Evie didn't want to look at anyone. She gazed out of the window. The streets were almost deserted: a late-night reveller heading home in a cape and top hat, his cane clicking on the pavement; a cat, slinking past the dustbins of a restaurant and an old man, poking around in the top of the rubbish, his fingers exploring the remains of other people's leftovers.

Torn

'Evie?' Bernard flew through the front door and into the flat. 'Evie, where are you? Are you all right?'

He found her in the kitchen, sitting in her underwear. The long grey dress was lying on the table in front of her and she was slowly and carefully ripping it to shreds with his nail scissors.

'That's Daisy's dress!'

'She's given it to me. And I no longer need it.'

She took the scissors, stabbed the point into the pale silk, high up by the glittery bodice, then she ran the sharp edge of the blade all the way down the material, creating a ripping sound.

'A wonderful noise, don't you think?' She glared at him, flushed and furious. At the corner of her eyes, tears were starting to appear.

He glanced at her hair, 'Evie, give me those scissors.'

'Don't worry, I'm not planning to sabotage my looks, just any future outing with you. But now I'm going to bed.' She stood up and, pushing past him, stalked out of the kitchen.

The ruined dress lay on the table, tattered and frayed: a ravaged bird's nest. He stood and looked at it, mind numb, heart racing. What a disaster. His first real evening out with her and she'd been completely humiliated. Why hadn't he stayed with her? He hadn't even noticed when she'd left. It took his friends, Archie and Harold, to draw his attention to it.

'I say, Bernard, where's your lovely wife, I was hoping for a dance,' Archie had moaned.

'Yes, it's a bit rum, old chum,' Harold added.

Only then did he look around and notice Evie was missing. Daisy explained about the treasure hunt, the jokes at his expense, how Evie had gone white after the second clue and green after the third. It was a disaster. How could he put it right? What could he say?

He tiptoed cautiously through to the bedroom. She was lying on the bed in the dark, facing the wall.

'I had a bit of a reputation,' he started, stumbling over the words, 'before I met you, I mean. But not as bad as many other men.'

There was no movement from the bed, but he could imagine her eyes, wide open, staring into the darkness.

'I swear I've been completely faithful to you.' A pause. 'Since the day we got married.'

There was a small sob in the dark.

'I love you, Evie.'

Silence.

'I promise I'm not betraying you with anyone else. I would never trick you like that.'

'You tricked me over Phoebe. You told me she was your maiden aunt.'

'Look Evie, I admit that before I met you, and even for a little while afterwards, I thought that life was a game. Now…' But he couldn't think what his life was now. He could probably paint it, but he couldn't say it. 'Now, it's – well now it's real.'

Silence from the bed.

'You're the first real thing in my life. The only real thing.'

An Interesting
Escape Route

North Lodge, Key Lane, Colyton, Devon
Friday 10th December 1920

Dear Evie,

I have just read this week's edition of Country Lives. *I knew you had married a clown; I now realise you are living in a circus. Surely that's too much for anyone of sound mind? I understand that the current employment situation makes it almost impossible for you to get a job, so I have taken the liberty to peruse other channels on your behalf.*

Many years ago, longer than I care to remember, I studied Law at Queen Mary's College, London with a certain Frederick Harper. As luck would have it, this same Frederick is now Professor of Law at Cambridge University, while his wife is Vice-Principle of Newnham Women's College. I have written to Professor Harper and told him about you – your matriculation from Colyton Grammar with the highest honours, your unstinting service as a post lady during the war and your current incarceration in Pimlico. He has offered you a place to study under him, just for a year, starting next autumn.

Cambridge doesn't honour its female graduates with an actual degree – you only get a certificate, and after one year of study this would only amount to a pass. However, it would give you an experience of academic life, and with a husband like Bernard it's only a matter of time before any legal knowledge you acquire comes in useful.

In order to get in, you will have to take what is known formally as the 'Previous Examination', and informally, as the 'Little Go', but you will pass it with ease (Latin and Maths, but no Greek). A few week's cramming should do it and I can help with the Latin. But first, Professor Harper suggests that you go up to Cambridge for the month of January and try a few Law lectures, to see if student life would suit you. His generosity in this regard reflects his decent character, as well as a rather large debt of gratitude he owes me from his own student days.

He and his wife live just two minutes from Newnham College and have a lodge in their garden. This is currently let to a Miss Hilda Braithwaite, a rather eccentric botany student, and the professor has offered you a peppercorn rent if you agree to share with her. I think he feels she needs looking after and I have assured him that you are an experienced lion tamer.

I will leave you to consider the offer, but don't tarry too long, I think it's a good one and an interesting escape route – if Bernard can 'spare' you?

Your father X

Evie sat in her drawing room, looking out of the window onto the rainy street. The letter lay beside her. Over on the bookcase, the phone started ringing, its shrill trills piercing the air. It would be Daisy, apologising profusely. 'I had no idea,' she would say. Or Lavinia: 'Are you feeling better?' The ringing stopped. The room was quiet again, just the tick of the clock on the mantelpiece; a strange Arts and Crafts clock some friend of Bernard's had made them. It had thick wooden numbers but charming hands carved in bronze: two little birds, chasing each other round the polished walnut face.

Time flies. Who said that? Anyway, it didn't. Time dawdled through the day, the sun creeping slowly around the windows of the drawing room, stopping now and then to highlight the dust on the sideboard. *Tempus fugit*. Was that right? Her Latin was rusty. '*Amo, amas, amat*,' she said out loud. 'I love, you love, he/she loves.' Except he/she probably didn't.

'Milk, fresh milk!' She heard the rattle of the milkman's handcart in the street below. She had been suspicious of the milk cart initially, especially when she saw the sign on it: *London's Safest Milk*. But then the milkman told her that the milk came up from Devon on the night train. After that, she always went down to greet him with her empty jug and watched him ladle the creamy milk into it. But not today. Today she stayed seated on the sofa and gradually his cries got quieter and quieter, until they died away.

The doorbell rang. Evie stayed where she was. The clock ticked. Another ring. She got up and glanced in the mirror over the sideboard. Her reflection bounced back at her – a small, pale face, multiplied in the jauntily angled panels of glass. A modern mirror, but not a modern face: lank, shoulder-length hair, dark rings under the eyes. The doorbell rang again. Evie gave in and went down to open it.

Benedict Cavalier stood on the doorstep, smiling uncertainly.

'You!' said Evie, before she could stop herself.

'Can I come in? I'd like to speak to you. You see, I did the treasure hunt too.' He smiled again, a lopsided smile, and gestured behind her into the hallway. 'May I?' he said with the strange mix of confident vulnerability that was Bernard's hallmark. For the first time, Evie recognised the similarities between father and son.

'Bernard's at the studio.'

'It's you I've come to see.'

'You'd better come in then.'

He stepped gingerly over the doorstep. 'Any chance of a coffee?' he asked, quick to capitalise on the advancement in his fortune, just as Bernard would.

It was only as she was pouring the coffee in the kitchen that Evie remembered she'd left the letter on the sofa. She picked up the tray and hurried back through to the drawing room.

Benedict was admiring himself in the mirror. 'What a clever man your father is.'

Evie flushed with anger, 'It's the height of rudeness to read someone else's mail.'

He looked at her ironically, one eyebrow raised. 'Desperate times call for desperate measures. Besides, I think it's a great idea.' He grinned at her cheekily, '*Carpe diem*!'

Evie banged the tray down on the coffee table and hot coffee bounced out of the cups onto the lace tray cloth.

'Don't leave him,' he said quickly. 'Have a break. Go and study. But don't leave him.'

She could hardly believe it: his teasing, his nosiness, and now this desperate plea.

'You must be livid,' he continued, 'those silly verses.'

'I'm a laughing stock,' muttered Evie.

'No, you're not. You see, I was in the car behind you, the yellow convertible. I dropped the second clue in the fountain. So clumsy of me!' He sat down and took a slurp of coffee. 'We won, of course!' He smiled at her blithely, 'A box of Cuban cigars.' He took another slurp, 'Do you have any sugar?'

When she came back with the sugar bowl he was on his feet again, re-examining himself in the mirror. Was his incessant preening a sign of vanity or nervousness? Or maybe it was restlessness – yet another trait he shared with Bernard.

'So, are you tempted?' Benedict asked, bounding back to his seat.

'Of course.'

'Good.' He spooned some sugar into his cup and stirred it thoughtfully. 'But how will you afford it?'

'I have a nest egg.'

'A nest egg!' he laughed. 'Charming, charming.' He stirred his coffee again, chuckling to himself, took a gulp and looked at her. 'I have a better idea. I'll pay, if you let me sculpt you.'

'I don't even know if I'm going yet.'

'But if you do?'

'That's very kind of you, but I couldn't be so indebted—'

'Oh, but you could. I can afford it. Besides, you remind me of someone.'

'I'm not sure Bernard—'

'What's it got to do with him?' He drained his coffee cup and stood up. 'Think about it,' he said. 'But don't tarry too long,' he added with a grin. 'I'll see myself out.'

Flying Pheasants

'It's the perfect crime!' laughed Daisy, pushing aside her half-eaten sandwich and lighting a cigarette. 'Posing for the father without telling the son. It'll even things up.'

'Will it?' Evie frowned at her friend.

'Why yes. It's a great way to get your own back. You'll feel better about everything afterwards and it'll help patch things up between the two of you.'

'Maybe, but am I going to walk into problems with Benedict? He says I remind him of someone.'

'Oooh! Both creepy and delicious. I wonder what Freud would say!'

'I don't know – I don't know much about Freud.'

'Neither do I but isn't that what everyone says these days. You're supposed to just reply *Freud would have a field day* and smile knowingly. You don't have to actually read his books. If it's quirky, or whacky, Freud will have thought of it and written a book about it.'

'But I don't want to pretend to know things. I want to know them. Which brings me to the second conundrum – should I go to Cambridge?'

'You're a full-time job, Evie. Soon I'll be able to give up all my charitable pursuits and focus solely on you.' Daisy took a long drag on her cigarette, then she noticed Evie's miserable face. She leaned forward and touched her friend's hand. 'Cheer up. This is a nice problem.'

'Is it?' Evie took a gulp of tea. 'The question is, can I trust Bernard, even for a month?'

'I don't know.'

Daisy's maid appeared: 'Mr Whittington-Smyth, ma'am.'

Toby came bounding in with two dead pheasants hanging from a bit of string. 'Hello ladies! Look what I've got – well, shot actually!'

'I hope they're not for me,' said Daisy. 'Cook won't touch them.'

'Oh.' Toby looked momentarily deflated then he smiled at Evie. 'Please take them, Evie. Bernard loves pheasant.'

'No thank you.'

'But they'll be marvellous!' Toby swung them round, whirling them up and over his head by the string. The pheasants whizzed past, wafting Evie's face with a morbid breeze, making the chandelier shake.

Evie jumped up. 'I don't want them, Toby! I don't want to hang them or pluck them or put them in the oven, and all for a man who may or may not come home for supper.'

'Right.' Toby looked really deflated now.

'Sorry,' said Evie, glumly.

'Not at all,' smiled Daisy. 'It sounds like you've made your mind up.'

A Sitting Duck

The morning of the sitting, Evie was unusually bright at breakfast, almost brittle in her brightness, her voice crisp and tense. She was worried Bernard would see through her cheery demeanour, but he took it at face value, relieved she seemed happy again.

'How lovely you look today!' he cried. 'I think I'll just do a morning in the studio and come home early.'

'Don't alter your timetable for me,' said Evie hurriedly. 'You should use all the daylight while you can.'

'How thoughtful you are! How lucky I am to have such a supportive wife.' He pulled her to him and kissed the top of her head.

Evie frowned.

'Oh Evie, don't frown. Now you've got two lines on your forehead.' He stretched his hand out and reached towards them, as if to iron the creases away.

Evie tossed her head back, out of his reach. 'I'm not a sketch, Bernard. You can't rub the imperfections out.'

She was smiling but he could sense her annoyance. The frown lines got deeper.

'They're quite pronounced, Evie, like two train tracks.'

'Get out!' she laughed. 'Go to work, leave my frown alone.'

'All right, I'm going.' He trotted out of the kitchen. 'I love you anyway!' he called from the hall.

As soon as she heard the front door swing shut, Evie rushed to the mirror. Bernard was right. There were two dark lines, wheeling up from the top of her nose and into her forehead. Where had they come from?

But there was no time to consider her worry lines. Evie put on her coat, brushed her hair and set off for Benedict's studio on King's Road. She walked quickly and purposefully along the pavement; she had to get there before she changed her mind. Once she was there, it would be too late and too embarrassing not to follow through.

Half an hour later she was ringing the front door bell of Benedict's beautiful town house. Almost immediately Jones, the butler, opened it and came out on to the street.

'Good morning, Miss Evie, how delightful to see you. Mr Cavalier is expecting you, in his studio.' He led Evie along the street a few paces and then through a gate in black wrought-iron railings and down worn stone steps to the basement.

'Down here?'

'Mr Cavalier likes to separate work and pleasure, and having a basement is so convenient.'

Jones knocked on the small wooden door and then retreated back up the stairs again.

'Come in!'

Evie opened the door and found herself in a small studio: wooden floorboards, splattered with plaster, and white walls covered with shelving. Life-sized statues crowded the corners; statuettes and broken moulds cluttered the shelves. Otherwise the studio felt less chaotic than Bernard's, although there was the same feeling of creative possibilities.

Benedict, who had been bending over a box of pencils, looked up to greet her. 'Evie! Thank you for coming and, most especially, for being on time. I have lit the stove to heat the room. You can undress behind the screen. When you're ready, come and sit on the couch, and we'll begin.'

'Undress!' Evie blushed beetroot. 'I wasn't expecting to take my clothes off!'

Benedict, who had turned his attention back to his pencils, looked up again. 'But I always sculpt nudes.'

'Then you will never sculpt me,' said Evie hotly. 'I'm sorry, but there's been a mistake. I can't possibly sit for you nude.'

'But a sculptor needs to see the frame of a sitter's body. Do you think Michelangelo would have wanted to sculpt your sturdy boots and Liberty frock?'

'I think we are wasting each other's time, Benedict. I would never in a month of Sundays sit for you without my clothes on.' She turned to go.

'Wait a minute. We have a deal, remember. It's a pity if you won't sit *nu* as the French say, but I'm sure we can come to some arrangement. What about if I lent you something a little lighter? I have a kimono for girls like you. It would provide plenty of cover, but still give some idea of what lies beneath.'

'I don't think so.'

'It would mean that your statuette would be clothed, but your body would at least make sense under it.'

'Still no.'

'Only your legs would be naked.'

'My legs?'

'To the knee.'

'Where is this kimono?'

Benedict disappeared behind the screen and reappeared with a silky dress. The black material was broken up by pink silk flowers and a red silk tie-belt dangled from the waist.

'See, it's perfectly safe,' he smiled, holding it out to her.

Evie took the kimono from him and disappeared behind the screen. She started to undress, but just as she got to her stockings, she was seized by a paralysing fear and stopped.

Benedict started talking again. 'It won't take long, just a few sketches. I can do the rest on my own. And no one will know it was you.'

His voice was low and quiet. Evie stayed where she was, hidden behind the screen, one stocking on, one in her hand.

'I don't think,' she began.

'Don't think, Evie. There's no need to think. I'm the one who's got to do the thinking.' His voice was soft and gentle now, like a hypnotist. 'Come on,' he said, almost tenderly.

She slipped off the other stocking and put on the kimono, wrapping the tie belt round and round her waist and securing it with a very tight knot.

'Ready?'

She could sense he was stretching his hand out. She felt like a bird in a tree, shy and startled, and he was the bird tamer coaxing her out of it.

'We'll start in a sitting position I think, so if you want to come and sit on the couch first.' His voice had changed again, more normal now, but still quiet, as if he thought any sudden sound would send her fluttering away.

Evie emerged slowly from behind the screen.

'Good, now come this way.' Without looking at her at all, Benedict led her to the couch. 'Let's see, legs crossed to begin with. How's that? Comfortable? Good.' He chatted away, like a medic about to perform a necessary but unpleasant procedure, talking to fill the silence of dread and anticipation, putting his patient at ease. 'That's perfect. Hold that pose.'

He picked up a sketch book, chose a pencil and began measuring perspectives with the meticulousness of an architect, then scribbling in his sketch book. The care he took to get it right made her feel more like a building than a body; as if she was a monument that was going to be copied exactly. He finished measuring and became engrossed in his drawing, only looking up from time to time, as if checking she was still there.

'Are you always so professional?'

'Usually, not always.' He smiled, 'But even Benedict Cavalier would hesitate to flirt with his son's wife.' He spoke without lifting his head from his sketch book, as if he was worried his joke might alarm her.

The room got warmer and Evie started to relax. She looked around at the statues and statuettes, puzzling out the process that brought them into being: sketches becoming a clay sculpture then a wax replica and finally a bronze casting. Such an interesting process – the sitter's body getting heavier and heavier through the different stages, slowly solidifying into a second self. Suddenly the idea of being duplicated appealed to her, like giving birth to a smaller Evie.

'It feels so strange,' she confessed, 'sitting for you when Bernard doesn't want to use me as a model.'

Benedict was quiet for a few moments, head bent over his drawing, then he looked up. 'That's a pity. Forgive my indelicacy, but a painting of you would command a high price.' He glanced at her anxiously, unsure how she would take the compliment. 'And that's important when you're trying to earn your living through painting. I mean art is uncertain, fashions come and go. One minute you're *in* the next, you're *out*. Believe me I know.'

'Is that why you're in the wine trade?'

'Was in the wine trade. I've more or less wound the business up. But, yes, you're right. As a penniless sculptor, I didn't appeal to the ladies, whereas as an affluent wine importer with a side-line in sculpting...' he grinned sheepishly. 'Besides, I had a son to bring up.'

'Tell me about Bernard's mother.'

'Sophia?'

'Is that her name?'

Benedict put his pencil down and looked at her. 'He hasn't told you her name?'

'No. It's lovely.'

'She was a lovely girl.' He picked his pencil up again and scribbled away, keeping his eyes on his drawing. 'She was from Dublin. She modelled for me. That's all I know.'

Evie digested the scant information. Just a few clues, the rest a blur, like looking at a face through a rain-streaked window. 'The only thing Bernard told me was that you found him on your doorstep,' she ventured. 'That must have been a shock. Why did you take him in? I mean, you didn't know if he was yours.'

'No, I didn't know for certain. But he looked just like Sophia, tall, long limbed, red-haired. She'd modelled for me about nine months earlier. Everything seemed to fit. I took a chance.'

'Out of pity?'

'I think it was more out of vanity. You see I'd sculpted so many people, so many beautiful women and bright young men, but I didn't have a copy of myself. And I was optimistic. I was almost certain my son would be taller than me and I hoped he might be better in other ways too – more dynamic, more creative.'

'And are you disappointed?' laughed Evie.

'Yes and no. Hold still.'

'Did you love her?' The words were out before she could stop herself. The warmth of the room, the surreal dream-like situation she was in, all combined to make her say exactly what she was thinking.

He paused, pencil mid-air, 'Perhaps. Not enough to try to find her again. But I think we had a lot in common.'

'Bernard and I have nothing in common.'

'Oh, but you do. The same quick temper, the same desire to question convention.'

'Oh no!' exclaimed Evie. 'I'm very conventional. I'm an ordinary, middle-class girl.'

He raised an eyebrow. 'Then why are you sitting here, in my studio? Why do you want to go to Cambridge? Why did you marry Bernard in the first place?'

Evie was quiet, considering his accusation.

He grinned at her, 'Bernard confronts society head on, but you attack from the side.' A pause. 'I expect great things of you.'

Evie laughed, 'Goodness!' She sat back and her eyes followed the cornicing around the edge of the ceiling. What an extraordinary man: so many different emotions flickering through him like sunlight on leaves; light and shade. 'Who do I remind you of?'

'Never mind.'

The front doorbell rang. Evie gave a start. Benedict stopped sketching and listened. They heard Jones exclaim loudly: 'Mr Bernard, sir, what a pleasure! It's so fortunate you've come. I need something moved in the drawing room and your father can't risk his back. Would you mind helping me?'

Evie jumped up as if she'd been burnt.

'Keep calm,' said Benedict. 'Jones will keep him upstairs for a while.'

Evie leapt back behind the screen, tore off the kimono and threw on her clothes, suddenly all fingers and thumbs, laddering her stockings in her haste. Then she turned for the door.

'Wait, your laces,' he said, bending down to do them up. 'Now listen, when you go up the steps to street level, turn left, not right, then he won't see you from the drawing room.'

His instructions made the sitting seem suddenly sordid, as if something dreadful had happened between them and now it was critical that Bernard wouldn't find out about it. She left without a word, tip-toeing up the stairs that led up from the basement studio, then turning left and scurrying along the street like a mouse along a skirting board. Her heart was in her mouth. She just wanted to run and run, back to Devon, scampering along the railway tracks, back home to her parents.

Instead she hurried back to the flat, locked herself in the bathroom and ran a long hot bath. She would wash away the morning – all of it. Benedict's teasing, his compliments, his accusation that she was like Bernard. She filled the bathtub as high as possible, then lowered herself into the water. It was mind-numbingly hot. She lay gasping in the steam, trying not to think about anything at all, trying not to look at her reflection in the dripping tap.

A few minutes later the front door of the flat opened. Bernard. She quickly ducked her head under the water.

'Ev-ie!' He almost sang her name, like a shepherd on a mountain, calling to his favourite sheep. 'Ev-ie!' The call reverberated under water. She came up for air.

'I'm in the bath.'

'Let me in!' he cried, rattling the door handle.

She reached an arm out to unlock the door, dripping water over the floor. 'Careful, it's wet,' she said, keeping her voice even.

Bernard came bounding in and plonked himself on the edge of the bathtub. 'Lovely!' he said, admiring her. 'I've just been to Benedict's. Oh, Evie! I think you're so sweet!'

Evie blushed from the roots of her hair to the tips of her toes. 'Benedict told you?'

'He did! And I'm delighted.'

'Really? I thought you'd be horrified.'

'Horrified!' he laughed. 'No, not at all. I don't care what people say. We love each other, that's all that matters. Besides you've got to use it, not let it go to waste.'

'Use what?'

'Your brain. Cambridge is such a good idea. And I'm very touched you talked it through with my father first. It's so sweet of you to confide in him.'

The gears in Evie's head shifted backwards and forwards, the cogs whirring so loudly she was sure he could hear them.

'He explained it would only be for a month initially,' he continued, 'and if I can't cope without you, you can just come home.'

'Can I?' Evie felt a mixture of relief and fury. So, Benedict had told Bernard about Cambridge. It was lucky he didn't know the real reason for her visit, but it was infuriating to imagine the two of them discussing her future, pushing her around like a prop on a stage.

'The thing is,' he confessed, 'I've found it rather difficult to organise myself since you've been in London. I mean, it's a bit like doing a jigsaw, working out where all the different pieces of my life go now. I feel like I've lost the plan of it all.'

'And I'm the extra piece,' said Evie. 'A piece from another jigsaw, the bit there's no room for.'

Bernard looked disarmed. 'Don't say that Evie, it's not true. What I meant is, I have a pile of commissions to do and now Carruthers is talking about another exhibition. So maybe a month apart would help us both. We could get together at weekends. I could come up to Cambridge, or you could come back to London—'

'It's a great idea,' interrupted Evie. The bath water felt suddenly cold. She stood up. 'Now, if you'll excuse me, I want to get out.'

The Sculptor

As soon as Bernard left, Benedict went straight back to his studio. He wanted to start fashioning Evie in clay while she was still fresh in his mind, while her essence still hung around him in the air. But it was difficult. Instead of concentrating on the task in hand, his mind kept racing back to that other model, the one Evie reminded him of. It wasn't just the slim figure and blue eyes that evoked a memory of Sophia; it was the faraway look, the frankness, the latent anger, like steam drifting lazily out of a volcano. These shared character traits added to his confusion. And what a dreadful confusion – confusing his son's wife with his son's mother.

Sophia, the girl he'd put out of his mind for years and years, had now reappeared in Evie's form as if to haunt him. And the haunting was painful. It brought up guilty feelings he'd thought were safely buried. He had treated Sophia badly and let her down. He'd never tried to find her and now, well it was almost certainly too late. He should have looked for her at the time. If only she'd rung the doorbell when she'd left Bernard on his doorstep – but he understood why she hadn't. She couldn't risk him saying no. How dreadful it must have been for her, dealing with everything on her own: giving birth and giving up the baby. And poor Bernard, brought up without a mother, not even knowing what she looked like. It was all due to his own selfishness. He'd done 'his duty', but not an iota more.

Benedict started to knead the clay, pressing his fists into the soft material, imagining it as a dough that would eventually rise. There was a skill to getting the clay just right: bearing down on it with all his weight, but not flattening it completely; pushing it down, then drawing it back again.

As he worked, he thought back to his conversation with Evie. He'd claimed that he and Sophia had a lot in common. But what exactly? A love of beauty and pleasure perhaps, a desire to live in the moment without considering the future. And if he and Sophia both shared this philosophy, then Bernard had been given a double dose. But this way of life didn't suit Evie. As he kneaded the clay, drawing and pressing, checking for lumps and bumps, Benedict remembered her horror at being asked to undress. He reached for the sketch book and flicked through the pages. A nude of Evie would be difficult, but not impossible. He could rub out the kimono, join the dots. She would forgive him – eventually.

Tea for Three

'Cassie!' Daisy waved Miss Richardson over to the table she was sharing with Lavinia. Fortnum's was crowded and the two girls were squashed beside the window. Cassie walked slowly over to her old friends, carefully picking her way past the other tables, so as not to snag her lacey, cream dress.

'How lovely you look!' cried Daisy, jumping up to kiss her.

'Indeed you do,' smiled Lavinia. 'I think you've lost weight, is that right?'

'Yes, no, well – a bit.' Glowing with pleasure, Cassie waved the compliments away.

'Do sit down,' said Daisy. 'We've ordered you a Lap Sang.'

'We're just dying to hear your news,' said Lavinia, 'It's been so long.'

'Too long,' chorused Daisy.

Grinning like the Cheshire cat, Cassie sat down between the two girls.

'First things first,' said Daisy. 'Cassie, we need to thank you very much for writing such clever clues for our treasure hunt.'

'Oh, did you like them?' Cassie's grin grew wider.

'Liked them? My dear, we loved them!' exclaimed Lavinia.

'It's such a pity that people didn't see them,' sighed Daisy.

'I'm sorry?' Cassie looked confused.

'Well, right at the beginning of the hunt, the second clue went missing, you know the one in the lion's mouth? I think it blew away or something.'

'Oh.' Cassie's smile faded.

'Never mind, we made hundreds of pounds on the night, and that's the main thing,' said Daisy brightly, 'and all thanks to you.' She squeezed Cassie's hand.

'We'll make sure you get a ticket next year,' smiled Lavinia.

Lavinia and Daisy chatted away about the ball and what everyone was wearing. Cassie listened uneasily until tea arrived and the three ladies were distracted by the distribution of cups and saucers.

'No Miss Evie today?' ventured the waiter.

'Not today, and not for a while I'm afraid,' smiled Daisy. 'She's going to try the delights of Cambridge.'

The waiter bowed sadly and disappeared back into the melee.

'I didn't think London would suit Evie Brunton,' ventured Cassie.

'Cavalier,' corrected Daisy, 'but you're right. She's too bright for us.'

'That's not what I meant,' said Cassie quickly. 'Anyway, I can't say I'm sad she's going.'

'She'll only be away a month,' said Lavinia. 'But I'm not sad either.'

'Really?' Cassie's smile was back.

'Really,' said Daisy. 'To be honest, we're both getting sick of her.'

Cassie leaned her lacey elbows on the tablecloth and leaned in excitedly. 'How come?'

Daisy, who had just lifted a teacup to her lips, put it down again. 'Well, I know this sounds a bit sour but—' she paused and glanced around her, 'haven't you noticed how, if Evie is around, the rest of us get almost no attention – from men I mean.'

'They're attracted to her like bees to a honey pot,' added Lavinia gloomily.

'I'm not sure I'd agree with you,' began Cassie.

'Well, you obviously haven't see her recently,' said Daisy. 'Perhaps it was different in Devon, but I can tell you she is the toast of the capital.'

'A real Helen of Troy,' added Lavinia, looking gloomier than ever.

At this point the waiter reappeared and the conversation moved on to other topics. Shortly afterwards, Cassie told her friends she would have to leave.

'What a pity!' cried Lavinia. 'But it was lovely to see you again.'

'Goodbye, dear Cassie,' said Daisy. There were kisses all round and then Cassie picked her way back across the restaurant.

'I don't think she'll bother Evie again,' said Lavinia, as she watched Cassie disappearing around the corner. 'Shall we order more tea?'

'Actually I need to go home and get changed. I'm meeting Toby for dinner.'

'What – again?' laughed Lavinia. 'He seems terribly keen on you.' A pause. 'Isn't it about time…?'

'I can't rush at him, you know.'

'I know. Sorry.'

'Don't be.' Daisy stood up and kissed her friend on both cheeks. 'Tea's on me.'

Champagne for Two

What the deuce was he to do? Toby stood at the cocktail bar of Brown's, tapping his fingers nervously on the marble counter, waiting to order his third half bottle of champagne. Behind him sat Daisy, looking particularly lovely, although a little tipsy.

It was a mistake to have chosen Brown's. Bernard had proposed to Evie here, and every time Toby leaned forward to pop the question, an image of his friend flashed before his eyes. Bernard, rushing into the cocktail bar, rucking up the carpet in his haste, kneeling before Evie, then jumping up and whirling her round the room in a demented waltz. It had been a clumsy but charming proposal, so typical of Bernard. And tonight, *he* was being clumsy as well: talking incessantly about himself when all he wanted to do was lean forward and say the words that kept getting stuck in his throat.

Half an hour ago, Daisy had disappeared to the powder room and, in a moment of desperation, he had taken the ring out of its velvet box and dropped it into her half-drunk champagne. She would surely notice it, and it would do the asking for him. But it was another mistake. The diamond was so clear, it was positively see-through, and it was so big that it had wedged itself at the bottom of the champagne flute and refused to budge. Daisy had raised the glass to her lips again and again, and the ring had stayed where it was, the diamond winking at him, and only him, in the candlelight.

He returned, grim-faced, to the table.

'Is there something wrong?' asked Daisy.

He seized the opportunity. 'It's just, I think you've got something in your glass.'

'Yes, champagne!' she laughed. 'You're spoiling me as usual.'

'Would you mind if I had a look?'

'No!' She laughed.

'No?' He looked devastated.

'I mean no, I don't mind. Whatever's wrong?'

'Oh. Right. Well, excuse me.' Toby put two fingers down into the champagne flute and wriggled them about, but they couldn't quite reach the ring.

'Would you mind if we got a bit of help?'

'Yes!'

'Yes?' Toby looked overjoyed.

'I mean yes, I would mind. I don't want the barman fishing around in my drink as well.'

'Oh, right.' He looked dejected again.

'Look, Toby, whatever it is, someone will find it after we've gone.' A pause. 'Actually, I'm feeling a little peckish.'

He took a deep breath. 'It's your ring, Daisy. I mean – your engagement ring,' the words were coming out in a rush, 'I was too shy to ask, so I dropped it in, while you were powdering your nose, but it's got stuck and I—'

'Dear Toby,' Daisy reached across the table and grabbed his hand. Her eyes filled with tears, 'I thought you'd never ask!' She started to cry.

Evie had cried as well. Why did girls cry? But the question was drowned out by so many others. *When could they marry? Where would they live? What sort of honeymoon? How many children?* Toby's mind whirled, doing its own demented dance of joy. His future was filling up, as if a draftsman was designing it at breakneck speed, drawing lines and angles, corners and curves, creating something miraculous.

'Dear Daisy,' but now he was crying too and he had to let go of her hand in order to find his hanky and blow his nose.

The waiter arrived with the third half-bottle. He fished in the flute with the ice tongs and caught the ring. It came out with a great clunk, splashing the table with champagne.

Daisy took one look at the diamond, the size of an ice-cube, and cried harder. Toby mopped her cheeks with his hanky and then the table top, and everything tasted of champagne.

1921

Leaving

In the end, Evie almost missed the train. At the last minute, Bernard had suddenly wanted to sketch her, sitting on her suitcase, with her hat and coat on.

'This is ridiculous. And I'll look like an émigré, or a refugee.'

'You'll look lovely. It'll remind me how lucky I am.'

'What, that I've gone?'

'No, that you're coming back again on Friday.'

'Are you going to prop me up on the mantelpiece, so I can glower over you like a governess and remind you to be good?' She meant to be ironic, but they could both hear the accusation in her voice.

'Put your frown away.'

'Why should I?'

'I don't like it.'

'I'm nervous, Bernard.'

He dropped the sketch book and rushed over, cupping her face in his hands, kissing her cheeks. 'Don't be nervous, Evie. It'll be great. You're on the edge of something really exciting. I'll have my art, you'll have your learning. It'll even things up.'

She nodded weakly. He was right. The way things were, the scales were weighted firmly in his favour. She was like a child left on one end of a see-saw, suspended mid-air. She needed to find a way back down to earth.

Slightly behind schedule, they dashed to the station.

'Have you got your ticket?'

'Of course. I bought it days ago.'

The train to Cambridge was in the platform and she jumped aboard. She flung her suitcase in a compartment, then came back to the door and stood by the window. They looked awkwardly at each other, suddenly paralysed by the situation: two strangers with nothing to say. He started glancing up and down the platform as if he was looking for someone; she examined the door handle on the inside, checking it was shut properly. After what seemed like an age, the train began moving slowly away.

'See you on Friday!'

He said something back but she couldn't hear him. He started to walk quickly, then lollop beside the train. For a few steps, he kept alongside, beaming in at her, then the train picked up speed and he began to lag behind. She craned her neck; his run slowed to a trot, then a walk. Finally, he gave up and turned away.

The Comet

Clutching the key to her new home, Evie made her way across the darkening garden. She should have got a taxi. She'd arrived at the Harpers' exhausted after dragging her suitcase across town, and they hadn't even offered her a cup of tea. They'd just enquired politely after her father, accepted a cheque for a month's lodging, then given her a timetable of first year law lectures and a key to the lodge in their garden.

Evie traipsed over the lawn, crisp with frost, and knocked on the door of the lodge. It looked charming from the outside, almost like a church, and she wondered if it had once been a family chapel with its low roof and arched windows. The sun was setting and the windows glowed orange, but there was no movement within. Her fellow lodger was obviously out. Evie turned the key in the lock and went inside.

The place was in near darkness. She fumbled around for a paraffin lamp, lit it, then looked around. The lodge was just one long room. There were two beds at opposite ends, with patchwork bedspreads that reminded Evie of her old room in Devon. Then there were two bookcases, bulging with plant books; a wooden table and two chairs; a small stove with a kettle on top of it and a basket of wood beside it. A sink skulked in a corner, full of dirty pots; a bar of soap and a nail brush balanced on the rim. No toilet. Outside, presumably. Plants sprouted on every available surface: the window sills, the kitchen table, the bookcases – flowers, seedlings and test-tubes of roots wrapped around each other like long strings of intestines.

The most interesting thing about the room was the walls. They were painted a midnight blue and dotted with dozens of stars. Streaking across the night sky was an enormous comet with a golden head surrounded by a corona of flames, like a fiery daisy. An angry tail trailed behind it; a dragon's tail with tongues of fire instead of scales. Evie stood and stared. What on earth did it mean?

The next morning, she opened her eyes to find a face peering at her. It belonged to a woman in her late twenties with pale skin, hazel eyes and a bird's nest of brown hair.

'Oh good, you're pretty,' the woman said.

'I'm sorry?' Evie was struggling to get her bearings.

'A flower is always nicer,' declared the woman. Then she offered a hand, as large as a trowel. 'Hilda Braithwaite,' she grinned.

'Evie Brunton, I mean Cavalier.'

'Make your mind up!' laughed Hilda. Her hand was rough and lined and there was soil under her closely cropped finger nails. 'Sorry to wake you, but I wanted to say hello as I have to dash out to a lecture. Plant anatomy! I meant to get back to welcome you last night but I got carried away by the new moon – it's the perfect time for collecting specimens.'

Wide awake now, Evie sat up in bed. 'Before you go, I wanted to ask you about the comet.'

'Oh, do you like it?' Hilda smiled modestly.

'I love it, but why?'

'It's inspired by a quotation: *A learned woman is thought to be a comet that bodes mischief, whenever it appears.*'

'Who said that?'

'Surprisingly, a woman. Bathsua Makin. Except she *wrote* it. Way back in 1673. She was being ironic.'

'Heavens!' said Evie.

'And now you are!' grinned Hilda.

Evie hadn't meant to be, but she smiled back.

'Right, I'm off.' Hilda waved vaguely in the direction of the sink. 'Don't touch the pots, I'll do them later.' She threw a green velvet coat over a long dress covered with tulips, tied a red scarf around her neck and dashed away. Evie glanced over at the dirty dishes. It was home from home.

Natural Laws

That first Monday in Cambridge was completely free with no Law lectures on the timetable and Evie decided to walk into town and have a good look around. Besides, there was nothing for breakfast. She threw on some clothes and set out into her new world.

First stop was a glance at Newnham College, where Professor Harper's wife was Vice Principal and where Evie would live if she started as an undergraduate in the autumn. She walked cautiously down the drive leading to the stately red-bricked building, broken up by large windows, reminiscent of an enormous doll's house. Girls about her age were buzzing out of it, like bees from a hive: some walking, some running, some on bicycles. They were clutching books or bags, chatting and laughing, calling over their shoulders to other girls flying out behind them. They were dressed in a multitude of ways, some in fashionably short dresses, others in long skirts; some coated up for a cold day, others in woollen cardigans and scarves. A motely but colourful crew – not an academic gown amongst them.

'Who's holding the cocoa party tonight?' called a girl on a wobbly bicycle.

'It's Marjorie's turn!'

'Let's hope her mother's sent a cake!'

They dashed past Evie, full of fun and excitement. She stood and watched them disappear down Sidgwick Avenue, suddenly longing to be part of it all. She imagined them all squashed into Marjorie's room that evening, hugging their cocoa cups, discussing some theory late into the night.

She wandered on, down Silver Street and over the Mathematical Bridge, where she got her first view of the River Cam. She stood on the wooden bridge and looked down at the water. A punt slid slowly and silently under the bridge, the oarsman standing erect on the platform at the back. She watched it move majestically out of sight, listening to the rush of water and the clunk of the oar on the river bottom; silence as the boat moved forwards, propelled by the oar, then the rush of the river again as it raced to catch up. Then she walked through the arch on the other side of the bridge and into Queens' College.

From that moment, her day became a blur as she was plunged head first into a medieval world. Cloistered courts, quadrangles, sundials, moon-dials, timbered structures, weathered stone, towers, spires, turrets, ancient wooden doors leading heaven knows where. Everything was a jumble of history, squashed together in narrow streets then suddenly opening out onto extensive lawns which stretched down to the river. The warm stones of the buildings, the green of the grass, the brown of the water all melded in her mind. Breakfast was completely forgotten. She wandered on past King's College, Clare College, Trinity Hall, each college closed in on itself at the front, jealously guarding its treasures, then fanning out at the back, onto the Cam. How Bernard would have loved it; there was so much to paint. She tried to memorise it for him, imagining his eyes darting around, taking in every gargoyle, every stained-glass window.

The next day she had a Jurisprudence lecture at ten o'clock. She didn't even know what the word meant and decided to get there early so she could sit at the front. But when she arrived the lecture theatre was almost full. She squeezed into the back row and gazed around.

The hall was crammed with male students. In front of her, rows and rows of young men, clothed in black gowns and mortar boards, bent over their notes. As soon as the elderly professor came in, they all started scribbling like mad, glancing up at the blackboard, pausing to chew on their pencils then bowing their heads and scribbling again. The rising and falling of their mortar boards gave Evie the impression of hundreds of slates falling off a roof. At the front, the bespeckled man spoke too quietly and wrote too quickly, rubbing off his learned comments almost as soon as he'd chalked them up.

'*Lex iniusta non est lex*,' he finally mumbled. 'A good point to end on. Something for you to think about for next week, and please remember we will be finishing Aristotle and moving on to Thomas Aquinas and his four kinds of law: eternal, natural, human and divine.'

The lecturer turned to clean the board and the Latin phrase disappeared. Evie threw her pencil down in exasperation.

'*Lex iniusat non est lex*. In case you missed it.' She looked up. The mortar board in front had turned around. Its wearer had a round, pleasant face. 'An unjust law is no law at all,' he explained.

'Of course,' said Evie.

'Aren't you going to write it down?'

'I'll remember it.' Evie shut her note book before he could read her jottings.

'Jurisprudence is terrific, isn't it?' he enthused. 'There's so much to think about.'

'Yes!'

'My name's Paul Drabble,' he smiled and held his hand out. 'And you're Miss—?'

'Evie Cavalier.'

'Pleased to meet you, Evie.'

They walked companionably out of the lecture theatre and into a quadrangle. As they emerged into the watery sunshine, a whole posse of male students, sitting on a low wall, started laughing.

'*On a tree by a river, a little tom-tit,*' one of them began singing, standing up and spreading his arms wide like an opera singer.

'*Sang willow, tit willow, tit willow,*' chorused the other students. They stayed sitting on the wall but they all smirked in Evie's direction.

'*And I said to him, dicky bird, why do you sit,*' bellowed the soloist.

'*Singing willow, tit willow, tit willow,*' the others howled in reply.

'Pay no attention to them,' said Paul, 'they're a crowd of clowns.'

'But why are they singing that song and looking at me?'

'It's from *The Mikado*,' he explained. 'It's Gilbert and Sullivan.'

'I know where it's from,' replied Evie with irritation, 'I just don't know why they're singing it.'

'Titular degrees,' said Paul. 'It's because women can't get a degree at the moment, just a certificate, but there are moves afoot for them to obtain, if not the full degree, then at least a "Titular" degree. But "Titular" is just a title, not the real thing. *Tit* is a sort of dig. They're just reminding you of what *they* consider to be your inferior status.' He emphasised the *they*, as if he was keen to distance himself. 'I'm awfully sorry,' he added.

'I see,' said Evie. She glanced at her watch, 'Well, I have a reading list as long as my arm so I'm going to go into town and find a bookshop.'

'Don't you need a chaperone?' Paul looked around him. 'They're usually hovering at the entrance like vultures, waiting to carry off any unaccompanied lady.'

'Really? Well, no, I don't. I'm not staying in a college, I'm in digs. Besides, I'm not even registered as a student yet.'

'Oh. No chaperone required. Then I must take you out for dinner one day.'

'Perhaps.' At that moment, Evie was much more concerned with how she was going to walk past the chorus of men and maintain some semblance of dignity. 'Well, nice to meet you, Mr Drabble. I'll no doubt see you at another lecture.'

Evie smiled, turned away from him and, as majestic as a galleon in full sail, she steered her way across the quad towards the giggling band of students. She was not just a galleon, she was also the figurehead: she was Boadicea, frowning out at the foaming sea. Waves of male laughter washed over her, but the singing stopped. Evie sailed straight ahead, ploughing through their mirth and they parted before her, peeling off like wheeling gulls, allowing her through. Only when she had disappeared around the corner did the song start up again.

Letter from Home

3, Warwick Mews, Pimlico, London, SW.

Monday 10th January 1921

Darling Evie,

I trust you got to Cambridge all right, it feels odd not being able to talk to you on the telephone to check. I hope your lodge isn't too primitive. I imagine the whole town is just steeped in history – how I would love to sketch those gothic towers!

Talking of painting, I've been very busy in the studio, working flat out on my new commissions. You would be proud of me if you could witness my prodigious output! If I get lots done when you're away, then we can enjoy the time that you're back home.

It feels very strange in the flat without you, especially at night. Toby has already taken pity on me and given me supper.

Only a few more days till Friday and then I can take you in my arms again.

Missing you dreadfully!

Your husband, B. xxxxxxx

The door flew open and Hilda burst through, blown in by a January gale. She was carrying a large bag of cauliflowers.

'Evie, you're back. How was your day?'

'Mixed.'

'Oh dear, did you get "titted"?' tutted Hilda.

'Yes.'

'Don't worry, you'll get used to it. Idiot men, they can't seem to enunciate words with more than three letters. They're running scared because there's a growing campaign for women's final exams to be recognised. They're worried that, if we get equal status, we'll get better results.'

'Equal status, I see. So, we don't have it at the moment. Is that why men wear caps and gowns and women don't?'

Hilda waved the comparison away. 'Who needs a cap and a gown? We only need knowledge.' She glanced at the letter Evie was holding, 'From home?'

'Yes,' said Evie, trying to hide her disappointment.

'Bad news?'

'He hasn't asked anything about my lectures. It's as if he's forgotten why I'm here.'

'*He* being hubby I presume?' Hilda rolled her eyes. 'Probably too dense to understand, either that or he's jealous of your beautiful mind.' She paused to consider Evie. 'Perhaps it's just as well you married before embarking on an education. To quote Bathsua Makin again: *No one will want to marry an educated woman, because she will mock her husband and make a fool of him.*'

'More irony I presume!'

'Yes, but you could be in trouble if you get really brainy.'

'Perhaps I'm really brainy already!'

'You may have potential, darling, but you are at present a virgin in the education department. However, very soon you will be seduced by your books. Then you will mature and ripen, your whole body will swell with the fruits of your labours in the library, and—' Hilda paused dramatically, 'when you return home you will give birth to a monster.'

'A monster? What will it do?'

'It will strangle your marriage.'

'I don't think Bernard would like that!'

'He wouldn't *like* it? And what else does this Bernard not like?'

'Any sort of greens, peas or beans. But perhaps peas are beans?'

'No, they are a different, although both are legumes. The genus of peas is Pisum, whereas the genus of a bean is Phaseolus. So, the common bean is phaseolus vulgaris.'

Evie smiled ruefully, 'Bernard would definitely describe beans as vulgaris.'

'Then he will not be welcome here – I'm a vegetarian.'

Although she had given her roommate the ammunition, Evie suddenly felt guilty that Hilda was taking pot shots at her husband. 'Actually, Bernard is a brick, allowing me to come here – sparing me.'

'Sparing you! You sound like a slave – a slave to the kitchen!'

Evie glanced over at the sink full of her roommate's dirty pots.

Hilda picked up a broom, 'Kneel before me!' she commanded. 'I'm going to make a free woman of you.'

'What?'

'Come on,' Hilda giggled.

Evie knelt down on the wooden floor and Hilda dubbed her on both shoulders with the broom handle. 'I hereby free you, Evie Brunton-Cavalier, from the shackles of marriage. You are now a free woman – free to study, free to expand your mind.'

'I'm Evie Cavalier.'

'Yes, but you were Evie Brunton. Why not Evie Brunton-Cavalier?'

'Why not Evie Cavalier-Brunton?'

'Because that is neither alphabetical nor sequential. You were a Brunton first, weren't you? Cast your mind back to the days when you couldn't cook.'

'I still can't.'

'Good, good. There's hope for you yet.'

And so, freed from a lifetime of drudgery, Evie Brunton-Cavalier spent the evening reading Aristotle's *Rhetoric*, peering at his theories in the dim light of a paraffin lamp. When she finally fell, bleary eyed, into bed, she had the most beautiful dream. She dreamt she was flying in a sky full of stars. She looked below her to see the earth as a ball of blue. Then she looked up to see a comet, racing towards her, getting nearer and nearer until her eyes were burning.

Visit Home

Friday came around more quickly than Evie thought it would. On her way to the railway station, she took a shortcut along the banks of the Cam, and there she met the Gilbert and Sullivan fans again. They were rambling along the river, decked out in their dark gowns, flapping their arms around as they talked, like chattering starlings. Suddenly they noticed her. She felt caught out; it was hard to look majestic carrying a suitcase and she felt lopsided and clumsy. The starlings seemed to sense she was handicapped.

As she passed them, the ringleader took a book from under his arm, raised it in front of his face and started chanting loudly, 'Tit, tit, tit, tit, tit...' like a deranged monk.

Evie kept walking, but then, after a few paces, something snapped inside her. She dropped her suitcase on the towpath and sprinted back to the tittering group. She grabbed the young man's book and, before he could stop her, hurled it with all her might right into the middle of the river. The book landed with such force it sank without a trace.

He stared at her in disbelief. 'You throw like a man,' he said.

The starlings looked at one another. Then, as a flock, they moved off; not too quickly, but quickly enough.

Evie returned to her suitcase and picked it up. Her hands were shaking so much the catch started rattling. She held her head high and continued along the river, but the jangling fastenings betrayed her disquiet.

Perhaps because of her encounter with the starlings, perhaps because she suddenly realised how much she'd missed him, Evie was hoping Bernard might be at the station to meet her. But when she alighted at Liverpool Street, the platform was empty. She didn't mind. No, really she didn't. Bernard was obviously busy; he was almost certainly finishing something important, or perhaps he was making sure that the flat was absolutely perfect. She dared to picture it full of flowers.

As she approached Warwick Mews, she glanced up and saw a figure flitting backwards and forwards past the windows. There was an extreme urgency in its movements as if it was a large bird that had got trapped in the drawing room. Back and forth it flew until it suddenly glanced out of the window, a look of profound panic on its face. She opened the front door and heaved her suitcase up the stairs. The large bird came flying down to greet her.

'Evie!' It held its wings out, either to embrace her, or to shield her from a nasty shock. Evie pushed past the bird into the flat.

Once inside, it was hard to assess exactly what had happened. A burglary? Perhaps thieves had been looking for jewels so valuable that it was worth emptying every drawer to find them. Or a revolution? A small one, concentrating in the bedroom but with an outpost in the bathroom. Or perhaps it was just the work of a modern artist left to his own devices for four nights on the trot.

'I kept losing things,' he explained miserably.

'I see.' She walked coolly past him into the kitchen.

This had also been a battle zone, but there had been a victory of sorts. Every pan and piece of china they owned was dripping on the draining board, piled high like the Leaning Tower of Pisa. As she watched, a plate and two cups moved precariously within the tower.

'Anything for dinner?'

He hesitated, 'Not at this precise moment.'

'What, no food at all? Not even an egg?'

He shook his head in mild disbelief, as though there had been stacks of food, but it had all mysteriously disappeared.

Evie set her mouth into an expression of regal detachment and picked her way back through to the bedroom. She changed her frock, powdered her nose and slung her pearls around her neck.

'Where are you going?'

'That's all right, darling. Don't worry at all. I'll manage,' smiled Evie, stealing a line from his own script.

'But where *are* you going?'

'I thought I'd pop round to see Daisy while you...' she gestured vaguely to the piles of clothes on the bedroom carpet, then she stalked down the stairs and out of the flat.

Once safely at street level, Evie leaned against the front door, blinking tears out of her eyes. All she wanted was a hot bath, a cup of tea, a piece of toast – and Bernard. Instead, she'd have to make small talk with Daisy, just so she could be guaranteed something to eat, just so she could win the 'set'. And even if she won the set, she still had to win the match. It was so tiring, but she couldn't afford to lose a point.

A Tutorial

Evie was glad when Sunday evening arrived and she could escape. The weekend continued to be exhausting as she and Bernard jostled to re-establish some sort of status quo, sparking against each other like two flints. Inside the flat they endured every kind of weather: sunshine, showers and one really big storm.

It was a relief to be back in Cambridge, but as she unlatched the Harpers' front gate and started to walk around the house to her lodge, Evie noticed a head peering out of the window, looking out. She slowed her pace. The back door opened and Mrs Harper stood in the doorway, long skirt and shawl silhouetted against the light like a Victorian paper doll.

'Evie, is that you? Professor Harper would like a word.'

Evie followed her into the house and along a corridor to a door at the end of it.

'He's in there.' The brusque, unfriendly tone did not bode well for her interview with the Professor.

'Come in!' called an elderly voice when she knocked. Evie was suddenly transported back to Benedict's studio. He was the last man who had grandly asked her to step into his presence. But there was a sharp contrast between his warm studio and the Professor's cold study. More importantly, there was no screen; although there was a chair and the Professor wearily indicated that Evie should sit on it.

'There has been a rumour, only a rumour mind, of an incident down by the Cam on Friday.'

The Professor had obviously decided to omit the niceties and get straight to the matter in hand.

'Really?'

'Apparently a fresher lost a book in the water. A young woman with blonde hair snatched it from him and flung it into the middle of the river.'

'Was it an unprovoked attack?' Evie asked.

'Completely unprovoked. I mention it because I suspect you might be implicated in this debacle.' He took off his glasses and jiggled them around in his right hand, in the manner of a prosecutor waiting for a confession.

Evie took a deep breath, 'Professor Harper, I have very much enjoyed my first week attending lectures. And I have already learnt many legal concepts, in particular the tenet that a man, or a woman for that matter, should be considered innocent until proven guilty.'

'Yes, yes,' Professor Harper sighed and shook his head. He tried another tack. 'Your father and I go back a long way. I wanted to help him by giving you a taste of university life. I was also hoping you would help contain the wayward antics of Hilda Braithwaite.'

'I fear that Hilda is a law unto herself,' Evie began.

'Well, that may be. But I must warn you that if Hilda's antics continue and,' a pause, 'if any other rumours come to my attention, Mrs Harper and myself may have to consider engaging a chaperone for the lodge.'

'I see,' said Evie.

'How like your father you sound, Mrs Cavalier, but you don't appear to have inherited much of his common sense.'

His scathing assessment wounded Evie to the quick, but she wanted to enjoy another three weeks of law lectures. She nodded, got up and left.

She stumbled across the dark lawn and staggered into the lodge. No Hilda as usual. She would be out gathering her herbs, or whatever it was she did at night. Evie threw her suitcase on the bed and knelt down to take off her boots. She glanced up at the comet; it seemed brighter than ever. What had happened to her this past week? She had lobbed a book into a river, taught her husband a lesson and infuriated a professor. Was it all the fault of the comet? Had it really unleashed its mischief?

A Garden Rose

The second week in Cambridge went even quicker than the first. Evie immersed herself in lectures and books and tried to forget about the tempestuous time she'd spent in Warwick Mews. She and Bernard had agreed that she would spend the second weekend in the lodge and he would come up for the day on the Sunday. One day together seemed safer than two. Remembering that Phoebe lived close by, Evie wrote to her on Monday and invited her for lunch on Saturday.

Only if I can bring it, Phoebe had written back, on Tuesday.

My roommate is a vegetarian botanist, Evie warned her in Wednesday's mail.

Lovely, Phoebe replied on Thursday.

Phoebe arrived on the Saturday, laden down with a basket. 'I understand you're a botanist?' She smiled at Hilda Braithwaite.

'I am!'

'Then hopefully you will like what I've brought for lunch.' Phoebe heaved her basket up onto the table. 'You see, it's all green!' she giggled.

'My favourite colour!' laughed Hilda.

'Good, good,' smiled Phoebe, starting to unpack. 'Now there's lettuce soup, that just needs to go on the stove to reheat, followed by courgettes stuffed with rice and mushrooms. We can eat those cold with a rocket salad.'

'How kind you are!' gasped Evie.

'Is there any pudding?' asked Hilda.

'Only if you like gooseberry fool!' laughed Phoebe.

'Gooseberries are my favourite!' cried Hilda. She did a mock swoon onto her bed. 'Evie, where did you find this angel?'

Phoebe and Evie grinned at each other. 'We're old friends,' said Phoebe.

'And have you met her eccentric husband, he who won't eat his greens?'

'Once or twice,' mumbled Phoebe.

Lunch was a triumph. The food was delicious and the conversation flowed. Phoebe seemed to know an awful lot about plants.

'Shakespeare loved them!' she enthused. '*O, mickle is the powerful grace that lies in herbs, plants, stones, and their true qualities.*' Phoebe waved her pudding spoon above her head.

'Marvellous!' cried Hilda. 'That must be the Friar in *Romeo and Juliet.*'

'*Within the infant rind of this small flower, poison hath residence and medicine power.*' Phoebe cackled the lines like a witch.

'You can't fool me, that's the Friar again!' shrieked Hilda. 'Same play. I bet it's even the same scene.'

'Bravo Hilda!' laughed Phoebe.

After a cup of Camomile tea, which Hilda and Phoebe relished and Evie swallowed out of politeness, Phoebe repacked her basket and said her goodbyes. Evie escorted her to the gate.

'It's been such fun,' Phoebe said. 'Evie, you must come over to Saffron Walden, it's no distance and Robert would love to see you again.'

'Thank you,' replied Evie warmly. She hesitated, 'Phoebe, we've never had chance to talk about, you know, that stuff with Bernard.'

'There's nothing to talk about. Besides, you and Bernard are perfect for each other.'

'Are we?'

'Oh yes! Now please don't mention it again.'

When Evie got back to the lodge, Hilda was dancing around the room like a gigantic fairy. 'Evie, what marvellous friends you have. Phoebe is simply tremendous!' She grabbed hold of Evie in a mock waltz and they did a few turns of the room before collapsing in gales of laughter.

'There's a game I play,' puffed Hilda, 'when I meet new people.'

'Oh yes?'

'I imagine what they'd be like if they lived in the plant world.'

'Sorry?'

'I have three classifications: flower, vegetable and tree.'

'Go on.'

'Well, Phoebe is a rose, a garden rose, slightly raggedy but with a magnificent smell.'

'I see, and what's her vegetable?'

Hilda laughed, 'Carrot. It's the teeth, I'm afraid.'

'And her tree is an oak,' said Evie, joining in.

'Exactly! Sturdy, vigorous, reliable.'

'And what am I?'

'Daisy is your flower,' said Hilda. 'You open and shut continually, depending on the atmosphere.'

'Interesting,' said Evie, uneasily.

'But if you were a vegetable, you would be a chilli, because I imagine you have a bite, especially if provoked.'

Evie laughed. This comparison was easier to swallow. 'And my tree?'

Hilda's face clouded over. 'I can't decide. I think you're more of a graft, you know a branch that's been cut from one tree and stuck onto something else, except it doesn't suit you.' She glanced over at Evie, who had wandered over to look out of the window. 'It's just a silly game.'

But it was true. Hilda had put her finger on the unease that had followed Evie all the way from Devon. She'd been taken from one tree and grafted onto another one and she wasn't happy. Was it London or her marriage that didn't suit her? She swung around to face her roommate.

'By the way, Bernard's visiting us tomorrow.'

Blowing Away

'*Enchanté.*' Bernard affected an enormously low bow, took Hilda's hand in his and raised it reverently to his lips. Hilda's arm went as stiff as a poker. She tolerated the kiss but then pulled quickly away.

'I'm so delighted to meet the wonderful Hilda!' he exclaimed.

'*Soyez le bienvenu,*' said Hilda tartly.

'*Soyez?*' Bernard looked puzzled.

'It's the subjunctive,' she smiled. '*Le subjonctif.* I assumed you'd have more than school-boy French.'

'Evie's told me all about you,' beamed Bernard, like a sun trying to poke through a cloudy day.

'And Evie's told me *all* about you,' retorted Hilda.

Bernard gestured to the night sky mural, 'Your comet is marvellous! You are certainly no amateur.'

'Oh, I hope I am, Mr Cavalier, because *amateur* means a lover of something, coming from the Latin verb *amare,* to love. Unlike many professional artists, I am passionate about my art.'

'Oh,' said Bernard. He gave up and turned away. 'I'm starving, Evie, let's go and find some lunch.'

'Lovely,' said Evie, looking for her coat.

'Or you could stay here and enjoy these?' smiled Hilda wickedly. She opened the cupboard and brought out a bowl of spinach leaves. She lifted one up in the air, threw her head back and dropped the leaf into her open mouth as if was a grape. 'Yum, yum!' she said, her eyes glinting at Bernard. '*Voulez-vous un apéritif, Monsieur Cavalier?*'

Bernard's face turned almost as green as the spinach.

'Go on!' said Hilda, thrilled at his reaction. She threw her head back again and let another bit of spinach slip slowly and seductively down into her mouth as if it was a jellied eel. 'Or I've got beans?' she suggested. 'Broad, green, runner or kidney?'

The joke would have been funny, in fact it would have been hilarious, if Bernard hadn't been the butt of it. Evie glanced over at him. He looked vulnerable and sad.

'Let's find a pub,' she announced, taking his arm and leading him away, like a mother shielding her son from a bully.

'What, lunch in a pub?' Bernard was beaming again. '*Au revoir, Hilda,*' he called cheerfully, over his shoulder.

'*Adieu, Bernard.*'

After the greasiest pie Evie had ever tasted and a glass of warm beer, she and Bernard wandered up the river.

'I just want to lie in a field and hold you,' he said.

'We'll have to go south then and it'll be a bit of a walk.'

They followed the Cam down towards Grantchester, eschewing the beautiful buildings she thought he would be dying to paint, heading for the quiet of the country. Eventually they reached farmland. No one around, just sheep and cattle. He pulled her down onto the grass and they lay and watched the water. She turned around to smile at him. His auburn-coloured hair blended perfectly with the bulrushes and he looked almost like a river creature. It was calm and quiet, just the sound of grazing. She hadn't felt so relaxed for a long time.

She realised that life with Bernard would work perfectly if it was just the two of them, without all those other people. When it was just them, it was fine. In London, she was the one who felt inferior; in Cambridge, he was the one that didn't make the grade. If only there was a half-way house where they could both be enough for the other one.

As if he'd guessed what she was thinking, Bernard said: 'I'm going to memorise your face and take my exams in *Evie* and I'm going to get a distinction, a first, a whatever. Knowing someone's face, completely, utterly, is the only thing that matters.'

'But my face will change.'

'Not to me. You'll always look like you do now.'

'Rubbish. Anyway, I'm more than just a face.'

'But Evie, you are your face, it tells me everything about you. Every memory, every fear, it's all there, in your face.'

'I'll be old one day.'

'You'll look beautiful old.'

She laughed, disarmed by his compliment, yet wanting to dismiss it. 'How do you know?'

'I can already see you old and I can see you as a child too. I'm an artist. I can see the past and the future in every feature. And when you're old, I will still see the Evie I fell in love with.'

Away from London he had so much time for her; he poured himself into her. This was the Bernard she'd fallen for. But she knew there were other Bernards too.

'We've done this the wrong way round,' she sighed. 'We got married and now we're getting to know each other.'

'Do you not like what you're getting to know?'

Unsure how to answer, Evie looked away down the river.

'Foxglove, cabbage, Bradford Pear,' announced Hilda when Evie returned from seeing Bernard off at the station.

'Good evening, Hilda.'

'I thought you should know.'

Evie sat wearily on her bed and pulled off her boots. Then she lay face down on the eiderdown, her head buried in her pillow. She would work the riddle out instead of giving Hilda the satisfaction of explaining it. Foxglove was easy. Foxgloves were poisonous and affected the heart. Cabbage? Well Hilda might have picked that because Bernard hated green vegetables, but it was almost certainly a dig at his intellect, or lack of it. But what about the tree? Bradford Pear. Evie had never even heard of it. She lifted her head up, turned around and caught Hilda's eye.

'Bradford Pear? What's wrong with Bradford Pears?'

The botanist glanced up from the plants she was repotting, 'They're not all bad. They grow fast and they have a nice shape and lots of blossom in the spring.'

'So what's wrong with them?'

Hilda grimaced, 'The blossom smells dreadful. Really horrible. Oh, and it's been bred to be sterile, although it does cross-pollinate with other species of pear. But, more importantly, the wood is weak. It splits easily in the wind, so when the first gale comes along, the tree will blow away.'

'Well, thank you very much!'

'I say it as I see it,' said Hilda.

'What a pity I didn't consult you before my wedding!' said Evie bitterly. '*Hilda Braithwaite, Botanical Analogies*.'

'It's just a game, Evie.'

'What – marriage? Or are we talking about life itself?'

Hilda didn't reply but Evie was really riled and spoiling for a fight.

'I look forward to categorising any man you bring back,' she snarled.

'There won't be any,' said Hilda, without looking up from her plants.

Evie lay in bed, staring up at the ceiling. When Hilda finally finished messing around with her pots and turned down the light, she fell into a fitful sleep and dreamt that Bernard was indeed a Bradford Pear, bending and twisting in a violent storm, and she was desperately clinging to his branches to stop him from blowing away.

Two in the Bush

As soon as the train pulled out of the station, Bernard felt a sinking feeling in the pit of his stomach. Her face was already fading. It was only half an hour since he'd been with her and already he was struggling to remember exactly what she looked like. When he'd lain beside her on the banks of the river, he was so sure that he'd memorised her completely. But now, when he closed his eyes, there were already holes in his memory. Was it two freckles or three on the bridge of her nose? How wide exactly was that gap between her teeth? And the angle of the arch of her eyebrows? He couldn't remember. He could usually remember people with astounding accuracy. But not Evie. He couldn't even remember her frown lines properly.

He blew on the glass window of the railway carriage so it misted up, then he quickly sketched her face with his finger. There. It was a caricature – still, it was perfect. But as he watched, Evie's eyebrows ran into her eyes and dripped down her nose which melted sadly into her mouth. He rubbed it off with the sleeve of his overcoat and started again. He blew gently on the glass and then quickly drew her with the tip of his finger. But the face turned into a crying clown and then just a splodge. He rubbed it out and started again. He worked desperately, like a student who has begun cramming for an exam with the realisation that they haven't studied enough. Again, and again he drew the face, and the miles went by and the gap between him and Evie widened.

The next morning, Bernard was just starting work when there was a ring at the door of his studio. He sighed, put his paintbrush down and stomped to the door. Penelope Armstrong stood on the door-step, dressed in a fur coat and cloche cap. She was holding a cigarette, elongated by its cigarette holder. It was a windy morning and smoke was billowing everywhere.

'Hello Bernard.' She stared at him with her large dark eyes.

'Hello Penelope.' Bernard spoke cautiously. She was too worldly-wise for his liking and he had the feeling that she held him, ever so slightly, in contempt.

'Can I come in?'

'No.'

'You're with someone?'

'I have a commission to paint someone's portrait.'

'Who?'

'Maureen.' A pause. 'Her father asked me to do it.'

'Then I shouldn't disturb.' There was a note of irony in her voice. She looked away down the alley and took a drag on her cigarette, blowing the smoke out of the side of her mouth. 'It's just, I'm worried about your father.'

'Oh?'

'He's been rather mournful of late.'

'Mournful?'

'Sad. Distracted. Maybe even a little depressed.'

'Oh?' But Bernard wasn't really interested; he didn't have time to worry about his father today, not with Maureen waiting for him inside.

'And there's something else.' She took a long slow drag on her cigarette, watching for the orange glow at the tip, concentrating on the task of not breathing, like an underwater swimmer.

'What?' Bernard said impatiently, drumming his fingers on the doorframe.

Penelope slowly exhaled, squinting up at him through the smoke. 'He talks in his sleep. One name. Over and over. *Sophia*. Sometimes *I'm so sorry Sophia*. Who is Sophia?'

'My mother!' exclaimed Bernard.

'Your mother!' Penelope looked horrified. 'But she must be so *old*.'

'None of us are getting any younger,' Bernard said nastily. 'Time waits for no man.'

Penelope's eyes glinted. 'You like sayings, do you? Well, I have one for you. A bird in the hand is worth two in the bush. Do you know that one?' She took another puff on her cigarette and blew it in Bernard's direction and suddenly he was lost in the swirling smoke, like a climber in the mist. When the smoke cleared, she had gone.

After Penelope's visit, a dark cloud seemed to hover over Bernard's session with Maureen and he couldn't concentrate. Eventually he dismissed her and went to see Carruthers. It had obviously been a busy morning because Carruthers was taking the opportunity to put his feet up and his head back when Bernard barged into the gallery.

'Bernard! What's wrong? You look like a bear with a sore head.'

'I am. Have you had lunch?'

'I have.'

'Oh.'

'What do you want apart from lunch?'

'Nothing. I'm at a bit of a loss, that's all. I can't seem to think straight today.'

'Missing Evie?'

'Probably. I seem to work better when she's in town.'

'I trust her absence is not going to set your exhibition back. I was hoping for an opening in the spring.'

'I'll be ready.' A pause. 'Fancy a drink?'

'No.'

'Right, well I'll go home then.'

Bernard wandered around the gallery for a few minutes, half-looking at the paintings, slapping his hands against his sides in exasperation, like a traveller who's waited too long for a train. Then he bumbled out of the gallery into the

159

darkening street. It was cold, too cold to light a pipe. Instead, he shoved his hands in his pockets and wandered along the road towards his mews.

He would go home and tidy up, there was always something to tidy up, then he might do some sketching, or write to Evie, or read a book. Did he have a book? Never mind, he would find one. He reached his street and glanced up at the dark flat. The windows looked black inside their white wooden frames and they glared down at him with dead eyes. He swerved away from the front door and turned back towards town.

Between the Sheets

Toby dashed out of the door of The Mansions, across the square into Berkeley Street and over Piccadilly. When Harold had phoned from The Ritz and asked if he could come over for a couple of cocktails with Archie and Bernard, he'd rushed straight upstairs to change and now he was on his way.

He raced up the steps to The Ritz, past the smart looking doorman and up the winding stairs behind the reception desk, into the Rivoli Bar. The lads were crowded around the barman, busy placing their orders for another round.

'Corpse Reviver for me,' said Bernard. He was holding onto the bar in a way that Toby knew well.

'Between the Sheets!' called Harold.

'I'll have a Bacardi Cocktail,' said Archie.

'Chicago!' cried Toby, coming up behind them.

'Toby!' The three men swung round and there followed a lot of handshaking and backslapping. Toby felt a surge of joy to be back with his old friends. He saw Bernard quite a lot, but not Harold and Archie and they were both great fun. Harold Fairweather, a part-time stockbroker, was full of freckles and cheeky jokes and Archie Meredith, a Welsh landowner, had recently sold his extensive estate outside Cardiff and taken up residence in Baker Street.

The barman started with the *Bacardi Cocktail*. He poured gin, Bacardi rum, lemon juice and grenadine into the cocktail shaker, shook it up and down and then tipped the foaming liquid into a glass. Next was the *Chicago*. Whisky, lemon juice and a dash of maple syrup; into the shaker and then into a glass for Toby, who lifted it straight off the counter.

'Chin, chin, boys, I'm catching up!' and he raised the drink to his lips.

'I say, Bernard, I think Maureen Fitzgerald is keen to bursting on you,' said Archie.

'I don't think so,' replied Bernard, still clinging to the bar, almost upsetting a bowl of olives.

'Come off it,' said Harold, 'she can't stop talking about you.'

'Well, it happens sometimes when I'm painting a portrait. A girl gets keen, just for a bit. It's the intensity of being painted I think. And spending a lot of time with someone in a small space.' He shrugged. 'It soon wears off again, once the portrait's finished.'

'Really? I'm not so sure,' said Harold, holding a hand out to take his *Between the Sheets* from the barman.

'She thinks you're exciting!' said Archie. 'Her friend, Priscilla, told me yesterday. Watch out, Bernard, walls talk in London. You don't want to upset that lovely wife of yours.'

Toby felt a niggle of anxiety. He hastily swallowed his cocktail. There was just a bit too much maple syrup and it left a sticky taste in his mouth.

'That was a strange one. How's yours, Bernard?'

'Top notch!' smiled Bernard, knocking back the *Corpse Reviver*. 'If this is what being dead tastes like, I can't wait!'

'Perhaps, if your next show is a flop, you could get a job as a grave digger,' teased Harold.

'As long as you get the perspective right!' laughed Archie. 'It would be dreadful if the coffin didn't fit.'

'I'll bear it in mind!' laughed Bernard.

'It happened once, at a funeral I went to,' said Harold. 'Great Uncle Ted's. He was enormous and, when the cortège got to the grave, everyone realised he wasn't going to get in the hole.'

'Crikey!' laughed Toby. 'What happened?'

'We left him at the edge and went silently away. It put a real damper on the wake.'

'I bet,' said Archie.

'Anyway, Bernard's next show won't be a flop,' said Toby, slapping his pal on the back again.

'Cheers to that!' smiled Bernard.

But everyone's glasses were empty, after all they were pretty tiny, so they ordered another cocktail. Harold and Archie had the same again but Bernard and Toby tried an *Alexandria*: gin, crème de cacao and a dash of cream.

As the barman was shaking this new concoction, a gaggle of girls walked in. Maureen was amongst them. She peeled off from the group and made a beeline for the bar.

'Look out,' smirked Harold. They all glanced round. Maureen was wearing a low-backed cocktail dress in a pale peach that complimented her grey eyes and strawberry blonde hair. She was heavily made up but striking in a way none of the men had noticed before. Her eyelids were painted with something glittery and she looked demurely at them from under the silvery eye-shadow.

'Hello Maureen,' said Bernard. The other lads mumbled into their drinks.

'Good evening,' she smiled and her eyes shimmered.

'Your eyes look bigger tonight,' said Bernard. 'You should have worn that silver stuff for the sitting.'

'I still could,' she said. 'I'll wear it tomorrow.'

Two Alexandria cocktails appeared on the counter of the bar. 'What would you like, Maureen?' asked Toby.

'Thank you, but I'll order with my friends. I just wanted to say hello.' She gazed at Bernard, from under her shiny lids.

'We're talking about wakes,' said Toby, keen to get rid of her.

'Oh, they're great fun in Ireland,' she enthused. 'Funerals are marvellous over there.'

'We're thinking of getting Bernard a job as a grave digger,' said Harold, 'if his painting career doesn't take off.'

'Why wouldn't it? He's a wonderful artist,' said Maureen.

'There we are, Bernard old chap, you have at least one fan!' laughed Archie. He winked at Harold.

'All is not lost!' Toby joined in, trying to sound jovial. 'So Bernard, when's Evie next back for a visit?' He looked pointedly at Maureen.

'Friday,' Bernard replied, lifting his Alexandria off the bar, looking only at his drink.

'And then she's just got one more week until she's home again,' continued Toby, still looking at Maureen. 'Is that right, Bernard?'

'Yep.' Bernard took a swig of his cocktail and a moustache of cream appeared on his upper lip.

Quick as a flash, Maureen grabbed a little napkin from a pile by the olives and came up close to Bernard's face as if to wipe it away. 'You've got something on your—'

Bernard swiftly rubbed his mouth with the back of his hand, smearing the creamy moustache over his cheek, moving his face away from Maureen and her bright eyelids. Maureen gave a little smirk and dropped the napkin back on the bar again. It landed clumsily, splaying outwards. There was a brief silence, then Harold started asking Archie about wakes in Wales.

'Well, I'll leave you gentlemen to your evening,' Maureen smiled. She glanced at Bernard, who was clinging to the bar again, and then she floated back to her girlfriends. The barman followed her to take their orders.

Toby downed his *Alexandria* and banged the empty glass back down on the bar with a sigh of relief as if he'd just completed a course of medicine.

'Well, that's my second drink finished, probably only time for one more.'

'Oh, Toby,' groaned Archie, 'why are you always in a rush?'

'I said I'd pop in and see mother later.'

'Your mother doesn't care what time you get back,' Harold reassured him.

'I'm under orders,' said Toby. 'Now, what's everyone having?'

Harold and Archie consulted the menu for ideas and got into a discussion about the different spellings of whisky.

Toby took his chance. He leaned towards Bernard, 'Your eyes look bigger tonight,' he said quietly in his ear.

He gave Bernard a shove; Bernard shoved him back.

'I get paid to notice things,' Bernard muttered, 'that's what artists do.'

'Well, right now, I think Evie would consider grave-digging a safer occupation.'

'Evie's not here.'

'Stop squabbling you two,' said Harold. 'I thought we were going to have some fun.'

'We are,' said Toby, suddenly longing to go home. 'But I'm sick of cocktails, let's have a bottle of champagne – my treat.'

'Hoorah!' said Bernard, all smiles again. 'No more cloying cocktails. Tobe, you're a brick.'

The champagne revived the four friends. They clowned around at the bar, making more jokes about funerals, wakes in Wales and dead things in general. The barman was clearly not enjoying the conversation much and kept wandering over to the girls' table to check on them.

'The ladies have asked if you would like to join them?' he announced on one of his return trips to the bar.

Harold and Archie shrugged. Bernard didn't seem to have heard.

'Not me, I'm afraid,' said Toby. He glanced at his watch, 'I really have to get going.' He slapped Harold and Archie on the back and gave Bernard a look of warning.

'Hold on, Toby, safety in numbers and all that—' began Harold.

But Toby had gone.

The Letter

On Friday, he was at the station to meet her. She ran along the platform and into his arms, throwing herself against him, wanting to melt into him and completely disappear.

'Darling,' he breathed into her hair. 'Thank God you're back.'

That night they didn't sleep at all. They clung to each other, like two capsized sailors to an overturned lifeboat. At dawn she dozed off, then woke to find him lying gazing at her. After a few minutes she drifted back to sleep. When she woke again the flat was empty. She wandered through to the kitchen. There was bread and milk on the table and a note: *Gone to deliver a commission. Back soon. I love you.*

She had just made a cup of tea and a piece of toast when she heard the flap of the letterbox. The post! She glanced at the clock. Half past ten. Goodness, she must have slept through the first delivery! She ran downstairs. An envelope lay on the doormat and she bent down to pick it up. A quick glance showed a handwritten address. Good. Not a bill then. She turned the letter over to open it and walked upstairs again. By the time she was back in the drawing room she had torn open the flap and pulled the letter out.

Friday 28th January 1921

Dear Bernard,

I was awake all night, thinking about what you'd said. I don't care a jot if you're married. And I'm not worried about Cynthia either. They can't love you like I do.

What we have is too special to throw away. I know it will be harder when Evie is back, but I can cope with seeing you less, as long as I can still see you.

Please don't leave me,

Maureen

Time went into slow motion. Everything slurred and slowed to a stop: the noise of traffic outside the window, the birds ticking around the clock. Evie stood up and the letter fell onto the floor. She stooped to pick it up, but her hands had grown enormously big and the letter had become terribly small. She couldn't seem to grasp hold of it. The moment extended. Evie stayed where she was, waiting, but the silence continued, dragging itself outwards, like a stretched piece of toffee and her hands carried on ballooning into boxing gloves. She shut her eyes and waited. A comet shot past her eyelids, then everything returned to normal again. The traffic rumbled past; the clock ticked. She cautiously opened her eyes. Her hands had shrunk back to their usual size, but she couldn't risk picking up the letter again. So she left it lying where it was and went to find her suitcase.

Empty

Bernard ran up the stone steps two at a time, which was quite risky considering what he was carrying. A huge bunch of flowers under one arm, and, in his hands, a brown paper bag full of eggs. He was grinning in anticipation of her look of sleepy surprise, blonde hair sticking up in the air like a baby chick. He had to put the bag of eggs under his chin while he fiddled with the door handle.

'Ev-ie!' He was the cock crowing in the morning, waking her with the sound of her own voice. Everything was *Evie* now. It was all about *Evie*, every breath, every beat of the heart.

He raced into the kitchen to dump the eggs on the table and then ran into the bedroom with the flowers. It was empty. He was surprised she was already awake when they'd both slept so little.

'Ev-ie!' He was now not so much a cock as a goatherd. He'd lost his goat, somewhere in the flat, but he would find her. He tried the bathroom. It was empty.

Bernard's heart began to beat just a little bit faster than normal, but he kept his smile on; he wanted to look really pleased when he found her again.

'Ev-ie!' He went into the drawing room. Empty. And there was a strange atmosphere in there, as if something had happened. The clock was ticking slower or was it faster; he wasn't sure but a feeling of dread crept over him, like a cold, insidious mist. He sat down on the sofa and then he saw it – a letter, lying on the carpet.

Bernard knew he had perfect eyesight. Years of working in a studio and he still had no need for glasses. Many of his contemporaries now gazed at the world with a tired myopic squint, especially on sunny days, yet his own sight was one hundred percent. But when he finally picked the letter up, he couldn't seem to read it at all. The words had all crashed into each other, as if every sentence was a different train and they had all collided on a hill, creating a carnage of letters that he couldn't make any sense of. Only one word was legible, the one at the end, on its own – Maureen.

The Wolf

The telephone rang and rang. Benedict was getting impatient. Finally, just as he was about to put the receiver down, someone answered.

'Hello?' a small voice stuttered.

'Bernard, I'm phoning to speak to my daughter-in-law. You've been selfishly hogging her all weekend and I'm dying to know about Cambridge. Could I have a word?'

Silence.

'Bernard, are you there?'

Then came a strange sort of moan, the sort of noise a wolf would make if it was caught in a trap.

'Bernard?'

The noise continued. Then Benedict realised that the moan was a name – Maureen. He replaced the receiver and turned to his butler.

'Jones, I'm afraid I'm going to have to ask for an enormous favour. I need you to go to Bernard's flat, collect him and bring him here. Immediately.'

'Is Mr Bernard in some kind of distress?'

'Imagine if you will, Leonardo da Vinci putting his foot through the *Mona Lisa* in a moment of madness. Can you imagine the distress?'

'Indeed I can, sir.'

'Now double it. Double the stupidity and you double the distress.'

'Oh,' said Jones.

Dear God, thought Benedict, after Jones had set nobly out into the dark like the good Samaritan. How on earth was he going to get Bernard out of this one? He shook his head, trying hard to remain the judgemental parent. But inside, a different man was wringing his hands in despair, trying to desperately wash away his own guilt. In his heart, he knew that he was almost certainly the one to blame. He'd carelessly thrown his own chance of happiness away; why should he be so surprised to see his son doing exactly the same thing?

Hollow

Strange how the earth was still spinning – revolving slowly but surely on its axis as if nothing had happened. Much later that night, when Bernard finally crawled up Benedict's stairs, pushed open the door of the spare room and lay stretched out on the bed, he realised that everything else was carrying on as normal. It was becoming increasingly obvious that the world would not end, not tonight anyway. Which meant he would have to wake up tomorrow and face it all again. He was already dreading the morning, when the bad dream would continue. And the moment of awakening when, just for a few seconds, he would have forgotten what had happened – a few carefree moments before the memory of the letter would come crashing down on him.

And then the shame would start again. Today it had poured like rain into the drawing room through a hole in the roof. There was no stopping it. It rained on him until he was soaked right through and then more than soaked – until he was saturated with shame. Then it started solidifying, stiffening like starch, so he could feel his arms and legs hardening. And after everything had set on the outside, everything on the inside started to burn away, as if he'd been put in a furnace so hot it made his innards melt.

He didn't get into the bed; he couldn't bear to have the sheets touch his skin. Because under the skin there was nothing left – nothing inside his body at all. He was just a mould now, a mould of a man. A life-sized mould like the ones in Benedict's studio. Inside he was empty, completely hollowed out – not a bone, not a rib, not a sinew. The only reason he could walk around was because his skin had grown very hard and extremely fragile. A tap, even a gentle tap, would crack it. When, after hours of scolding, Benedict reached out to touch his arm, Bernard moved it quickly out of reach, worried it might crumble.

He lay on the bed, a hollow man, nothing but an empty shell, brittle to the touch. He couldn't blame Maureen. It wasn't the word Maureen that had done the damage; it was the other word – Cynthia. He could have explained Maureen away as a girlish crush. It was the second name that betrayed him. It was the fact that there were two women in the letter that really ruined everything.

Gone

'Are you feeling any better?'

Evie could hear her roommate padding around the bed and she could sense the concern in her voice, but she couldn't face her. She kept her head under the blanket and lay completely still.

'As long as you're not dead?' A pause. 'No one died of a broken heart, Evie.'

Under the blanket, Evie winced. *She means to be kind*, she told herself.

'I've got to go out now, but if you're feeling peckish later there's soup on the stove.' Hilda padded round the bed again. 'Right, well I'm off.' A pause. 'I hope you get better soon.'

Evie heard the sound of a scarf being pulled off a coat hook and wrapped round and round a neck, then the swish of a door opening and closing again. She was gone.

Gone. An interesting word, the hard 'g' creating a finality that suited the meaning – echoing the definitive shutting of a door, or the click of a telephone receiver. In French, it was *parti,* or *allé* but both sounded more positive somehow: there was the feeling of new departures and new adventures couched within them. *Gone* didn't just mean *left*, it meant *missing*. *Gone* conjured up the image of a mother bird looking into an empty nest, or a drunk tipping up a wine bottle to see if there was just one more drop inside. *Gone* was when a train left a minute before you got there, *'I'm*

afraid it's already gone, Miss,' leaving an empty platform
with a yawning gap onto an empty track that made you feel
so dizzy you had to rush into the waiting room. But *gone*
without the 'g' was even worse. It meant one, as in the
opposite of two, as in one person. If you put an 'l' in front,
you got lone and then you just needed that extra 'a' to
complete the jigsaw.

Three days and still no word from Bernard. Did he feel
too guilty to contact her or not guilty enough? Still there was
no point lying moping. She was missing her law lectures.

She got up, got dressed, wandered into town to find a café
for breakfast and then walked to the university. Jurisprudence
today. Her favourite. But when she got to the lecture hall the
doors were shut. An old beadle was standing outside.

'I'm afraid there's no room today.'

'No room, what do you mean?'

'We had another influx of students at the weekend.'

'I don't understand.'

'Amazing how those soldiers are still coming back. The
war ended more than two years ago, and they're still returning.'

'And?'

'And they're studying law.'

'I'm studying too.'

He smiled at her uncertainly, 'We have to prioritise, Miss.
But you could try again next week...'

Evie was completely flabbergasted. She walked slowly away
from the hall and found a bench to sit on. She sat in a daze,
trying to digest this new information. And if the lecture halls
were full, what would she do now?

'So, you're late as well!'

She looked up to see the cheery Paul Drabble bending over
her. 'Not late, just—'

'So, how about that dinner?' He peered into her face, his
warm brown eyes twinkling.

'That's kind of you, but I'm not sure about dinner. Perhaps
lunch one day.'

'Lunch then, as long as it's today,' he smiled. 'You see, I'm very keen to get to know you.'

'It's not a very good day to get to know me.'

'Why ever not?'

'I'm tired and—' she hesitated, 'sad.'

'Then I absolutely must insist on cheering you up.' He led Evie masterfully out of the quadrangle. 'I know a lovely place for lunch in town and I can tell you a bit about the buildings we pass on the way.'

She'd been fasting for days, too distressed to eat. Suddenly, despite her breakfast, Evie felt desperately hungry. Lunch at a nice restaurant was just too tempting. She needed a bit of pampering. Her heart was bruised, no, in fact squashed – completely flat, as if a steam-roller had run right over it.

The restaurant was lovely: white tablecloths with glittering table-ware; ladies looking elegant in tea-dresses and hats; fans whirring overhead for an American feel; palms in pots for French chic. They sat beside the window. The low winter sun streamed in through the windows and danced a jig in the glass chandelier. It felt like a reprieve – a break from the lodge and thinking about Bernard.

Paul Drabble may have been very keen to acquaint himself with his lunch date, but he was even keener to tell her about himself. During the starter, he recounted tales from his idyllic childhood in Shropshire; during the main he regaled her with stories from his stellar career at Shrewsbury School where he was captain of cricket; then, as pudding approached, he realised he had almost but not quite forgotten the reason for their lunch.

'Your turn, Miss Cavalier. I'm sure you're much more interesting than me.'

'Well, yes and no. I haven't been to a private school or anything, although I have worked for a bit. But I suppose the most important thing of interest is that I'm not really a Miss Cavalier. I'm a Mrs.'

Mr Drabble placed his elbows carefully on the table, either side of his raspberry pavlova; then he rested his chin on his hands and stared at Evie in puzzlement. He looked like a philosopher chewing his way through Plato's *Republic*. 'Good heavens!' he said eventually. 'So, you're a widow.'

'No—' began Evie.

'Of course, the war,' he continued, talking over her. 'Tired and sad. Isn't that what you said? How dreadful for you. I'm so sorry. It's just, I mean you look very young so I assumed, well that you hadn't been,' he paused, 'married.' He picked up his spoon and attacked his meringue with great ferocity, then he looked up at her again. 'I'm afraid this changes everything, Evie. I'm sorry about your husband, really I am, and I think you're lovely. It's just, well, I think I should come clean. The thing is, I'm not really interested in—'

'Tainted goods?'

'I don't mean it like that.'

'Oh, but you do.' Evie spoke quietly but there was a fierce look in her eyes.

'I would like an inexperienced wife,' he said lamely, 'that's all I mean.'

'Who said anything about becoming your wife? I thought we were just having lunch.' She pushed her pudding away.

'You see,' he seemed desperate to explain himself, 'I have a strong moral compass—'

But Evie had had enough. She jumped up and grabbed her purse. 'It was kind of you to buy me lunch, but I'm going to go home now.'

'Are you sure? Oh dear, I hope I haven't chased you away. Should I see you back to your lodgings?'

'There's really no need. I have my own compass,' she smiled.

Once she was safely away from the restaurant, Evie's expression changed. Her countenance took on the look of a Medusa so fierce it would have turned Paul Drabble to stone. She ran along the pavement muttering to herself. *An unjust law is no law at all.* That was the first thing he had said to her. And yet the rules he used to govern his own life were incredibly unjust. He had immediately assumed she was a widow; because the idea of a married woman dining with a single man was beyond his comprehension. But, in his eyes, a widow was spoiled, used, second-hand.

Evie kicked a stone into the road, narrowly missing a parked car. The unfairness of it all, when men could do as they pleased. She remembered Maureen's letter. *I don't care a jot if you're married.* One rule for men, another for the so-called 'fairer sex'. And his dig about 'a moral compass'. Which point on the moral compass was it when male students called their female colleagues 'Tit'?

She stormed along the street. She'd had enough of Cambridge. She still had a week to go, but she couldn't bear to stay a minute longer. She would go back to her lodge and pack. And then she would leave, for good. She'd claimed to have her own compass. Now she would have to use it. But where would it take her? Where on earth would she go next?

She marched back to the lodge and crashed around it, throwing her things into her suitcase, discarding a pair of shoes to make room for Aristotle. Just as she was about to set off, Hilda's dirty pots and pans caught her eye. She hadn't said goodbye. She tore a page out of her notebook and wrote three words.

Honeysuckle

Onion

Maple

Then she wrote a tiny *P.T.O.* at the bottom of the page. On the back, she wrote:

Nocturnal

Sharp

Sweet beneath the 'bark'.

She turned the paper over again, left it lying on the kitchen table and set out.

Two Letters and
a Telegram

Tuesday 1ˢᵗ February 1921

My dearest Phoebe,

Well, the inevitable has happened. I have discovered that Bernard has had an affair, and not just with one girl, but two. I'm an absolute idiot and I hate my idiocy almost more than I hate Bernard's infidelity. I should have known, but like an ostrich, I kept my head firmly buried in the sand.

As far as I'm concerned, our marriage is over, or at least so damaged as to be almost irreparable. My heart is torn in two, but worse than that, my ego is badly dented. I fear the dent will take much longer to mend. I can't go back to Bernard, but I can't stay in Cambridge either.

I hate this university's attitude to women and yet I've absorbed more in its lecture halls than I've learnt my whole life. Cambridge has taught me to think for myself – it has given me permission to make my own mind up. And I have learnt the most important lesson: I know almost nothing. Still, I have the rest of my life to change that. Books will be my new love now. They at least are dependable.

I might go home for a bit and then I'll probably travel. Everyone seems to these days and I have a nest egg I can draw on. I know it's eccentric to disappear on one's own, but perhaps I am eccentric, or at least a misfit. I feel as if my whole life has been heading in the wrong direction. At least abroad I can reset my compass and work out a way out of this mess.

I envy you your Mr Hazlitt. You have an equal relationship; I've only ever been Bernard's appendage. He is the artist, I am the adoring wife, or worse, the quiet muse, the stay-at-home inspiration, kept out of the way.

I must stop, I'm becoming bitter and invective.

Phoebe, I hope our paths cross again,

Evie xx

Tuesday 1ˢᵗ February 1921

Dear Bernard,

I owe you an apology. I opened your post again, this time by accident. I'm also sorry for running away without giving you a chance to defend yourself. To be honest, I just couldn't face you. Besides there seemed so little to say, apart from the obvious – we've made a terrible mistake.

I think once, and not so very long ago, I loved you. Perhaps you even loved me. We had a physical love anyway: erratic, jealous, sometimes tempestuous. But that passionate torrent seems to have suddenly dried up, for me at least. And there's nothing behind the waterfall – I've looked.

I hate failure and I hesitate to say this is the end. But I for one need a definite break. I've decided to go away for a while, perhaps a long while. Don't try to find me, don't try to write – if I change my mind I'll get in touch.

Evie.

TELEGRAM TO:

MISS DAISY PRITCHARD 79 CHARLES STREET
MAYFAIR LONDON SW

2.2.1921 WATERLOO

GOING AWAY. LOTS OF REASONS. LOOK
AFTER BERNARD. EVIE.

A Visit from Daisy

She should have worn different shoes. The ones she'd been trying on when the telegram arrived were new, expensive and just not up to the job. They were shoes for standing around at a cocktail party and were not designed for walking anywhere. The heel of the right shoe fell off just as she reached the studio; Daisy slipped the shoe off and used it to bang ferociously on the door. The shoe made the most terrific noise, so it was worth the sacrifice.

No one came.

'I know you're in there!' she yelled.

Still no one. She banged again.

Eventually the door opened a crack and Bernard's face peered out. He looked dreadful, swollen eyes and a puffed-up face.

'I've had a telegram from Evie!' Daisy reached into her pocket, brought it out and waved it in front of his face. 'Going away. Lots of reasons.' She stuffed it back in her pocket. 'How many reasons, Bernard?' She spat the words at him and he retreated slightly, back inside. 'And don't think I'm going to look after you!' she continued. 'You dreadful, horrible man.'

Bernard's face reappeared, as if he wanted or needed to hear the torrent of abuse, like a man in the stocks, welcoming whatever is thrown at him because he believes he deserves it. Behind him, Daisy could see the dark studio.

'Who've you got in there today?'

'No one.'

'Oh no one!' shrieked Daisy scornfully. 'Of course not. Ha, ha, ha, ha.' She gave an over-rehearsed laugh, like a wife in an opera who has just discovered her husband's latest ruse. Then her voice changed. 'Well, whoever she is,' she shouted into the darkness, 'she's a fool. And she'd do well to stay away from you!' Daisy's voice had started strong, the voice of a righteous judge, but as she went on, another voice appeared, a voice full of hurt on behalf of a friend.

'I think you'd better come in and see for yourself.' He opened the door for her, then turned and went back inside.

One shoe off, one shoe on, Daisy hobbled in after him. But there was nobody there. Just a canvas balanced on an easel: a picture of Maureen, half-finished.

'She's got clothes on,' observed Daisy.

'Yes. Her parents commissioned it.' Bernard sighed. 'No more nudes, it'll be still lifes from now on.'

'So, is it Maureen?'

He sighed again. 'I had a very brief fling with Maureen. And then, well in the past, long before my marriage, I used to flirt with Cynthia. And the other day, while she was sitting for me and I'd had too much to drink...' His voice trailed off.

'You betrayed Evie!'

'Evie was away. I thought I could cope. But I couldn't.' He gestured helplessly towards the picture of Maureen. 'I'm the fool, possibly the most foolish man alive, but I'm not the heartless villain you think I am. I've made two terrible mistakes and,' his voice trembled, 'I may never recover from them, but I love her.'

'Damn you, Bernard. I'm getting married in the spring – and now she won't be there.'

'Surely she'll be back by spring?' gasped Bernard.

'I think she'll go to Europe,' Daisy said, half to herself. 'She was always talking about France.'

'Does she like France? If I'd known—'

'But that's the point. Don't you see? You hardly knew her. And now she's gone.'

Not the Best Man

'Would you like another half, sir?'

Toby glanced down at his empty beer glass.

'Not just now. I'm waiting for someone. Thank you, anyway.'

'That's fine, sir.'

The barman went back to washing glasses and Toby went back to playing with his beermat. Bernard was late as usual, but for once Toby hadn't noticed. He was too busy working out what he should do. This was obviously the night to break the news to Bernard. It was the perfect opportunity – they were only meeting for a drink, so there would be no silent dinner to plough through afterwards; and they were on their own – no Harold or Archie to distract them. They were meeting in Bernard's local pub so there would be no one they knew swanning over to ask for a 'light' or enquire after Toby's mother. Well then, he would just have to bite the bullet and tell him straight. But how? How did one tell a chap that one no longer wanted him to be one's 'best man'?

It was wretched for Bernard. First Evie had disappeared and now it would look as if he was deserting him too. But it wouldn't look right to use a man known as a 'philanderer' to witness his marriage to Daisy. It gave everyone the wrong impression – especially Daisy. Not to mention Daisy's parents...

'Sorry I'm late.'

Toby looked up startled. Bernard had appeared. He looked like death warmed up – his complexion completely white with black rings under his eyes.

'I fell asleep. Not really sleeping at night, so I tend to nod off during the day...'

'Would you rather leave it?'

'No.' Bernard caught the barman's eye, 'My usual, but no chaser.'

'Certainly, sir. On the tab?'

Bernard nodded, then turned to his friend, 'Toby? My shout for once.'

'I'm fine.' Toby couldn't bear the thought of Bernard buying him a drink, he felt guilty enough.

Bernard went up to the bar and picked up his freshly-poured pint. He raised the glass to his lips and started to drink it down, greedily, thirstily. Toby could hear him gulping the beer like a fish. When it was half gone, he turned and came back with it to Toby.

'Cheers,' he said, without smiling.

Toby didn't know what to say.

'I'm glad you've come,' Bernard began, as if the meeting had been his idea, 'because I wanted to let you know that I don't want to be your best man anymore. Or at least I'd rather not. I mean, I don't think I'm the best man for the job.'

There was a silence while both men miserably considered the unintentional pun.

'That's fine,' said Toby, eventually. 'I'll ask Archie or Harold.' He hadn't got round to working out an alternative. This was the outcome he'd been hoping for, but instead of being relieved, Toby felt terribly sad.

'It's just, I'm not a very good example, right now.'

Again, Toby didn't know what to say.

'I've let everyone down. Especially Evie.' Bernard lifted his glass and drained his beer.

'Why, Bernard?'

Bernard shrugged. 'I don't know. It's that thing, isn't it, that artist's self-obsession – a ridiculous assumption that I deserved things without having to look after them, just because I paint. I mean I wanted the girl, the beautiful girl and the nice home to put her in. And then when I'd got it, when I had it all, I wanted more. I wanted to go out and leave the beautiful girl at home. I wanted to know she was there, waiting for me. And, for a while she was. Then, suddenly she wasn't. And it's all my fault.'

'It must be hard,' said Toby.

Bernard gave a twisted sort of smile. 'Another drink?'

Dried Up

After Evie left, everything got harder – much harder. The paint almost dried up in the tubes and he had to stamp on them to get anything out. The brushes seemed to be constantly stuck together and no amount of careful washing could stop their ends splaying outwards. Even if a brush was new, it quickly got gummed up like all the others. The paintings themselves seemed to take an age to finish; each canvas stretched away into the distance like a field of snow. He worked slowly and clumsily in one corner, gradually scratching his way across the surface.

And then the pictures took an age to dry; the bit of paint that he managed to get onto the canvas always tried to slip off again. It would stay slippery for days and then it would turn tacky, sticking to his fingers if he dared to touch it. All this meant that it took a long time to finish a painting but, even when it was finished, it still looked half-baked, as if what he'd wanted to say was only half-said; as if he'd stopped mid-sentence or turned his back on the viewer halfway through.

Despite his unsatisfactory results, or perhaps because of them, Bernard worked harder. Besides, there was nothing to go home for. The flat seemed to have grown in size and it was now much too big for one person. Every footstep echoed eerily as if he was in a cathedral and it was easy to get lost in the enormous drawing room or the unending corridor. The only good thing about being at home was the telephone. There was always the chance she might ring. He got the telephone wire extended so it could sit by his bed and he would sleep with one ear cocked all night, like a mother listening for a baby's cry. The telephone rang quite a lot, but always in his dreams. He would shake himself awake and stumble to pick up the receiver in the dark.

'Evie, is that you?' But there was never anyone there.

Of course, *he* could have called *her*. There was a window of at least a few days when she would almost certainly have gone home. But the thought of speaking to Mr or Mrs Brunton made his blood run cold. What could he say to the parents of a young bride betrayed by her husband so early in her marriage? And right now, they would be very angry and they might say something that would make things more difficult in the long run. 'Don't contact her again, don't phone, don't write, don't visit.' That's what he would say, if he was Evie's father.

And he could have written to her in Devon. But writing terrified him, because none of his feelings stood still long enough to describe them accurately. He was on an ice floe, moving quickly along a coastline he didn't recognise. Whatever he wrote today would be different tomorrow. Putting down his thoughts in black and white didn't seem possible when they were just a blur.

So, instead of contacting Devon, he waited for her to come back from it. Twice a day he made a pilgrimage to Waterloo station for the afternoon and then the evening train. Twice a day he would buy a platform ticket and wait hopefully on the platform where the train from Seaton Junction was due to come steaming in. It became a ritual: arriving at the station in plenty of time; running like a mad man if he was even slightly late; checking the platform number even though it never changed; finding the best possible position so he could see everyone who got off. Then he would stand and wait.

The last minute was always the slowest. If the train was delayed, he would wring his hands and get irritated and jumpy. Finally, he would hear it puffing along the track and his heart would beat faster and faster and then there would be a squeal of breaks and it would be in the platform and everything would speed up: the steam from the engine, the slamming of doors, the rush of porters, the dash of travellers. This was the hard bit, trying to check every single passenger, looking for a flash of fair hair among the crowd of people making for the exit. They came quickly, like the tide rushing up the mouth of an estuary, and it was easy to get swept away.

Sometimes he stood strong and firm, like a breakwater, letting them race past; sometimes he would swim along beside them. Once or twice, he was sure he'd seen her and he'd run after a young woman carrying a suitcase, racing up behind her, tapping her on the shoulder, almost tripping her up in his eagerness. But the face that turned was always unfamiliar. He would back off, apologising, retreating, disappearing down the platform the way he'd come.

After a few weeks, his pilgrimage stuttered and then stopped. He confined himself to the studio and there he painted all day and most of the evening. And slowly but surely, like a child labouring over his homework, he produced the work for his next exhibition. It took weeks. And, when the paintings were finished, when he laid them all out along the walls of his studio, he realised that he didn't like a single one.

He marched out of the studio and down the street to the Tate. He stood for a long time in front of *The Wrong Envelope*, but she didn't look round at him. Despite *her* indifference, *he* felt an overwhelming mix of emotions: the shock of the haircut; the beauty of the mole it revealed; the anger in the long pale neck; the tension in the hands holding a letter of rejection – a letter destined for someone else. Knowing how the letter had hurt Evie brought back all the shame and guilt he had felt at the time. It added to the remorse he already felt, layering itself on top, like a fresh coat of paint on a canvas already thick with it. And if he looked at her for long enough, her hands seemed to tremble.

He rushed away, out of the gallery, back to his studio. The new pictures were leaning against the wall; every one as dry as dust, as if he'd painted them with sand. A strange fury swept over him: a realisation that the beauty of *The Wrong Envelope* originated not from him, but from her.

He raked around at the back of his studio and found another picture: an enormous canvas, the biggest he had ever painted. It was a life-size portrait of Evie. Evie in her old life, Evie the post lady, soaking wet from a rainstorm. He dragged it out and leaned it against the chaise longue. He considered it for a few moments, gazing at her blue serge jacket, her cheeks flushed from the rain, the light dancing in the raindrops dripping from her hat. Then he took his biggest and thickest brush, covered it with white and began to paint over it. He started slowly and carefully, beginning in the middle of the picture where Evie's hands were opening her postbag. He gritted his teeth and smeared white paint onto the canvas, over the top of her long, pale fingers. It looked dreadful – a white streak, ruining everything. He recoated his brush and worked his way up the painting, up the buttons on her jacket, up to her neck and over her face. After her face disappeared, the brush took on a life of its own, flying in all directions – up and down, left then right, until the painting was completely white.

He thought that would be it, that he would finally be free of her. But as soon as the canvas was blank, another picture started appearing on it, slowly tracing itself on the fresh coat of paint. He stood watching the lines draw themselves, sketching out another figure. A new Evie was replacing the old one: bolder, wilder, more arresting – so beautiful it was frightening.

A Modern Eye

'So glad you could come.' Carruthers spun around with the champagne bottle, poised to fill up the art critic's glass. He was pretty sure that this was the reviewer from *Country Lives*, the one who had written such a wonderful piece on Bernard's first big show.

'Is there another room?'

'I beg your pardon?' Carruthers was confused. 'What do you mean another room? This gallery only has two rooms.'

'Oh.' The critic looked around in bemusement. 'In that case, which bit is *modern*?'

'Well, all of it I suppose,' said Carruthers, but his heart was in his mouth.

The reviewer glanced at the gallery walls, 'Old hat, if you ask me.'

'I do hope you're not being a little hasty with your judgements,' said Carruthers quickly. 'Mr Cavalier has a fine reputation—'

'Had. These nudes are deadly dull and the still lives are, well, rather flat.'

The stinging assessment sounded frighteningly like a line from a review. Carruthers gulped, 'How could we help you change your mind?'

The reviewer thought for a minute. 'There were two portraits in the last show – two very interesting girls. One had long hair, the other short. At the time, I thought they were two different people; now I'm not so sure. There was an intensity in both pictures and a feeling of tension and excitement that I don't see here.' His eyes flitted around the gallery again as if they might have missed something. 'Where is she now?'

Carruthers gulped again, 'Perhaps you should ask the artist himself,' he said, gesturing to where Bernard was standing chatting to another reviewer.

'Another time.' A pause. 'Well thank you,' he said, handing his glass to Carruthers. 'I'll be off.'

'So, Bernard, how do you think that went?' asked Carruthers, as the last art reviewer disappeared into the evening.

'All right, I think.'

'The critic from *Country Lives* wasn't so sure. He didn't seem to think it was very *modern.*'

'We can't expect everyone to be one hundred per cent positive.'

'No,' said Carruthers, doubtfully. 'Do you happen to have anything of Evie?'

'Only one thing, but it's enormous. Anyway, I did it for me.'

'You mean the life-sized picture of her as a post lady? That would be marvellous. Any chance we could add it to the exhibition?'

'I painted over it.'

'You painted over it!' Carruthers put one hand over his eyes.

'I painted the new one over it.'

'Is it of Evie?' Carruthers looked up, hopeful again.

'Yes, but you wouldn't know.'

'Well, that's no good then.'

'Yes, it is, I mean it is good. But I was planning to hold on to it.'

'Look Bernard, I know you're missing her, but can I remind you that you can't pine on an empty stomach. You need to eat. We both do.'

There was an uneasy silence, during which Bernard's stomach started rumbling. 'I'll go and look out that picture,' he said eventually. 'But I'll need a van to get it here.' He put down his champagne glass and started lumbering towards the door.

Carruthers watched him. 'How is Evie, anyway?'

'Don't you mean *where* is Evie?'

'You don't know where she is?'

'Nope. Somewhere in Europe. That's all I know.'

'And how do you know that?'

'Daisy gets postcards.'

Postcards. Little squares of time and place; two times really – the period when the city was built and then the moment when the tourist visited. Postcards. Strange objects, flying back from another country – from hot to cold. And always the same message: *This place is sunnier, older and prettier than home.* And then the same smug line: *Wish you were here!*

When the first postcard appeared on Daisy's mantelpiece: a picture of La Tour Eiffel; Bernard knew instinctively it was from Evie. He was having coffee with Daisy in her drawing room and, although he'd never taken sugar with his coffee before, he suddenly fancied some.

'Of course,' said Daisy.

But instead of ringing for the maid, she'd gone herself. And she was a while.

Bernard had rushed over to the mantelpiece, picked up the card and quickly turned it over.

Paris. Sun 13th Feb

What rain! Funny, I never imagined Paris wet. But it doesn't matter, because for the last few days I have been lost in the Louvre. Extraordinaire! Evie xx P.S. How's Bernard?

The last line was so sweet it went straight to his heart, like a dagger. Then Daisy had reappeared with the sugar, but the words were already engraved upon his memory. And a few days later, there was another one. La Baie des Anges, Nice. Beautiful houses swept round a pebbled beach and a bright blue sea. Again, the sugar was missing and Bernard needed some for a 'pick-me-up'. Again, Daisy took her time fetching it.

Nice. Wed 23rd Feb

Guess what, Daisy – I've seen Matisse! Can you believe it, I passed him on the Promenade des Anglais! I was too shy to speak, but it was thrilling. He lives here now, and no wonder. I have never seen such light – dancing on the sea, dancing in my mind. I don't think I can ever leave! Evie xx P.S. How's Bernard?

By the time Daisy was back with the sugar bowl, he'd memorised the message and it sat in his heart, alongside the one from Paris. At night, he would recite them to himself the way other people said their prayers; the words felt warm and comforting in the dark night of his bedroom.

The next time, it was a picture of Florence but, when Bernard tried to pick it up, it opened out into a concertina of pictures, each one a different painting from the Uffizi. His hands trembled with excitement. Evie's spidery writing went on and on as long as his arm.

Florence. Thurs March 17th

Dearest Daisy, Well, I finally made it to the most beautiful city in the world. I adore Italy, but it doesn't seem to agree with me and I've been a bit off colour lately. Much better today. I've just been to the Uffizi and am now sitting in a café in the Piazza della Signoria. The sun is shining of course – this is Italy! An occasional pigeon flies in to pinch bits of cake, but otherwise everything is perfect. I can't begin to describe the Uffizi

Suddenly, Daisy was back. 'Get your hands off, Bernard!' she cried.

But it was terrible not being able to finish the letter, not knowing what Evie liked about the Uffizi, and also, not knowing if she'd finished her message in the usual way. Soon after that, Daisy and Toby got married and suddenly Daisy was too busy to ask Bernard round for coffee. Besides things weren't quite the same between him and Toby, and Bernard felt awkward dropping in on them. So, where was Evie now?

A Cheque

717, King's Road, Chelsea, London, SW.
Sunday 10ᵗʰ April 1921

Dear Evie,

I hope this letter finds you well. I am writing for a couple of reasons, but firstly I wanted to tell you about 'A Modern Eye', Bernard's latest exhibition at the Carruthers Gallery.

Unfortunately, most of the pictures in the exhibition are less than average. To quote Country Lives: *'dull nudes and flat still lifes.' However, there is one marvellous picture – of you I'm afraid, called* Girl in a Bath. *The painting is enormous and completely beautiful. There is no face, or not a recognisable one anyway, but it is quite obvious that, whoever the bather is, the artist is completely in love with her.*

At the opening yesterday, there was much murmuring about the picture as people tried to guess who the girl might be. One of Bernard's models, a girl called Cynthia, got drunk and demanded to know why Bernard had never painted her like that. It was very awkward and in the end she had to be ushered out of the gallery. She pointed at Bernard as she went and shouted: 'Never again!' like the bad fairy in Sleeping Beauty. It was quite a drama.

I'm sending this letter to Devon in the hope that it may be forwarded on to you as I understand you're travelling. I think it's a marvellous idea, but your nest egg must be suffering. I'm going to send a cheque to your father, made out to you, for the sum of £500, in the hope that he will deposit it on your behalf. I'll tell him that it's money you lent to Bernard. Mr Brunton won't like that story – but he'll believe it. Don't worry, it's not 'damages', it's payment for a job you did for me once. It would break my heart were you to spend it wisely.

Missing you and hope we will meet again soon,

Benedict

Unopened

The letter was waiting for her when she went down for breakfast, propped up against the coffee pot. The envelope was a mess: her Devon address crossed out and the address of her Florence pension scrawled over the top in her mother's hesitant hand. As for the writing underneath, at first glance, she thought it was Bernard's, but when she picked the envelope up and hurriedly turned it over, she saw Benedict's address on the back. What did she expect? She'd warned him not to contact her. She'd told him not to write. Besides, what could he say?

The Ponte Vecchio seemed the best place to do it. The Arno flowed at a tremendous rate under the bridge so the river would carry it quickly away before she could change her mind. She stood in the early morning sunshine, leaning on the stones of the parapet. People rushed past her, calling to each other in Italian, their melodic voices blending with the rush of the river, soothing her, causing a hypnotic confusion of sound that allowed her to lean over and drop the letter into the water. A blur of white, then it was gone.

The Times

'Where on earth has it got to?' Mrs Brunton was ransacking the cupboards for sugar. Behind her a saucepan full of apples boiled angrily on the stove. Mr Brunton sat serenely having his breakfast, *The Times* spread out on the table in front of him.

'Oh dash it, I'll have to nip out and get some.' Mrs Brunton took the pan off the range and picked up her shopping basket. 'Back soon.'

'Yes, dear.' Mr Brunton listened for the click of the back door and then the back gate. At last – peace and quiet. He perused the *Foreign News*, then the *Court and Circular*. Finally, he turned to the *Arts* section.

TATE ACQUIRES SECOND CAVALIER PAINTING

The Tate gallery have just purchased another picture by the London artist Bernard Cavalier. The painting, entitled simply Girl in a Bath *was exhibited at the Carruthers Gallery, Cork Street, earlier this month. Mr Taylor, Head Curator at the Tate, said he was very excited to be able to acquire such an important work by such a young artist.*

Speaking to The Times *yesterday, Mr Taylor said: 'Cavalier is the British answer to the late Impressionists. Bathing is a theme previously tackled by Cézanne and*

Degas. Cavalier has brought an energy to the subject that is both new and familiar. Firstly, the enormity of the painting – six feet by four, gives the bather a gigantesque stature, dwarfing the viewer and plunging him headfirst into the intimate scene. Secondly, the way the bather is engulfed in waves of light creates a refracted jumble of limbs that is both balletic and unsettling. Her face is featureless, yet Cavalier manages to convey an expression of both abandon and despair – a feeling that the bather is being swept away, not just by the bathwater but by life itself.'

After the runaway success of his first show, Cavalier became something of a phenomenon in the capital. Interest in the artist had been waning in recent months; now this new picture has caused a new flurry of excitement...

Mr Brunton tore out the page, screwed it up into a tiny ball and stuffed it in the rubbish bucket under the sink, hiding it under some apple peelings. Mrs Brunton looked quizzically at the mangled newspaper, when she got back from the shops.

'Marmalade,' he explained. 'It got covered in marmalade. I had to rip a page out.'

'I hope you're not wasting it, I've only two jars left.' A pause. 'I notice Bernard has got a new show, I wonder if Evie knows.'

'I hope you're not intending to go?'

'Not on my own, dear.'

Fish out of Water

The annoying thing about Bernard's latest exhibition was that there was only one good picture in it. Of course, this one picture was marvellous and would soon join *The Wrong Envelope* at the Tate, securing both Bernard's reputation as an artist and his own as an agent. But a painting could only be sold once, and if it was the only good painting, then that didn't leave much hope for the others.

Carruthers leaned back on his chair, lifted his feet up onto his desk, put his head back and shut his eyes. Almost immediately, the gallery door opened with a loud ding and an elderly gentleman walked in. He was tall, with a pronounced stoop, grey hair but an attractive face: a long straight nose that divided it exactly in half with a pleasing symmetry. He looked like a retired accountant, a man who was careful, particularly with money. There would be no sale this afternoon. Carruthers sighed as he heaved himself up off the desk and went to greet him.

'Is the artist here today?' asked the man.

'I'm afraid not. He's at the studio, but I could get someone to fetch him if you wanted?'

'No, no,' said the man. 'That won't be necessary.' He turned as if he was about to look at the first painting, then glanced back. 'Thank you, anyway,' he smiled.

Carruthers realised that he had just been dismissed. How intriguing. He disappeared into the second gallery and then he poked his head back around the corner. The man had returned to the door and was making furtive gestures with his hand to someone on the other side of the street. As he watched, a lady, in her mid to late fifties, came stealing across the road. She had a round, tired looking face. Her hair was greyish, but it had almost certainly once been blonde and it was tied up in a bun. She was wearing dowdy clothes, but there was a vague dreaminess about her that was rather appealing. So, who were these two people who wanted to avoid, rather than meet, the artist? Carruthers came back out of the second gallery, into the first and approached the couple.

'Oh, I thought you were on your own!' he said, feigning surprise, 'but you've brought your wife Mr—?'

'Smith.'

'Mr Smith.' Carruthers smiled at the man and then beamed at his wife: 'Delighted to meet you, Mrs Smith.'

Mrs Smith gave a pretty little giggle.

'And do you know the artist, Bernard Cavalier?'

Mr and Mrs Smith glanced uneasily at each other as if they weren't sure if they knew him or not.

'Don't worry, most people aren't sure if they really know Bernard. He's an enigma, even to me.'

Mrs Smith smiled nervously but Mr Smith was already busy looking at the paintings. He worked through them meticulously, starting with the one by the door and then moving on to the others: one by one; slowly, steadily; in the correct order; scanning, inspecting, digesting, like a spider might approach a web full of flies. He could only remember one other person who had viewed an exhibition in this way – Evie Cavalier, or Brunton as she was when she first came to London. Were these Evie's parents? He inspected them again. Evie's blonde hair might come from Mrs Smith, along with that dreamy air. And the symmetrical features and long straight nose could be from Mr Smith, together with the organised and comprehensive inspection of the paintings. Yes, Evie was almost certainly an interesting mix of these two people: tall and fair, floaty yet methodical.

Partly because he was intrigued, and partly to annoy Mr Smith, Carruthers followed the couple around the gallery like a guardian angel. Mrs Smith skated across from right to left and back again, glancing over her shoulder at previous paintings and looking on to the next ones, as if she wasn't sure where to begin but didn't want to miss anything.

'Do you like the still lifes?' he asked, catching up with her in front of a picture of a vase of daffodils.

'They're,' she hesitated, searching for the right word, 'a bit still,' she finished apologetically.

What a perceptive comment! Carruthers couldn't feel wounded by it; it was so 'spot on'. He remembered how Evie had made similarly disarming observations on her visit to Bernard's previous show. So, this is where she got her incisive ideas – from her delightfully dithery mother. What an intriguing family. He couldn't wait to see her reaction to *Girl in a Bath*.

There was a loud 'hummmph' from around the corner. Mr Smith, who was following the map in the catalogue, had got there first and was standing glaring at the naked bather. An obvious reaction from a conservative father. Carruthers didn't waste any time assessing it. Instead he waited with baited breath for Mrs Smith to wander around the corner. Eventually she appeared and looked up at the enormous picture of her daughter – all legs and arms and bath water, everything dancing with an extraordinary fluidity. She stood, rooted to the spot, staring.

He sidled up to her, 'This one isn't so *still*, is it?'

'No.'

Then, to his dismay, enormous tears appeared in the corners of her eyes and ran down her cheeks, transforming her into one of those angels that gaze on the sorrows of the world and silently weep. Carruthers hurried away.

He sat at his desk until he heard the doorbell ding again. Then he got up and wandered back through to find Evie's father still standing there, perusing his guide book. He looked up.

'I don't suppose you know a reasonably priced hotel? Reasonably central, with decent rooms and good beds, not too soft, not too hard, and a reasonable breakfast?'

'No,' said Carruthers. Then he had an unreasonable idea. 'Why don't you stay with the artist, Mr Smith?'

'I don't think so,' said Mr Smith. And then he was gone.

Less than a minute later, the doorbell dinged again. A tall, thin woman – what Carruthers normally termed a 'spindly spinster', came in, except she wasn't a spinster because, leaning on her arm, was a balding man in a dog collar.

'Good afternoon,' said the balding man. He had a pleasant face and a humpty dumpty smile and Carruthers warmed to him immediately. 'I don't usually have to lean on my wife,' he explained, 'but London is so exhausting and my legs feel weary.'

'Oh dear,' said Carruthers, amused by how a man could use the word *weary* when he wasn't yet forty.

'We just had to come, you see we are friends of the artist.'

'I see.'

'Which means we have neither the brains nor the funds to buy anything.'

'No matter.' Carruthers waved his hand magnanimously, as if forgiving them.

'My husband is also an artist,' smiled the girl.

'Not at all, I tinker. But we haven't introduced ourselves. I'm Robert Hazlitt and this is my wife, Phoebe.'

'A charming name – Phoebe,' said Carruthers.

'Isn't it?' agreed Robert. 'A charming name for a charming girl,' he said, looking into her eyes, rimmed with spectacles.

Phoebe blushed and looked terribly pretty, all of a sudden.

'Well, I must leave you both to browse.'

'Please don't. We will need all the help we can understanding this "high art"!' Robert grinned cheekily.

And so Carruthers accompanied the couple on their tour of the first gallery and tried to breathe some life into the still lifes and they listened politely to his observations on light and shade and Robert murmured 'Quite, quite,' in all the right places.

When they went into the second gallery and saw *Girl in a Bath* they both gasped.

'Absolutely marvellous!' cried Robert.

'Heavenly!' cried Phoebe.

'But my darling, it could have been you!' hooted the vicar, and he collapsed on top of his wife, making a strange sort of braying noise, breathing in and out like a demented bellows.

'I don't understand,' began Carruthers.

'Phoebe is an old *flame* of Bernard's,' the Reverend Hazlitt explained.

'Really?' Carruthers was astounded.

'Correspondent,' corrected Phoebe.

'Imagine the look on my parishioners' faces if we put that up in the vicarage!' Robert guffawed, throwing his head back, releasing more bellowing brays, or braying bellows. Carruthers joined in, it was impossible not to. They brayed and bellowed for a couple of minutes and then Robert looked thoughtfully at the picture.

'I knew he was a fool to let Phoebe go – but Evie too?' He shook his head and grew serious.

Carruthers felt suddenly stricken with worry, as if the clergyman had lifted the curtain on a tragic play. 'And how would you define a fool, exactly?'

Robert shrugged his shoulders, 'Someone who throws all their blessings away.'

1922

New Love

When did it happen, this extraordinary love – sensual and fierce, yet pure in its passion, like a flame that burnt everything up, making it hard to remember the way things were, *before*. But it didn't matter, for now everything was *after*. After London. After Cambridge. After Bernard.

With Bernard, she had measured her love out carefully, weighing it by the ounce, believing it to be as precious as gold, taking bits off the scales again if she felt she had doled out too much, tutting if she thought an extra sliver wasn't appreciated. Now she threw love about, spade loads of it, like a fireman stoking a fire on a train, shovelling it into the furnace, feeling the train speeding away, carrying the two of them far from everything else. Evie had never felt like this before. No one had ever consumed her soul like this – completely.

The Ghost

Benedict Cavalier had many theories about Art. He liked to expound them at the end of a dinner party when the men retired to pass the port, or the snooker room was filled with the pleasant smell of cigar smoke. His favourite theory was that the most creative ideas always hit the subconscious mind before the conscious brain. Some artistic visions, he argued, were so arresting, so life changing, that the subconscious could feel them approaching, just as animals could sense an approaching storm.

One afternoon in early January, Benedict sensed one of those moments. He was sitting in Fortnum's, waiting for Penelope, when he felt a slight zing in the air, a feeling of tingling down his spine and a strange sense of déjà vu. He waited expectantly for the astonishingly brilliant idea or realisation that usually accompanied these spooky feelings, but nothing happened. Slightly disappointed, he relaxed again and looked absent-mindedly around him.

Penelope was late and it was becoming a habit. She used to be slightly late, then the *slightly* changed to *quite* and then *really*. Today she was really late and he knew there was probably a reason, but he couldn't face poking around to find out why. He had either done something wrong or not done something right. That was the annoying part, having to guess that he was in trouble, and then guess why.

Still, there were worse places to be kept waiting and Fortnum's was sparkling today. He loved the restaurant for its perfect fusion of past and present: the timeless waiters with their silver trays and the fashionably dressed ladies, short bobs swinging jauntily around long necks. Necks were delightful; he just couldn't get enough of them. And then there was the piano and clarinet duo, playing 'Beale Street Blues', bringing a bit of modern America into old London town, the clarinet slurring its way up and down the melody like a lazy cat.

He cocked his ear to listen, leaning back in his chair, reaching into his pocket for a cigar, when suddenly, out of the corner of his eye, he saw a tiny fist. It poked in and out of a Moses basket, and it seemed to appear and then disappear and then reappear again in time to the music, as if the clarinettist was a snake charmer and the little clenched fist was the head of a snake. It was an intriguing sight and Benedict paid close attention. He had already experienced the feeling of anticipation, the warning of *déjà vu* and he was primed for a full-blown artistic vision, although it had never happened in Fortnum's before. There was no one sitting with the baby, the mother was presumably powdering her nose or paying the bill. Benedict thought he would take a peek at the little mite.

He got to his feet, ambled over to the basket and peered inside. And there, right before his eyes, in broad daylight, was a ghost: the ghost of his son, Bernard. The same long limbs, folded up in the basket, the same shock of flaming red hair, the same plump, rosy cheeks. It was the perfect fusion of past and present; the old Baby Bernard had been somehow reincarnated into this new little chap. He stared into the basket and the baby stared back with the same eyes and in the same unflinching manner that had been Bernard's hallmark. Benedict's heart did the most dramatic somersault. This was either a ghost or Bernard had a baby boy. But it couldn't be a ghost, could it? Which meant it was real. But why hadn't Bernard told him?

'Sorry, sorry, sorry!' Penelope came sailing towards him, arms outstretched, making a noise so people would notice both her and her new mink coat.

Benedict turned to greet her, 'Hello, darling.'

'Well, what do you think?' Penelope gave a little twirl.

'Lovely darling,' and then his head turned back towards the basket.

But the baby had gone. He scanned the restaurant, craning his neck around all the pillars and potted palms. No baby. Then he suddenly saw the basket being carried out of the restaurant and down the stairs.

'If you could excuse me for just one second, my dear.'

Benedict gestured vaguely to their table and shot after the baby. But the place suddenly seemed to be teeming with people. Bags, coats and waiters kept getting in his way, and by the time he had extricated himself from the throng he was at least half a minute behind the basket. He raced to the stairs and then saw the lift. Which one: lift or stairs? Which was quicker? There was a growing sense of panic welling up in his chest and it was only when he got into the lift that he knew why. If Bernard hadn't told him he had a baby boy, it was quite possibly because he didn't know he had one.

In his rush, he pressed *Up* instead of *Down* and the lift started lumbering slowly up to the next floor, creaking its way up the lift shaft like an old man going upstairs. His panic increased. When they got to the next floor there were four women, two children and a pram all waiting to get in. Benedict squeezed out of the lift, pushing past them all, and ran for the stairs. Down, down he ran, reaching the landing with the restaurant and then down, down again, across the busy shop on the ground floor and through the swing doors onto the street. But there was no sign of a baby. The ghost of Bernard had completely disappeared and taken his mother with him.

The realisation that he had lost both mother and baby hit him hard, as if he had run into a wall. Benedict leaned against a street lamp, fighting for breath. A terrible pain was starting in his chest and shoulders. He hunched himself up against the lamp post as if trying to protect his chest and, when that didn't work, he slid to the ground and bowed his head into the centre of the pain, willing it to stop. But the pain got worse and soon he was lying on the ground, bent over himself like a comma, his head curling into his body. He could hear people running up and the sound of talking and he knew he'd been taken ill – very ill. And a bit of him, the *déjà vu* bit, stood outside himself and watched the scene unfold, observing the ambulance arrive and take Benedict Cavalier away. And the bit that was left stood and puzzled over the incident and tried to work out why.

That night, in Charing Cross Hospital, Benedict was haunted by two ghosts. An impossibly tall woman came floating up to his bed, carrying a baby. She put it onto his chest, then turned and floated away again. The baby immediately started growing bigger and bigger until he could hardly breathe.

'Sophia!' he cried, but his chest was crushed by the enormous child and his cry came out as little more than a whisper.

'Don't worry, sir, we'll have you home in no time,' said a voice beside his ear.

'Jones, I need to talk to Bernard.'

'When you're stronger, sir. When you're safely home again.'

The Fortune Teller

For a long time after her return from Europe, Evie missed Nice. At night, the curtained window of her tiny room would transform itself into the shuttered window of her Pension in Nice's old town. She would lie in bed and remember the dark Mediterranean, lapping a few yards behind the shutters. She would think about the way the sun rose and blinded everything with its perfect whiteness; a slow blindness, gradually gaining in intensity, until it was hard to fix the colour of things. Even the sea, a pale blue at dawn, would dissolve into silver. For the rest of the day nothing was still; everything was dancing and, if you half shut your eyes, you could see why. Great rays of light were slanting down on the city, like spotlights on a stage, illuminating the dancers.

That first morning, she'd been woken ridiculously early by the marché aux fleurs. She'd lain in the dark, listening to the low chuntering of conversation, the purr of delivery vans and the sound of trestle tables being dragged along cobbles. Then suddenly, as if a curtain had gone up, the air was filled with cries. She leapt out of bed and flung back the shutters. There was the flower market, full of life and colour and, beyond it, the sea; still pale blue but starting to metamorphosise into a mermaid's tail of silver scales. She leaned on the crumbling windowsill and drank in the light, feeling it seep right through her, into her bones.

Evie knew she wasn't the first English girl to fall for the Riviera. The smart London set came in droves, mainly to Cannes and Antibes, but some were bound to float on to Nice. She had read about them in *Country Lives*: the Gambling set, the Polo set, the Golf set, the Tennis set. Evie didn't want to be part of any set; she wanted to be incognito. She flung on a loose frock and cardigan and found the marvellously broad brimmed hat she'd purchased in Paris. The hat was made of straw and punctured with flower patterns which created a confusing pattern of light and shade over her face. Safely disguised, she grabbed her guide book and her purse, left the dark Pension and made her way up the Cours Saleya; weaving her way through the market, past flowers, fruit and vegetables of every colour, and onto the Promenade des Anglais. Already the pebbled beach was dotted with deckchairs and on the deckchairs lounged tourists. Women in jersey dresses looked out over the transparent sea; men in baggy trousers, jackets and open-necked shirts sat beside them.

She was in no rush to find breakfast, but eventually, half way up the boulevard Gambetta, it found her: a quiet café, shaded by an enormous plane tree, its tables dotted around the roots that were working their way up through the pavement. Evie found a spot outside, half in sun, half in shade, ordered a coffee and croissant and settled down with her guide book.

After a few minutes, she glanced up. There was a change in the atmosphere. An old lady had come into the café, in a long skirt, worn shoes and a heavy shawl which covered her upper body and grey hair. She started to work her way around the tables, offering tiny buttonholes of flowers and little bags of lavender. Most people ignored her and carried on with their breakfasts. Evie followed suit, burying her nose further into her guide book, but she felt vulnerable. Perhaps the woman noticed, for she gave up with the other customers and made a beeline for Evie's table.

'*Une fleur pour une fleur?*' she asked in a croaky voice, holding out a posy.

'I'm sorry, I don't understand.'

Evie looked away, back to her book, her eyes dancing uneasily on the page, trying to find her place again. But she *had* understood. She was being dishonest and lazy, like a typical tourist, wanting to engage with a place on some but not all levels. The woman came closer, leaning right over her. Evie could hear the slight raspiness of her breath, but she kept on obstinately reading her guide book.

'Two is good,' said the woman, as if she was reading something in the book that Evie hadn't noticed. Her accent was strong, not French sounding, but a foreign accent of some sort. Evie stopped reading and stared at the page, frozen on one word, like someone who knows bad news is coming but can't escape it.

'Two is good,' said the woman again, 'But three is more. Three is…' she paused, searching for the word in English, then she gave up, '*trop.*' Another pause. '*Peut-être,*' she added. Then she quickly turned and left the café, as if she wanted to be far away before the prediction came true.

Evie sat, still frozen in her seat, half in sun, half in shade. She waited until the woman was out of sight then she flipped her guide book over and found the rudimentary dictionary at the back. *Trop.* Her eyes flew over the Section for the letter T.

Thé – Tea. *Do not expect a cup of tea like you get at home. The French serve tea without milk and far too weak. It's wiser to ask for coffee, especially in the South.*

Très – Very. '*Il fait très chaud aujourd'hui.*' – *It is very hot today. A useful phrase for beginning a conversation with local people.*

Trop – Too much or too many. *Use this term when you are bartering in a market. If you feel something is too*

expensive say: 'C'est trop.' The vendor will almost
certainly lower his price.

Evie closed the book and shut her eyes. Despite the rising
temperature on the boulevard, she felt very cold. She knew
exactly what the woman meant. *Two's company, three's a*
crowd. Horrible. A dreadful thing to say to a wife who has
discovered her husband is cheating on her. But she'd asked
for it: raising her guide book in front of her face as the woman
approached, as if shielding herself from a vagrant. She was
no better than the London set, snatching the sun without
giving anything back, without bothering with the locals.
Three's a crowd. Yet the prediction was only half true. For
there were four of them: Bernard, Cynthia, Maureen and
herself.

The old woman's words completely ruined her first day.
Evie spent the rest of it going up and down the boulevard
trying to find her; wanting to buy some, if not all of her
flowers, desperate to right the wrong and change the outcome.
Only as the sun set behind the Alpes Maritimes did she start
to feel calmer. The peut-être, she realised, added a strange
hopefulness. *Perhaps*, the lady had suggested, as if the result
was not yet clear, as if three people might *not* be too many
and it was up to Evie to decide.

Making Enquiries

'There's no use denying it. You have a son, I've seen him with my own eyes.' Benedict was back home in Chelsea, sitting up in bed, berating his son. Bernard was standing by the window, clinging on to the curtains.

'There's no mistaking him, Bernard, he looks exactly like you did, the same long limbs, the same shock of red hair, the same plump cheeks and blue, staring eyes.'

'But all babies look the same. It could have been anyone's.'

'That was *your* baby, Bernard, I would have known him anywhere. And there's only one thing to do now – find the mother.'

The irony of this comment was not lost on either of them. Benedict steadied his nerves with a few grapes and Bernard stared moodily out of the window.

'I think it's important to stay calm,' ventured Jones, who had come in with an Ovaltine for Benedict and discovered father and son in a stand-off.

'The fates that punished me have moved on to the next generation!' cried Benedict, waving the milky drink away.

Eventually, Bernard managed to extricate himself by promising to find both the baby and the mother, by hook or by crook, in the next twenty-four hours, or sooner if possible.

He wandered along King's Road, gloomily considering his predicament. Creating a baby out of wedlock was one thing; creating a baby out of wedlock when one was in wedlock was quite another. And it made him look very careless when he was sure he'd been very careful. Anyway, he had to face facts: there was a baby – his father had seen it. He would have to do something.

Bernard considered his options. There were only two: Maureen or Cynthia. He would go and see both girls and ask, as delicately as possible, if there was any chance they might have given birth to his child. But how did one ask such a question delicately? He raked through his memory, recalling all the possible phrases he could use for the task ahead.

Bun in the oven sounded cosy and conjured up warmth and baking. But Maureen's family had a cook and he didn't think Cynthia was a baker. *Up the duff* had shocked his wife when he had used it to question Phoebe. *Gooseberry bushes* sounded painful and *storks* sounded infantile. Finally, he hit on the word *expecting*. It had an ambiguous ring to it. It could be used in the past, present or future and, if he got in a tight corner, it could be used with other innocuous words, like: 'Are you expecting rain?'

But there was no chance of rain today. The sky was a strange grey colour and there was a taste of snow in the air. It wasn't falling yet, but it was waiting up in the clouds, biding its time. Bernard stuck the tip of his tongue out; yes, he could almost taste snow.

He trundled along the pavement, working out a strategy 'on the hoof'. Maureen or Cynthia? Both were possible and, strangely enough, there were clues to suggest that either girl might be implicated. Maureen had recently returned from an extended stay with relatives in Ireland. She had been away for at least a month and was only just home. An extended stay away seemed highly suspicious. Surely this was exactly what girls 'in trouble' did? They went to a safe house, where no one knew them locally. Bernard gave a small groan. Oh, let it not be Maureen! And Cynthia had got married recently. Out of the blue. Just like that. He hadn't been invited to the wedding but another artist friend had gone and told him it was a riot. So why had Cynthia got married, if she wasn't expecting a baby? Oh, let it not be Cynthia!

Bernard got gloomier and gloomier, but gloom was better than despair. Much better. Despair was what he would feel if he stopped trying to solve the 'baby mystery' and considered the bigger picture. Despair was what he would feel if it turned out he had done something so hurtful that Evie would never want to see him again. So he stuck with gloom and arrived, looking as sober as a judge, at Maureen's door. The maid answered the bell.

'Is Maureen at home?' enquired Bernard, desperately hoping she wasn't.

'Yes. Is she expecting you?'

There, the magic word, *expecting*. It was a sign that he should use it in his difficult quest. And it was a message from the heavens that everything would all be all right.

'No but,' Bernard was thinking on the hoof, 'I would like to see the portrait I painted of her in situ.'

'You'd better come in then.'

The maid led Bernard through a tiled hallway and into the morning room. It was a bright room, south facing; a family room, with a card table and two comfy sofas. There were two Maureens in there: one on the wall, looking rather lascivious, and one at the table, looking rather moody, her head in a book. Both Maureens looked up as he came in and stared at him. There was, unfortunately, someone else in the room as well. General Fitzgerald, Maureen's elderly father, was sitting on one of the sofas, reading the newspaper.

The general was a no-nonsense sort of man. Tall and dark haired, despite his advanced age, with bushy sideburns and a distinguished monocle, he had been very clear in his instructions concerning his daughter's portrait. He wanted a modest picture of his eldest daughter, nothing showy, nothing gaudy. Demure. If it was satisfactory then he would ask Bernard to paint the other three. He had paid in advance and had given Bernard a delivery date. *Delivery date*. The word took on a whole new meaning as he stood before the man who might well be a grandfather.

'Good morning,' Bernard began. 'I'm so sorry to disturb. I was just passing and was curious to see what the portrait looked like in situ.'

'Huummph,' humphed General Fitzgerald. 'It wasn't quite what I was expecting.'

Bernard glanced up at the picture, 'You don't like it?'

'You have made my daughter look like,' the general glanced at the real Maureen and chose his words carefully, 'an actress.'

'Oh,' said Bernard. He could sense he was already on borrowed time, but the general had given him a route forward.

'And were you expecting?' he smiled hesitantly at Maureen, who closed her book and glared at him. 'For the picture to look like that?' he finished lamely.

There was a pregnant pause. 'No,' she said.

Another silence. Oh well, he may as well be hung for a sheep. 'And were you expecting in Ireland?' he asked, addressing the portrait rather than the girl.

The general's monocle fell off, 'I beg your pardon?'

'I mean, was Ireland what you were expecting?' Bernard's voice trailed off.

Maureen was too shocked to speak but the general stepped into the breech.

'Let's get this straight, young man. My daughter is not expecting, nor was she expecting, nor will she be expecting, not until she is married, and hopefully not for a good while after that.'

'Of course, of course,' agreed Bernard hurriedly.

There was another silence, which seemed to last for almost nine months. During the silence, Maureen excused herself and stalked out of the room and the general angrily rustled his newspaper.

'Are you expecting snow?' Bernard ventured, eventually.

'What I am expecting, is for you to leave this house immediately!'

'Of course, of course.'

'And I hope you're not *expecting* anyone to show you out.'

'No. I'm not.'

'And my daughter will not be *expecting* to see you in the future, either the near future or the distant future.'

'No,' agreed Bernard.

Cynthia, he decided, as he walked quickly away from Maureen's, would be much easier; much more straightforward. She was from a class that could take things on the chin. She didn't stand on ceremony and she wouldn't like euphemisms, so he could be perfectly straight with her. But there were still complications. She had recently married. And she lived in the East End. The East End was a long way to go to find a baby. It felt like a pilgrimage traipsing over there and, like a true pilgrim, Bernard prayed constantly: 'Please no, please no, please no.'

It took a while to find 101, Sidney Street. All the red-bricked terraced houses looked the same – dilapidated. And some had numbers and some didn't. He wandered up and down, passing two little boys trundling wooden toys along the cracked pavement, their faces almost completely obscured by over-sized caps: 'Yer all right mister?' He located the house eventually, walked up to the front door and knocked on the peeling paint.

'Here's trouble,' Cynthia muttered, eying him through a crack in the door.

'Hello Cynthia. Are you on your own or is your husband there?'

'If you've come for any hanky-panky then I can tell you I'm through with all that. I'm a married woman now. Respectable.'

'Oh no, no, no, no, no, no, no, no,' said Bernard. 'I haven't,' he added.

'I ain't doing no more modelling for you, either. You don't paint me right.'

'I know, you told me.'

'Do you owe me money then?'

222

'I need to speak to you about something.'

'Well my husband's 'ere. Sleeping. He's night shift at the docks. Better not wake him up.'

'I'll be as quiet as a mouse.'

Cynthia shrugged and opened the door. Just over the threshold lay an enormous Alsatian, dead to the world. Bernard stepped nimbly over the dog and followed Cynthia down a corridor into the back room where a fire smoked in a tiny grate. She motioned to a chair. It looked quite flimsy and he sat down gingerly.

How to begin? He glanced at her. She was such a beautiful girl, with her long black hair and her pale, delicate face. But in her home environment she looked harder: less vulnerable; more difficult.

'Congratulations on your marriage.'

'What d'yer want?'

'Well, I was just wondering if there was a particular reason for your sudden wedding?' Bernard tried to speak vaguely, academically, as if he was researching the phenomena of hasty marriages.

'Sudden!' cried Cynthia.

In the hallway, the Alsatian gave a little snarl in its sleep.

'Sudden!' she cried again. 'I've been waiting for Billy to pop the question for four an' a 'alf years. If you call that sudden, then yer a slower man than I thought.'

'Oh.' Bernard recalibrated. 'So you didn't get married because you had to?'

'What?'

'Because,' Bernard made helpless gestures over his stomach.

'Are yer saying I'm getting fat!'

The dog gave a growl, then a yelp, then fell silent again.

'No, no, no, no.' Bernard was whispering now. 'I mean did you get married because you were in the family way? I mean, because you were having my baby.'

Cynthia looked at him with incredulity. 'Your baby!' She paused and looked around dramatically, as if the room was full of people and she wanted to involve the audience. 'No thank you!' She glanced at his tall sturdy frame. 'Those long legs! No thank you. I'd rather give birth to a giraffe. And that head. Crikey. Like a melon it would be. No thank you.'

'Oh.' Bernard didn't like her insinuations. 'But babies are usually fairly average in size, I don't think—'

'Not your baby, Bernard. Believe me, your baby would be a monster!'

Bernard could hear a stirring in the bedroom immediately above them.

'So, that's a no?' he wanted to double check and then vanish.

'God spare me the very thought of it!' cried Cynthia.

'God spare you what?' Cynthia's husband was on the landing. He sounded as grumpy as a bear disturbed half-way through hibernation.

'There's a gentleman here thinks I've had his baby.'

There was the noise of someone thumping down the stairs. Bernard jumped up and shot back down the corridor, leapt over the dog and flew out of the door, slamming it behind him. Then he took off down the street, as fast as his giraffe legs could carry him.

Once he was safely back on Mile End Road, he slowed down and got his breath back. Horse-drawn carts clipped by, pulling barrels of molasses from the Caribbean, then a Breton onion seller wobbled past on an overloaded bicycle, garlands of onions around his neck.

Bernard felt very relieved; not only had he escaped the jaws of an irate husband and his Alsatian, but he had also run the gauntlet of both Maureen and Cynthia and come through unscathed. Neither woman was the mother of the mystery child. Well then. He smiled up at the sky where tiny flakes were starting to whorl and ambled along Mile End Road. He would walk to Whitechapel and get the District Line all the way to Sloane Square. But after a few paces he remembered why he was going there – to face his father. And

Benedict would not be happy with the result of his morning's work.

Bernard swerved into the red-bricked Blind Beggar pub. He bought a pint of ale and a chaser and sat in the window, watching the comings and goings on the road outside. There were so many different nationalities squashed in the narrow streets around the public house: emigrés, migrants, refugees, all trotting past the window; all industrious, all hopeful. A man walked past with a basket of live ducks, another with a sack of flour, slung over his shoulder. Then a little boy came by, probably only four or five years old. He was wearing a sweet little shirt with no collar and a dark, rather grubby pair of trousers. His feet were bare. Bernard watched him run along the street, on his way somewhere. And that was the moment he started to miss him: the son he didn't know he had; the son he hadn't wanted but who he suddenly longed for. He downed his drinks and headed to his studio.

A View of the Cam

Bernard was always in a rush. He knew it, but he couldn't help himself. He even drew with his paintbrush, sacrificing accuracy for spontaneity. But by foregoing line and form, he could concentrate on colour. Today he had a particular colour in his head: a bright magenta pink. He knew he had to use it carefully, a few blobs here and there; crocuses, dotting their way up the tow path and humming in the grass beside the river. And now the magenta dots reappeared in the water, reflected and refracted by the gentle current.

A young couple were lying in the long grass beside the tow path. It must have been a cold day because they were wrapped in the same coat. The man had red, and the girl blonde hair. And there were other differences between them. The man had lifted his head up and was looking down at the girl as if studying her closely, whereas she was looking away from him towards the viewer and her eyes, though a vivid blue, seemed rather lifeless, as if part of her was absent, or perhaps she was just thinking about something else.

There were other objects in the picture too: cows and sheep and the distant spires of Cambridge, but they were all painted in a rather hazy way, not quite detailed enough to capture the viewer's attention, ensuring the viewer's eyes would be directed back to the vibrant crocuses, both the flowers on the bank and their reflections. The ones in the water were now blurred to such an extent that they had become wavy pink lines that stretched almost from one side of the river to the other.

After he'd finished the flowers and the reflections of the flowers, Bernard dipped his paintbrush one more time in the magenta paint and painted in the bottom right hand corner of the canvas: *For Evie.*

The Writer

It started like a niggly ache, a strange uncomfortable feeling.
Suddenly Evie wanted to write; not so much *wanted* but *needed*
to. One rainy day in Florence, she bought herself a notebook.
It was mid-afternoon, the shuttered shops were slowly reopening,
and she was wandering dreamily down the narrow, sleepy
streets. One of the shops caught her eye. Il Papiro, a stationer
selling hand decorated notelets and the marble paper for which
Florence was famous. It wasn't the only one, the city was full
of stationers, but there was something about the light, slanting
through a gap in the overhanging roofs and illuminating the
gold Papiro lettering that pulled her in.

Inside was a treasure trove of gorgeous hand-pressed
parchment: wrapping paper, notepaper, letter paper, cards and
sketch books, all decorated with traditional designs in every
colour, adorned with silver and gold. They all sang to Evie,
like sirens out at sea. *Write on me.* Evie spent ages poring
over them until eventually she chose a broad, thick notebook,
with a beautiful clasp and, in the clasp, a tiny lock and key.
She bought the book, rushed back to her pension and spent
the rest of the evening locking and unlocking it, staring at
the blank pages, closing them again, fiddling with the fastening.
The idea of actually writing anything was terrifying and she
hid the notebook at the bottom of her suitcase. Now she
turned the little key, opened the first page and began to jot
on the paper with her pencil.

STARS, COMETS AND DISOBEDIENT WOMEN BY EVIE BRUNTON-CAVALIER (FIRST DRAFT)

Introduction

Throughout the ages, only a few British women have made their mark on history. These few have stood out as being exceptional, perhaps the stuff of legends, whereas the history of women in general, ordinary women, has been left as a blur. Torch-bearers can leave a darkness after they pass, causing we who follow to stumble. They blind us with their shining light, emphasising our inadequacy, and then they are gone. We cannot even begin to imitate their greatness and so even learning about them is off-putting. It is possible that the history makers encouraged this exaggeration of their talents precisely to make them harder to copy. Female historical figures become legends and then fairy tales. Once fictionalised, they are out of our reach; we will never attain their greatness. Those that 'manned' the first printing presses realised this and the deception has continued up to the present day.

Some women shine like stars; others burn like comets. Stars are the famous women from history who have shone as a guiding light to inspire and encourage ~~other women~~ others. Some of these ~~women~~ stars burn so brightly that they are as dispiriting as they are inspiring. Some of them shine ~~very~~ faintly, as if they are light years away. Comets are more exciting. They don't just sparkle from afar, they bring their message right into our atmosphere with a terrifying directness. These are the women from the past who have a vision of the future: a vision of fire and instability. They come hurtling towards us and there is always the danger of collision. Rather than a twinkling star, which cannot really affect us, comets collide with our lives, burning *us, enmeshing us in their fiery tail and dragging us into the future.*

A gentle knocking on the door. 'Are you asleep, Evie? There's a parcel for you. A large one. It looks like a picture.'

Evie glanced at her watch – two hours gone just like that. Still she'd made a start. She quickly slid the notebook under her pillow.

'No, not asleep, just resting. Come in!'

Given Up Trying

It was a few days later. Outside the snow was falling steadily, but inside the master bedroom of 717, King's Road, the temperature was soaring. Benedict was lying in bed, staring up at his beautifully ornamented ceiling, his face bright red in colour. Bernard was pacing up and down between the window and the door, wearing out a priceless Indian rug.

'It's so hypocritical of you, when you made no attempt to find my mother. One rule for you, one rule for me. I have to abide by the Ten Commandments, but you did exactly what you liked.'

'And that's why I'm so determined that history won't repeat itself, that you won't make the same mistake.'

'I can't believe your sanctimonious drivel. *You don't want me to make the same mistake.* Don't you know that children always copy their parents? It's the only reality they know and they recreate it, just like you and me duplicate beautiful women. Except we do it for money and,' he smiled snidely, 'other things. Children do it because it's all they understand. I watched you as a child. I observed you working your way through girlfriends and, now I've grown up, I've copied you. But *you*, suddenly white as snow, sitting on your high throne of condemnation, you have decided that you find the results displeasing.'

Jones came in. 'A telephone call for you, Mr Bernard, sir.'

'I didn't hear it ring,' countered Bernard.

'If you could just follow me sir, you can take it in your father's study.'

Jones led the way downstairs and into a room at the back of the house.

'There is no telephone call, sir. I just wanted to take the opportunity of explaining that your father's heart is still very delicate. The doctor ordered complete bed rest and absolutely no sudden shocks or excitement. He needs calm and reassurance, not—' but Jones couldn't seem to think of the word.

While the butler was talking, Bernard glanced around the study. As a child, he had spent hours in here, pouring over books on painters, absorbing their techniques. He would open the bookcases, heave out the heavy volumes and drag them onto the floor for closer inspection, the sharp pages nicking his fingers, the shiny covers slipping off and away along the carpet.

And he remembered sitting on his father's knee while he answered his correspondence. He would watch Benedict's fountain pen at work, the scratchy nib scrawling its way along the paper, and wait for the confident dot after Benedict. There was always a pause before his father wrote the dot. Benedict would raise his pen up in the air like a conductor, and then bring it down with a dramatic finality on the paper – the last note of the symphony. That final dot meant they could go back to their games: dominoes, chess, hide-and-seek.

There were always bronze statuettes spread around the room: wonderful objects for a child, heavy and solid in the hand, like chunky wooden toys, almost unbreakable yet detailed. He would run his fingers over the lumps and bumps and the nudes provided him with an early anatomy lesson.

Today there was a new statuette, and there was a feeling about it, well her, that he half-recognised. Who was it? But Jones, having delivered his sobering warning, was leading him back out of the study. Bernard's memory grappled with the mystery girl for a few seconds, like a knitter searching for a dropped stitch, but he couldn't quite place her. He should have had a better look. Next time.

'If I could trust you to be a little gentler while I make Mr Benedict some lunch,' smiled Jones, uneasily.

'Of course.'

Jones disappeared into the kitchen and Bernard went slowly back upstairs.

When he got back to the bedroom, Benedict was sitting up in bed. He'd thrown off the covers and was fiddling distractedly with the gold tasselled belt of his silk dressing gown. He looked very gloomy but his complexion had returned to a more normal colour.

'I'm sorry I got a bit wound up,' began Bernard, scanning Benedict's face for signs of the father he used to like. If only they could just sit and discuss painting and sculpture. If only real life hadn't caught him by the scruff of the neck.

'It's time you grew up,' said Benedict, as if he'd read his mind and pushed away the memories, like a sick man rejecting a supper tray.

Bernard felt really wounded. When did his father drop the all-embracing bonhomie of a lovable rogue and adopt this holier than thou persona? Was there a day, an hour, a moment when the bohemian Benedict decided his son must absolutely *not* follow in his footsteps; an instant when, instead of encouraging his child to dance after him across the silver sands of life, he'd produced a stiff broom and swept away his traces.

'I can't find my child, and I may not be able to find my child, so it may not have a father. But I have never had a mother and that didn't seem to bother *you*. Not only that, but you didn't admit you were my real father till I really pressed you, until I forced you to tell me. You were happy to raise me, yes. But admit real responsibility for your actions – no.'

Benedict said nothing. He just smoothed down the bedsheet, as if ironing out invisible creases with his fingers.

233

Bernard knew he should probably stop. He had said a lot, maybe too much. There was no knowing how ill his father was and a bit of him was desperate not to leave on a sour note, just in case anything should happen to Benedict between this meeting and their next one. But most of him wanted to go on. After all it was true, and his father deserved to hear it.

'And you never went to any bother to trace *my* mother. She might have been ill, or hard-up. But you didn't care. You let Sophia down completely. I'm not sure I can ever forgive you.'

Bernard glared at his father and then he left, bounding down the stairs and out of the house, suddenly wanting to be far away from the whole sordid business and from the man who'd inspired it.

Up to his elbows in soapy water, Jones heard the thumping on the stairs. He wiped his hands on a tea towel and returned to his master's bedroom.

'Ah, good, there you are, Jones.' Benedict looked devastated but determined. 'There is a lot to do. But, with your help, a few phone calls, a few enquiries, we will find her.'

'Who, sir?'

'The mother.'

'Which mother, sir?'

A View of the Thames

He started with the sky, slapping on greys with his pallet knife, darker at the top, then getting gradually lighter. He returned to the pallet and added white and yellow, burnt sienna, turquoise and the tiniest bit of crimson, creating a silver which quickly became the river. His pallet knife twisted in all directions, daubing oil paint onto the canvas and scraping it off again. To create the buildings, he mixed different browns and a Paynes grey together with a dash of orange, then he slapped it onto the canvas on the other side of the silvery water. Some houses were tall and thin, others squat, but they all loomed over the Thames as if watching the scene. In the middle ground, he painted the sailing barges that gave London its timeless feel, brown wooden boats with ragged red sails clinging to the masts, their ropes deftly portrayed with a flick of the knife. He wanted to keep going but the paint had to dry. He forced himself out of the studio and wandered off down the street, fumbling in his pocket for pipe and matches, propelling himself homewards.

The next day he returned and took up his pallet knife again. He held it gently, dexterously, as if he was a writer working away with a feather quill. At the bottom left of the picture, he slowly and carefully painted a couple in the gloom, this side of the river. They were folded in on themselves: she, almost blotted into the dark of his overcoat; he, leaning back to look at her, one hand in her hair. The light from a gas lamp shone on her, but not on him; he was in shadow.

Boadicea

It had been difficult getting to grips with the typewriter. In the beginning, Evie had spent most of her time disentangling the keys and pulling bits of mangled paper out; unwinding or rewinding the spools of ribbon, inking her hands in the process – not to mention jamming her fingers on the carriage return. Now she was finally getting the hang of the eccentric machine and enjoying seeing her thoughts converted into black and white. The typeface gave her ideas much more formality and authority than her spindly handwriting.

Boadicea, Queen of the British Celtic Iceni tribe, is known by several different names: Boudica, Boudicca, Boadicea, or the Welsh, Buddug. Whichever way her name is spelt, Boadicea only means one thing: Vengeance. Any woman who has ever been slighted will have felt the overpowering desire for revenge. Boadicea wasn't just slighted; she was betrayed, degraded and insulted. However, she got her own back.

In AD 60, Britain was part of the Roman Empire and Boadicea's husband ruled as an independent ally of Rome. When he died, he left his kingdom to be shared between the Roman Emperor and his daughters. However, the Romans ignored his wishes and seized the whole of his kingdom. What is more, Boadicea was flogged and her daughters were raped.

Thirsty for revenge, Boadicea led the whole Iceni tribe in revolt. They destroyed Colchester and moved on to London, (or Londonium as it was then called). The army was 100,000 strong and the Romans had no choice but to evacuate and leave the city to the Icenis, who burned it to the ground. Boadicea and her army were eventually defeated, but not before they had wreaked terror on Romans and Britons alike.

History loves to look back at a brave woman with a fighting spirit and applaud her courage. However, a woman from the Twentieth century who behaves in an impulsive and violent manner, even if she has a just cause and understandable motives, is considered to be a treacherous saboteur.

And what if Boadicea suddenly and unexpectedly came back to life and revisited Londinium? Where would she live? Hampstead perhaps? And would the rebel freedom fighter while away her hours doing good works or would she join the Suffragettes? And, if she did, what horrors might the warrior who so many men love to champion inflict on the capital? I am neither advocating nor condoning political activism, I am merely drawing parallels between the celebrated and the vilified.

A gentle knocking. 'There's another parcel for you.'

Evie gave a start. She hit the carriage return by mistake and so hard that the paper crinkled.

'Could you just leave it outside the door? I'm rather busy.'
'Of course, would you like another cup of tea or someth—'
'No thanks.'
'Right then, I'll leave you in peace.'

Evie heard a rustle, a gentle thud on the carpet and then footsteps dying away. She made herself rescue the sheet of paper first. She pulled it carefully out of the typewriter, smoothed the creases out and added it to the growing pile of pages before jumping up and opening the door.

Lunch with Uncle Geoffrey

Cassie sighed. It was turning out to be a dreadful morning. All those days of snow when London had looked so pretty and now the icy rain had turned the crisp white pavements into a grey slushy mire that splashed her stockings as she clambered out of the taxi cab and walked up the steps to the Embassy Club.

The powder room was crowded and Cassie put her grey velvet purse down beside what she thought was a mink stole to peer into the mirror and powder her nose. Unfortunately, the mink stole turned out to be a Pekinese and the Pekinese slavered all over her purse, leaving a stain that looked like the River Nile: several tributaries at the top, near the clasp, running into a single stream that coursed its way down the middle of the purse to the bottom. To add insult to injury, Uncle Geoffrey seemed to have been delayed and Cassie was sitting by herself at a table for two, making sure that her purse was resting slavered side down on the white tablecloth.

Uncle Geoffrey was often late, but being late at the Embassy, where everything and everyone was reflected in the enormous wall mirror, was embarrassing. Uncle Geoffrey was her mother's brother. He was the indulgent uncle, the relative who always bought extravagant presents and paid for fantastical treats. Uncle Geoffrey was generous to a fault. He would understand that a girl stuck in London in January was needing a pick-me-up: a short but exciting trip to Italy.

Her father didn't understand. He thought one trip a year was enough. It was an old-fashioned attitude, medieval in its backwardness. If a girl was to blossom, then she needed warmth and light. She needed the gentle ruins of Rome and the soft nudge of an Italian waiter as he picked up her plate of half-finished spaghetti with a 'Mi scusi, signorina,' the stress on the 'ina' as if adoring the fact that she was still, incredible though it might seem, unmarried. A girl needed all these things to counter the cold chill of a London winter.

Cassie sighed, picked up her silver bread knife and used it to emphasise the fold in the tablecloth between her side plate and fish fork. She dug into the linen, watching the sharp line appear and disappear again as the knife tilled its way through the snowy cloth.

'We may as well order,' said a voice at the next table. 'I think this will be yet another no-show from Bernard.'

Cassie didn't look round but she pricked up her ears. There was only one Bernard.

'Is he still on the hunt?' asked a second voice.

'Nope. He's given up all hope of finding his baby.'

His baby. Cassie could hardly believe her ears. She glanced in the mirror and immediately recognised the men: Harold Fairweather and Archie Meredith. Harold was far too small. Archie was tall and dark but he had an unattractive hump, something to do with breaking his back in the war. In the normal way, neither man interested her in the slightest; today she hung on their every word.

'So what happened with what's her name? Mary? Maria? God help me, I can never remember the girl's name,' said Harold.

'Maureen. It was a *No* with a capital N from Maureen.'

'And Cynthia?'

'Saw him quickly off the premises.'

'Cynthia's a doll,' observed Harold.

'Yes,' agreed Archie, 'but she ain't the sort of girl one could take home to one's Mama.'

'Bernard ain't got a Mama,'

'No, but he has a Papa. And I don't think Benedict is best pleased with the way things have turned out.'

'And are there other suspects?'

'Apparently not. I don't think he's even talked to a girl since Evie disappeared...'

Then the waiter arrived to take their order and soon afterwards Uncle Geoffrey steamed his way across the dining room, large but majestic, like a transatlantic liner. Cassie put on her Third Class passenger face, trying to look both wounded and hopeful at the same time: wounded that fate had dealt her the blow of only one annual trip abroad; hopeful that he might offer the chance of another one.

But Uncle Geoffrey had other things on his mind. His horse had fallen at Cheltenham's New Year Flat races and would almost certainly not be able to compete at Ascot. And while he was spending a fortune on equine vets for his injured thoroughbred, his son, Barney, had been gambling recklessly on other horses and suddenly the family fortune didn't feel quite as inexhaustible as it used to.

'It will all be gone in another generation,' he mused, tapping his cigarette on his cigarette case.

'We all have our cross to bear,' said Cassie. It was a larger than average hint that all was not well with her, but Uncle Geoffrey had moved on to the worrying state of the family shares in Bolivia.

'Bolivia!' breathed Cassie, wistfully. 'I have such a wanderlust,' she sighed, 'although Italy would do.'

'You should stay at home and save your father's money,' said Uncle Geoffrey sternly.

Cassie realised she had picked the wrong day to tap her uncle for travel funds. She smiled and nodded as she listened to his financial warnings, but her attention flew back to Harold and Archie's table and hovered between the two men. She was an invisible hummingbird, drinking in the confidential nectar. They were discussing Bernard again in the way certain friends talk about other friends who are in any kind of trouble: pure glee wearing the thin suit of mournful concern.

'So, what will Bernard do now?' asked Harold, as he cracked a quail's egg on the back of his spoon.

'Who knows.'

'How dreadful – and poor Evie. What on earth must she be thinking?'

'Oh Evie's been travelling for ages. She probably has no idea her husband's in a pickle.'

'Surely estranged husband?'

'Who knows.' Archie bit into his langoustines with relish.

'And you're sure Bernard doesn't have a lady friend at the moment?'

'Not for months. At least nine! When he's not painting, he spends his time drowning his sorrows.'

'Poor chap, we must catch up with him. Does he still come here of an evening?'

'Most nights, I believe.'

The hummingbird listened quietly, and then her attention returned to Uncle Geoffrey.

'Well, I suppose I must follow your advice and postpone my longed-for odyssey to Rome,' she said, not uncheerfully. She moved the conversation on to her mother's rheumatism, which dreaded the damp, and her father's new interest in stamps from the Empire. During their main course. she regaled him with tales of the bats that had infested the attic, but when it came to dessert Cassie announced she had to go. There was someone she needed to see and would he mind awfully eating her *crème brulée* for her. Uncle Geoffrey did the only decent thing, which was to plough his way through two puddings, while his niece set off to run her pressing errand.

Views of the World

It was Sunday morning. The cold snap had continued all week and now it was starting to snow again, white flakes sticking to the windows like bits of tissue paper. Breakfast was over and Toby had taken his mother to church. Daisy stayed at the breakfast table, lit a cigarette, poured herself another coffee and opened the weekly newspaper that had just been delivered.

The Views of the World. It was a rag of course, but what fun to read all the latest gossip and see what everyone had got up to the week before. There were plenty of photographs and outlandish stories about murders and monsters that she knew couldn't possibly be true, but which she enjoyed anyway. Tittle-tattle, but everyone needed a bit of that. Daisy took a sip of coffee, added a bit more sugar, had a quick puff on her cigarette and then opened the paper.

CAVALIER'S CURIOUS QUEST

You've heard the sad story of Little Bo-Peep who lost her sheep? Well now the popular artist, Bernard Cavalier, also seems to have lost something and he's bleating about it all over London. Despite the runaway success of his exhibition last year, all is not well in Pimlico, for Mr Cavalier has fathered a son and immediately lost it! 'He doesn't know where to find it,' to quote the nursery rhyme, because he doesn't know who the mother is!

Cavalier is a married man, so his first port of call should have been his wife, but we understand that the beautiful Mrs Cavalier has been out of the country for months now – we can only wonder why. Meanwhile, the artist has knocked on one or two different doors to try and identify the mother and we imagine that he probably has 'a little list' of other possible suspects. It's tiring work, which perhaps explains why Cavalier is to be found most evenings reviving himself at the exclusive Embassy Club on fashionable Bond Street.

We are keen to help the famous artist in his search, so if any reader happens to know of the baby's whereabouts, or is even harbouring his son, then please do get in touch. And we have some advice for Mr Cavalier – try Euston Lost Property Office or Hyde Park Lost and Found; both are busy most week-days.

A love of young ladies runs deep in the Cavalier family. His father, the well-known sculptor, Benedict Cavalier, is frequently to be seen around town with a lady on his arm...

Daisy threw the paper down and put her head in her hands. Then she stood up and paced between the table and the window. Berkeley Square was slowly disappearing under the snow: large flakes twirling through the air, covering the ground in a thick white blanket. Passers-by struggled along the pavement, muffled in scarves and hats. They left perfect footprints in the new white world but, almost immediately, the snow rubbed them away again. And it was just the same with Bernard. He would make great strides in getting his life back in control, and then, just when he seemed to be on the straight and narrow, another mistake would throw him off course and his efforts seemed to melt away.

It was a few weeks now since Evie had written: a hopeful letter in which she'd said she was considering contacting Bernard and wanted to know whether Daisy thought it was a good idea. Daisy had stalled, unsure how to reply, watching for signs of progress in Bernard, seeing them appear then disappear again. Now this. She sighed and turned back towards the roaring fire. She would have to write to Evie and give her some sort of version of the truth; enough to warn her off without humiliating her too much.

19, The Mansions, Berkeley Square, Mayfair, London, SW.
Sunday 29th January 1922

Dear Evie,

Thank you for your letter. Sorry to be a bit tardy replying. I've been considering your question very carefully. On reflection, I think it would be better if you didn't try contacting Bernard for the time being. He seems to have got himself in a bit of a muddle recently. He is worried that he may have fathered a son with someone in London and has been asking around to see if he can find the mother. I'm afraid it's all a bit sordid and he has been the butt of a few jokes in the capital. I'm sorry to have to tell you this, but I would hate to see you caught up in the confusion. My advice is to leave him alone for the moment.

I wish I had something more positive to report. It feels like ages since I've seen you and I miss you so much.

Your loving friend,

Daisy xxxx

The following morning, a young woman visited *The Views of the World* office in Fleet Street. She was smartly dressed in a navy jersey suit with a plain tunic and patterned sleeves and skirt. It was sporty yet demure; smart yet functional, and the girl on reception felt rather jealous of her jaunty look, not to mention her long mink cape.

'Can I help you?' she asked.

'I have something to collect,' said the fashionable girl. 'I believe there is something for me from the Editor.'

'Can I have your name?'

'Richardson. Miss Cassandra Richardson.'

'One moment.' The girl disappeared and came back a few minutes later with a fat brown envelope. 'Here you are.' She glanced at the thickness of the envelope and a slight look of contempt flashed across her face.

Without acknowledging the receptionist further, Miss Richardson stuffed the envelope in her large leather handbag, pulled her mink cape tighter and stepped back out into the January morning. It was cold and grey in London, but Rome would be warm and sunny. She would start in Rome and make her way north to Milan. A longer trip, and hopefully a fruitful one. She crossed the road with a spring in her step. There was a smell of mimosa in the air.

Bad News

It had been a charming evening. The Embassy was usually quiet on a Monday, but tonight Harold and Archie had popped by and the staff were particularly attentive and his Beef Wellington was perfect. Bernard sat sleepily at the bar, hugging an empty whisky glass, steeling himself for the short walk back to Pimlico in the cold. There was a tap on his arm and he turned to find Jones standing beside him.

'Jones!' he smiled. 'And what brings you here so late in the day?' But as he spoke he silently answered his own question, for it could only be one thing.

'It's bad news I'm afraid, Mr Bernard, sir.'

'My father?'

'Yes.'

Bernard sat blinking at the bottles behind the bar. Most of them were hanging upside down, tapped for easy access by the bar staff. Just for a few seconds, Bernard's world turned upside down as well.

'Oh dear,' he said, when it had righted itself again. 'When did it happen?'

'This evening.'

'I didn't realise he'd gone downhill so quickly,' Bernard said, 'or I would have...' but he didn't finish the sentence.

'He got much worse yesterday, after the newsp—' but Jones didn't finish his sentence either. 'Well, perhaps you could come round tomorrow, sir. We can start planning the funeral.'

So he really was dead. The world turned upside down again.

'I will. Thank you, Jones.' As he spoke, Bernard noticed that his voice suddenly sounded more mature. Perhaps this always happened – the son taking over from the father, stepping into their shoes, picking up the baton and continuing onwards as head of the family.

He pondered this and many more things on his way home, examining his thoughts and feelings. He felt more philosophical than sad. But perhaps it was no great surprise. He and his father hadn't seen eye-to-eye for a long time. They hadn't confided in each other for years and recently Benedict had constantly tried to interfere in his life. It would almost be a relief not to have him peering over his shoulder. He was now a free man; the only catch was that he was also an orphan. Bernard stifled a large sob. Where had that come from?

He weaved his way back to Pimlico, desperately confused by the news. And the next day was no better. He woke up crying. He'd dreamt he was a child again and he was tearing across Hyde Park on Benedict's shoulders. They were laughing and Bernard could hear the sound of his father's feet thumping on the grass and feel the impact reverberate through his little body, making his teeth rattle. Benedict always made a funny noise when he ran, like a squealing piglet. Bernard loved it and tried to copy it. And so they ran on, two little piglets, laughing and squealing. They passed a tree and there was a young girl with long blonde hair, hanging upside down in it, singing to herself. The girl's legs were wrapped around a branch and her arms were stretched out, as if she was trying to touch the ground. Too late, he realised it was Evie. He turned his head to look back, craning his neck right round, but Benedict was carrying him quickly away and she was soon out of sight.

As he lay, remembering his dream, Bernard realised that he now had a means to try to win Evie back. He was no longer a disorganised artist with a rented mews in Pimlico and a messy studio. He had a town house on the King's Road and a very organised butler. They could live in Chelsea. Evie could go to university, hopefully in London, and he could paint downstairs in the basement. Jones would attend to their every need; Evie wouldn't even need to cook.

He hurried into the bathroom. He should shave – he needed to look smart for the man who was now his servant. But when Bernard looked into the mirror, he saw his father's face: the same cheeky mouth, the same determined chin, the same laughter lines around the eyes. He collapsed into the bath tub and lay there weeping, clinging onto the taps because he desperately needed something to hold onto.

After a few minutes, or was it hours, the phone started ringing. He heaved himself out of the bathtub and went to answer it.

'Bernard?' It was Toby's voice. 'I say old chum, have you seen *The Views of the World* this week? I'm afraid it looks very bad.'

'Sorry?'

'Well not it, *you*. You look very bad, Bernard.'

The Funeral

There was hardly anyone there. Just Penelope, dressed head to toe in black lace like a Spanish Madonna, Toby and Daisy, Jones, Mr James, the lawyer, and two old friends of Benedict's from school days whom Bernard had never met.

Perhaps it was the snow, falling steadily outside the windows of St Luke's, that put people off. Perhaps it was the nasty 'flu virus that was doing the rounds. Or perhaps – but Bernard couldn't bear to consider the possibility that no one in the smart, bright, moneyed set that Benedict inhabited could be bothered to show up for his funeral. Obviously what had happened was that *The Times* had printed the wrong date in the funeral notice. Or the wrong time, or even the wrong church. Bernard imagined all the people Benedict had ever known waiting patiently in a different church, wiping their eyes and sniffing into their handkerchiefs.

St Luke's was almost empty and that didn't suit its size. The building was massive, with seating for at least two thousand people and a high vaulted ceiling in a mock gothic style. Bernard looked up to the ribbed vaults. It was like being inside a whale, an enormous whale. Who was swallowed by a whale? Jonah? If only his knowledge of the Bible was better. He hardly went to church and no wonder, if it made you feel like you'd been swallowed. Whole. A dreadful feeling. And his father didn't go to church either. So why were they here, in this massive edifice, a few folk and a coffin, if not to emphasise the futility of life.

The vicar stood in the pulpit, droning on about Benedict, which was odd because Bernard was sure he'd never met him. His mind began to wander and he started to think about Evie. During the first few hours after Benedict's death, he'd allowed himself to entertain the vaguest hope that she might come to the funeral. Europe wasn't so very far away. She could have made it back in time. But then that article had got in the way and suddenly there was *no* chance of her coming, absolutely no chance at all.

The vicar droned on. Benedict had enjoyed a long, long life. So many exhibitions, so many awards. It was true he was a good sculptor; not the most modern or exciting, but certainly accurate and perceptive. And it was also true that he was a kind man. Was he really on the Board of Barnardo's? Bernard had no idea. He suddenly wondered if Benedict had left the charity a little something in his will. He found himself hoping that he had indeed left a donation, but just a small one, a generous gift rather than an extravagant one.

After the vicar had listed Benedict's skills and triumphs, he went on to catalogue his illness: the one big heart attack followed by a steady degeneration of the heart. Bernard found himself reaching for his handkerchief and blowing his nose two or three times. Finally, the Reverend praised his loyal butler, Jones. In the later stages of the illness, he had transformed himself from butler to nurse and from nurse to friend. It was very moving and Bernard would have blown his nose again, except he was overcome with guilt which somehow paralysed him and kept him staring glassy eyed straight in front of him, so his nose just kept running.

After what seemed like hours, they emerged from the church to go on to the Crematorium. The coffin was carried ahead, the black pallbearers sweeping slowly down the path from the church through the snow, reminding Bernard of a Danish painting. Then something terrible happened. A young man in an overcoat appeared from behind a gravestone with a notebook.

'Found yer baby yet, Mr Cavalier?'

Something snapped inside. Bernard raised his fist and rushed at the journalist. Jones and Toby dashed after him and grabbed his arms just before he reached the reporter. Bernard was swearing and shaking but they managed to keep hold of his arms and pull him away.

'Just clear off!' shouted Toby as they led Bernard back to the path. 'Get out of here!' The words rang out, clear as a bell, in the churchyard. And the gravestones stood like druids in their white hoods of snow, silently watching.

The funeral notice had invited everyone back to Brown's hotel but, after the Crematorium, Penelope announced that she had an appointment, and the school friends had a train to catch back to wherever they had come from. Toby offered to go to Brown's and tell them that tea was off and pay any monies owing. Daisy melted away into the snow and that left Jones, Mr James and Bernard.

'As things have turned out, this might be the perfect opportunity for you and me to have a chat,' said Mr James, smiling uncertainly at Bernard.

The idea of anything being perfect on an afternoon like this one was very appealing. Bernard agreed and asked Jones if he would like to come along but Jones said he had a lot of things to see to and disappeared.

A Box of Cuban Cigars

Funny how, in difficult moments, Bernard sometimes found himself caring more about how he appeared to others than how he felt inside. It had been a dreadful day, but now came the more agreeable part: the last will and testament of Benedict Cavalier, and he was the only heir. Bernard knew it was important not to look too smug as Mr James totted up the figures and told him exactly what his father was worth. He knew he had to look mildly surprised at the total amount and also rueful that his father was not still around to enjoy it.

In the taxi that they took to Mr James's office, Bernard pressed his face right up against the window, so the lawyer wouldn't notice, and practised the appropriate facial expressions: trying to look surprised then rueful in quick succession, like a cuckoo popping in and out of a clock. He was so busy practising that he didn't notice when the taxi arrived in Gray's Inn Road and it was the lawyer who had to root around in his pocket for the fare.

Everyone was terribly kind. The doorman, noticing they were both in black, bowed low and Mr James's secretary insisted on making them a cup of tea, it being such a dreadful day. Finally, he and Mr James were alone in an enormous office, lined with wooden cabinets and drawers. They sat opposite each other and a huge desk stood between them, covered with piles of papers, each pile tied together with ribbons.

'Now then, let's get down to business,' the lawyer smiled. He picked up one of the piles of papers, undid the ribbon and read from the top sheet.

'I, Benedict Horatio Cavalier, being of sound mind, etc., etc., do hereby bequeath to my only son, Bernard Horatio Cavalier, the following: the Degas statuette presently in the study—'

'Lovely,' interrupted Bernard. Degas was not his favourite; he preferred his father's Rodin, but perhaps he was leaving that to Jones and, gosh, the man deserved it.

'And the Rodin statuette on the mantelpiece in the snooker room.'

'Lovely!'

'And the snooker table, if he can find anywhere to put it.'

'Oh.' That was a confusing one, but perhaps Benedict had lost the plot a bit towards the end.

'And the Caravaggio inspired oil painting in the drawing room above the sofa, which is not actually by Caravaggio but by a disciple of Caravaggio. And a box of Cuban cigars.'

'Lovely, lovely, good, good,' said Bernard, gesturing gently and politely that the lawyer should continue.

But Mr James had placed the sheet back on the top of the pile of papers and was busy tying it up again.

'And what about the house?' asked Bernard.

'The house? Well, Mr Cavalier, it's bad news, I'm afraid.'

'Sorry?'

'Apart from the various sundries described above, you are not entitled to anything from your father's estate.' A pause. 'What I mean is you are *not* your father's heir.'

'I beg your pardon.'

'The late Benedict Cavalier has left his estate to someone else.'

'Someone else?' Bernard was too surprised to raise his voice. 'But I am his only heir.'

'You are his only child, but not his beneficiary.'

'But that's outrageous. I am entitled to his estate. I shall contest the will.'

'Yes and no, Mr Cavalier. You could contest the will, but,' the lawyer hesitated, 'I wouldn't advise it.' Bernard sat in stunned silence. Mr James took the opportunity to have a sip of tea. 'I wanted to let you know as soon as possible,' he continued, 'so as not to disappoint.'

'Disappoint! I have been disinherited by my father and you use the word disappoint! I can tell you I am much more than disappointed. I'm devastated, I'm hurt, I'm—' But Bernard could hear his voice breaking and stopped.

There was another silence during which the man who was a son, but not an heir, stared moodily at his tea and Mr James discreetly finished his.

'I demand to know who has stolen my inheritance!' said Bernard, eventually.

'I'm afraid Mr Cavalier insisted that the name of the beneficiary be kept secret.'

'But I'm his son. I'm entitled to know.'

'I'm sorry, sir, but I always abide by a dead man's wishes. If I didn't I would soon find myself struck off.'

'Is it Evie?'

'No, sir, it's not your wife.'

'Is it Penelope Armstrong?'

'No, sir.' The lawyer stood up, keen to quash any further attempts at a guessing game. 'It's been a lot to take in, and on top of the funeral. I suggest you go home now, Mr Cavalier. Try to rest.' To emphasise his point, Mr James opened the door and gestured towards it.

As if in a trance, Bernard staggered to his feet and moved towards the door. The secretary saw him out of the office and the doorman ushered him out of the building. He stood on Gray's Inn Road, staring at the traffic. He didn't know where he was. He didn't know who he was.

Grieving

After his conversation with the lawyer, the real grieving began. Bernard confined himself to his mews flat and there he wept, day and night. But it wasn't the money he was grieving for, although not having it was extremely inconvenient, and it wasn't the smart Chelsea house or the loyal butler. It was the fact that his father clearly didn't trust him at all. Benedict had obviously decided that his one and only son was not dependable, reliable or a man that could be counted on in any way whatsoever. Bernard was not sure that he would ever recover from this devastating analysis. Whether or not it was true was completely irrelevant. All that mattered was that his father had rejected him. Completely.

And Bernard also started grieving for his wife. He had nothing to tempt her back to London with now. And when Evie heard that her husband had been snubbed by his own father, she would realise that he really was the most worthless man alive.

Over the next few days, Bernard lost a stone in weight. He didn't eat; he didn't sleep; he didn't paint. Instead he sat in the drawing room and watched the birds flying round and round the clock. In his more lucid moments, he noticed how quiet it was in the flat and he wondered how his wife must have felt on her own all day. It was a bit like being in a library with no books, or a museum with no exhibits. The ticking clock was the only sign of life, that and the occasional ringing of a telephone.

Bernard sat in the drawing room and clung to his memories of Evie. He thought about her constantly. He wanted her so much that his throat started to close up and every swallow became so painful he could scream. And Evie started visiting: sometimes through the door but mostly through the wall, the one between the bedroom and the drawing room, although once he passed her on the stairs. Then one day he found her in the bath and that's when he knew he should ring Toby and Toby came straight round in a taxi, bundled him out of the flat and took him back to Mayfair.

The Rest Cure

'Say Aaaaaaaagh.'

'Aaaaaaaagh.'

The doctor pushed Bernard's tongue down with a little wooden spatula and peered inside his throat. Daisy and Toby stood in the doorway, like two anxious parents. Bernard tried not to gag.

'Much, much better. I think the infection has gone.' The doctor pulled the little spatula out again. 'And are you still having hallucinations, Mr Cavalier?'

'No,' said Bernard, gloomily.

'Good, good.' The doctor turned to address the parents, 'And is he sleeping well?'

Toby and Daisy nodded.

'And is he eating well?'

The nodding grew more vigorous.

'Excellent, then I pronounce the patient cured.' The doctor smiled, 'Who should I send the bill to?'

'Me,' said Toby.

While Toby and Daisy showed the doctor out, Bernard leapt out of bed. Cured! How marvellous – miraculous even, and only a few days ago he was sure he was dying. Recovered. Restored. Healed. One hundred per cent better. He threw off his pyjamas and pulled on his clothes, stopping only to glance in the mirror. A little thinner in the face perhaps, but still good looking. He stuffed the few things he had brought with him into his suitcase and bounded downstairs. He met Daisy in the hallway.

'Toby's taken the doctor to see his mother.'

'Nothing wrong, I hope?'

'No, not really. Just a cold, but he wanted to check she's all right.'

A cold. How dreadful. Thank goodness he was well; sickness was for the weak. He was a strong warrior: a Viking or a Pict – whichever was the tougher.

'Thank you so much for looking after me, Daisy, but I really must get going.'

'Why the rush?'

'I've got to find Evie.'

'But you don't know where she is.'

'I will travel the world if I have to!'

'You may have to,' smiled Daisy. 'A coffee before you go?'

'Wonderful!' Bernard beamed. He'd suddenly remembered the mantelpiece. He hadn't been in Daisy and Toby's drawing room for a long time. Over the last few months he had spent his evenings at the Embassy in a state of melancholia, and during his illness he had been confined to his mews flat and then Toby's guest bedroom, too weak to come downstairs.

He raced into the drawing room, followed closely by Daisy. The coffee was already there. A tray with two Wedgewood cups, a coffee pot, a milk jug – and a bowl of sugar.

'The maid is off today, so I'll be mother,' said Daisy. She started to pour.

Bernard's eyes shot to the fireplace. There were several cards on the mantelpiece: a notice for a dinner in Tooting, an *At Home* card from Lavinia, an invitation to the wedding of someone he didn't know and then, right at the end of the mantelpiece, a postcard. From Constantinople. He jumped up.

'No, you can't read it,' said Daisy. 'So you can just sit back down again.'

Constantinople! What was she doing there? It was so very far away. He could feel his insides unravelling.

'That's a long, long way to go,' he said weakly. 'I hope she's all right.'

'Oh don't worry about Evie, she's a real adventurer. And she's having a spiffing time. Really topping.'

Spiffing and topping sounded like strange words to describe a visit to Constantinople, but who was he to argue; Daisy had read the postcard and he hadn't.

'I feel rather worried about her. She seems to be getting further and further away.'

'Drink your coffee,' said Daisy kindly. But she didn't take her eyes off him.

They sat quietly, Daisy sipping her drink, Bernard lost in thought. Suddenly the doorbell rang.

'Delivery!' cried a voice.

Bernard cheered up immediately. 'You'll have to get that, Daisy, seeing as the maid is off.'

Daisy looked a bit anxious, but she got up and went to the door. Bernard seized his chance and raced over to the fireplace. He picked up the card, but just holding something that Evie had once held was almost too much. He gazed at the colour plate of the Blue Mosque with its tall, thin towers and behind the towers a cityscape and then the sea. The view was breathtaking and Bernard could hardly breathe. Would there be a PS this time? He braced himself and flipped the card over. But there was nothing on the back. No writing at all. The postcard was blank.

Daisy came back into the room to find Bernard standing by the fireplace. He was holding the postcard in one hand and drumming his fingers on the mantelpiece with the other.

'You wanted me to think Evie was away,' he said, 'but she clearly isn't.'

Daisy didn't reply.

'Which means she is almost certainly back in this country. But where?'

Daisy remained silent.

Bernard leaned on the mantelpiece, holding the postcard, considering the options. 'If she was trying to hide from me, then Devon would be too obvious. But where else could she go?' He was quiet for a minute and then suddenly his face lit up. 'Of course! She would go to Phoebe's. Phoebe and Evie get on well and Phoebe lives in Saffron Walden, near Cambridge, so Evie could return to her studies.' Having solved the mystery, Bernard glanced down at the decoy, 'You won't be needing this anymore?'

Daisy shook her head.

Bernard looked at her sadly, 'Why did you try to trick me?'

'Because you need more time, Bernard. Time to mature, time to grow up.'

He gave her a very reproachful look, then he stalked out of the drawing room. She heard him running up the stairs and then down again. The front door slammed shut.

A few minutes later, Toby bounded into the drawing room. 'Where's Lazarus? I want to take him out for lunch.'

'I'm afraid he got up, picked up his suitcase and walked.'

'What?'

'He's gone.'

Toby glanced over at the mantelpiece. 'To Constantinople?'

'Saffron Walden.'

'What, without saying goodbye?'

'He saw through our ruse, he's mad we tried to trick him.'

'What an ungrateful bastard!' Toby said. A pause. 'Well, not literally.'

'Yes, literally,' said Daisy.

Going to See Phoebe

All the way to Saffron Walden, Bernard turned Daisy's treachery over in his mind. She'd woven a web of deceit and he'd almost got caught in it. He drew a spider's web on the window of the carriage and then a tiny fly. And Toby, his so-called pal, had stood idly by. Dreadful. Only when he changed trains at Audley End did he start to forget about his friends' betrayal and begin to feel hopeful. Evie might be at Phoebe's. She might be almost within his grasp.

He'd forgotten what a dark, rambling house the vicarage was. It was set back from the road behind a red brick wall and hooded with mature trees. As he lifted the latch of the gate and walked up to the front door, the wind whispered uneasily in them, as if warning of his arrival. He rang the doorbell. After a couple of minutes, the door opened and Phoebe peered into the garden.

'I'm afraid the vicar is out,' she began.

'It's me, Bernard.'

'Bernard? Oh, my goodness, I didn't recognise you. You look older.'

So did she. Much older.

'Can I come in?'

'Of course.' She opened the door and he stepped into the hallway.

'It's so good to see you!' Phoebe opened her arms and gave him a sweet little hug, like a grandmother embracing a grandchild. She let go slowly, and her hands shook slightly as she led him into the parlour.

'Are you well, Phoebe?'

'I'm all right.'

The room looked very different from Bernard's last visit. Last time, the walls had been covered in dark flock wallpaper which in turn was covered with pictures of clergymen. Now, the walls were pale blue and festooned with watercolours. Some depicted gondolas in Venice, others the ruins of Athens. They were amateur but charming.

'Robert painted them,' said Phoebe, following his eyes. 'They were done mostly on our honeymoon.' She blushed with pride. Her face, which had looked pale and drawn, suddenly filled with life. 'Where did *you* go on honeymoon?' she asked.

'Oh, we didn't manage one,' said Bernard. 'We were too busy moving into our mews and I was very much in demand after my first exhibition...'

'I'm sorry you're having a period of separation.'

He couldn't think how to reply.

'Would you like some tea?'

'Yes, please.'

Phoebe disappeared and Bernard sat down on a chair, keeping his ears cocked for any noises from upstairs. If Evie was here, she would almost certainly be hiding. He gazed around the room again. The only piece of furniture remaining from the Reverend Carson's days was a loud clock on the mantelpiece. Last time he was here it had ticked 'Nit-wit, Nit-wit,' at him continually, until he'd almost thrown it through the window. He cocked his head and listened: 'Fa-ther, Fa-ther,' it ticked. But under the strains of the clock he heard something else, a faint clanging coming from a bedroom. What on earth could it be?

When Phoebe came back with the tea tray, Bernard decided to try an element of surprise. 'Phoebe, are you by any chance harbouring Evie?'

'Harbouring? She's not a ship, Bernard,' she said, sharply, 'but no, I am not harbouring your wife.'

He had never heard Phoebe talk like that before. Bernard sat in shocked silence while she poured the tea. 'I heard a noise from upstairs,' he said eventually.

'My father. He's bedridden now. He bangs on the pipes when he wants something.'

For some strange reason, a big tear squeezed itself out of the corner of Bernard's eye and plopped into his teacup. 'I was so hoping she'd be here,' he said.

'Well she isn't,' said Phoebe, more gently this time. She leaned towards him and lightly touched his arm.

But now her kindness was as hard to take as her sharpness and another tear plopped into his teacup. 'I've made so many mistakes,' he whispered. 'I've fathered a son, and I can't find the mother.'

The hand quickly withdrew. 'You've what?'

'I've fathered a son, but I haven't even met him because I don't know where he is.' He glanced at her, but she was looking away, hands busy with the sugar bowl, pulling the sugar spoon out and digging it in again, a look of great concentration on her face. 'I hope I haven't shocked you?'

She turned to him then, her mouth slightly twisted at the corners. 'Not shocked. But I find your carelessness extremely,' she paused, 'depressing.'

After that they drank their tea in silence. He couldn't think of anything else to say, or rather he didn't dare to say anything else. Only the clock spoke: 'Fa-ther, Fa-ther,' it ticked. Could she hear it too?

The telephone rang. Phoebe looked at it suspiciously for a few moments, then she picked it up. 'Hello? Oh Robert, hello.' She sounded so relieved to hear his voice. 'I've got Bernard Cavalier here. We're just having tea.'

Bernard winced to hear her use his surname.

'Would you? Thank you.' Phoebe put the phone down. 'Robert has offered to take you for a drink,' she said.

The 'has offered' sounded so formal and dismissive, as if he was a troublesome relation they had agreed to share the care of. How different to the tender hug she'd given him in the hall.

Bernard stood up. 'Well then, I'll go and find him. I suppose he's at the church?'

'That's right.'

For a moment, he thought she wasn't going to get up and was just going to sit in her chair and not see him out or say goodbye, but she got to her feet and accompanied him to the door.

'Goodbye Bernard,' she said. The door shut.

A Drink with Robert

'So, this is a pleasant surprise,' said Robert, not particularly pleasantly, as he carried two pints of ale from the bar over to the table in the corner where Bernard had plonked himself.

'Robert, I think I've upset Phoebe.'

'Why?'

'Well, I told her about my predicament – that I've fathered a son, but I can't find the mother.'

A storm of emotions crossed Robert's face: clouds of hurt, worry and anger, rolling continually over it. 'Yes, I think you probably have,' he said eventually, 'upset her I mean.'

It was too late to say 'Cheers,' the atmosphere being now rather tense, so the two men sat quietly and sipped their drinks.

'So you told Phoebe that?' Robert asked again.

'I might have implied it.'

'Oh dear.' Robert was silent for a while. 'Was that the only reason you came up?'

'I'm looking for Evie.'

The vicar didn't reply. Instead he gulped back his ale, as if he was trying to finish it as quickly as possible.

'I've been a fool,' mumbled Bernard.

Robert stared at his beermat.

'I messed up my marriage and now I've lost my son.'

'*Lost your son*?' Robert lifted his head and glared at Bernard. 'You have a strange approach to life and I'm not sure it works terribly well.'

'I'm in a dark place. Please, take pity on me.'

'Why? You don't appear to have any for others. I'm not sure you really care about anyone except yourself.'

'But I love Evie.'

'You love in a strange way, Bernard. You use love like a paint, splashing it around, slopping it on then sponging it off again.'

Bernard sat staring into space, his drink quite forgotten. 'I've been living like a monk for months,' he said eventually.

Robert looked momentarily confused, but then he smiled. 'I've met plenty of monks, Bernard, and you are not a monk!' He gave a tiny laugh.

Bernard joined in, even though the joke was at his expense, relieved that someone was laughing. The first laugh of the afternoon, but it was short-lived.

'Dear, dear,' said Robert, shaking his head. He drained his glass. 'And now I've got to get home.'

The two men stood up at the same time, their perfectly choreographed movements highlighting all their other differences. They left the pub and walked back towards the vicarage.

'Well, goodbye then,' Bernard said. 'Thanks for the drink. I'm sorry you couldn't help me.'

Robert seemed to relent, as if he'd remembered that, at the end of the day, he was still a vicar.

'Where would you go if you were Evie?'

'Devon.'

'Well then?'

Letter to Mr Brunton

3, Warwick Mews, Pimlico, London, SW.
Wednesday 22 February 1922

Dear Mr Brunton

I hardly dare put pen to paper. I'm sure you must hate me at the very least. However, despite our differences, you and I have one thing in common and this one thing is a priceless jewel. Your daughter is a pearl beyond price – a pearl that I have tossed away and am now, rather belatedly, trying to find again. It may be too late in the day for your liking, but there is a very small chance that it is not too late for Evie. She has forgiven me before. In my wildest dreams, I dare to hope that she may forgive me again.

I have tried writing to her in Cambridge only to have my letters returned. I have tried writing to her in Devon but have had no reply. There was a time when I thought I could live without her, but that's no longer possible. I'm sure she can live without me – live and thrive. I am, as ever, thinking only of myself.

Mr Brunton, I implore you to tell me where Evie is. I must see her. If she is with you then I beg you to allow me to come to Colyton and meet with her. If she is somewhere else then please, please, let me have her address, for I have a lot of explaining to do. If she is not with you and you don't know where she is then I am finished.

Your desperate son-in-law,

Bernard

As soon as Mr Brunton had finished the letter, he tore it up into tiny pieces and stuffed it back in the envelope. It was fortunate that he'd been the one to pick up the post. He got up out of his armchair and threw the envelope into the middle of the fire that blazed in the hearth of the parlour. The envelope ignited at once, burning with a bright yellow flame.

'The pure flame of ardour!' he muttered sarcastically, as he picked up the newspaper again.

Posthumous Sale

POSTHUMOUS SALE OF WORK BY

BENEDICT CAVALIER

ON FRIDAY MARCH 3RD 1922 AT 3PM.

PREVIEW 10AM – 12 NOON THE SAME DAY
CHRISTIE'S AUCTION HOUSE, KING STREET,
LONDON

The preview was teeming with people. As soon as he walked in, Bernard realised that this was the real funeral for Benedict Cavalier, and it was the ideal setting for a send-off. The room was lined with arched windows; the morning sun slanted in and the ten sculptures for sale were bathed in light, creating dramatic shadows, both of the statuettes themselves and the plinths they were resting on. The impression created was of the inside of a church and people looking at the work did so quietly and reverently, as if Christie's was, for one morning only, the sculptor's last resting place.

All those who hadn't come to his funeral now wanted a memento of the sculptor, a shiny piece of bronze to treasure for ever. And the preview provided them with a perfectly romantic day. They could be inspired by the late sculptor's work, float off to Brown's for lunch and then back for the auction. They could buy a statuette by Benedict Cavalier to keep on their sideboard and, when there was a lull in dinner-party conversation, they could nod at it and say, 'How we all miss Benedict.'

But it was irritating that these 'friends and supporters' were out in force on a sunny day in March when they were so obviously absent from a snowy day in February. Their quiet piety infuriated Bernard. He started walking noisily around, bumping into plinths, knocking into people, apologising loudly and profusely. In between, he hummed to himself or emitted little exclamations of surprise.

'Haven't seen that one before! Oh, wait a minute, this one's an old favourite.' In this manner, Bernard narrated the last ten sculptures created by Benedict, the ones he didn't live to exhibit himself. And people glanced around half sympathetically, as if he was an idiot son who they were tolerating solely out of respect for his great father.

Benedict's work seemed to be sharper towards the end, as if he knew that it was these last ten works he was going to be remembered by. There was a beautiful bronze of a pair of ballet shoes, exquisite in their detail, another of a pair of hands belonging to an older lady and one of a young girl looking up from a book. The rest were nudes. Bernard glanced through the catalogue. He knew all the names: Cynthia, Gertrude, Delia Plum. Golly he had even persuaded Nelly Ogden to sit for him. But there was one more: *Untitled*. Someone for him to guess – that would be fun.

He wandered over to plinth number ten and there was the mystery statuette he had noticed on his last visit to Benedict's. He crept up close, determined to identify the sitter. She was a nude, an attractively proportioned nude and she seemed oddly familiar. There was a feeling of uncanny familiarity. He glanced around; no one was looking so he gently put out a finger to touch her face. Then he absent-mindedly ran his finger around the back of her head. And that's when he felt it: a tiny bump in the bronze, a little lump on the nape of her neck. A mole.

Once Bernard knew it was there, he couldn't stop touching it. He ran his fingers up and down the small metallic dot. Then, before he could stop himself, he picked the statue up and hugged it to his chest.

A Christie's employee rushed over. 'Please put it down, sir, you are not allowed to touch the exhibits.'

'But it's my wife!' cried Bernard, hugging the bronze tighter.

The employee nodded to someone in a doorway who nodded to someone else and then a man in a smart suit appeared.

'Mr Cavalier, please put the statuette down.'

'But it's my wife.'

'It's not your wife, sir, it's a likeness, a copy. It is not her person, it's a work of art. And you do not own it. It is the property of Benedict Cavalier's estate.'

Bernard glanced around. The pious pilgrims who had earlier given him sympathetic glances were now starting to sneer. Bernard reluctantly handed the naked body of his wife over to the manager. The manager carefully repositioned it on the plinth, extracted a large handkerchief from his pocket and proceeded to polish Evie Cavalier, carefully removing the grubby fingerprints of her estranged husband.

Bernard stormed out of the preview and down the steps of Christie's, into St James's Park. He flopped down on a park bench and put his face in his hands. So, he'd sculpted Evie – nude! How dare he! And how dare *she*! She'd taken her clothes off and revealed herself to a man who was notorious with ladies. What a betrayal. Bernard could hardly believe it. He imagined Evie in Benedict's studio, nervously undressing behind the screen. It was disgusting, disgraceful.

He pulled his pipe tobacco out of one pocket and his pipe out of the other and sat on the bench. He bent over the pipe, teasing the twirls of tobacco into it, pushing them down and then lighting them with a match, puffing on the pipe until white smoke was billowing out, like a steam train. He inhaled deeply a few times, then he threw his head back and looked around. The park was quiet. Everyone was at the preview, staring at his wife.

When and why did it happen? He cast his mind back to those early days in London. Two images flashed into his mind: Robert with his head lolling on their dining table and Evie ripping up a ballgown. Then he suddenly remembered going to Benedict's one morning and being asked to move some furniture for Jones. It had taken a while. Afterwards, his father had appeared and announced that Evie wanted to go to Cambridge and wasn't that a marvellous idea. Perhaps that was the *when* and the *why*. Perhaps Benedict had offered funds for Cambridge *if* she posed for him. He'd effectively bought her. And both of them had kept him in the dark.

He tried to recall their conversation when he'd got home and found her soaking in the bath. She had looked lovely, he remembered that much, and she'd suddenly stood up, complaining the water was cold. Then he heard her voice, quite clearly, drifting over St James's Park: 'I'm the piece from another jigsaw, the bit there's no room for.' And he wanted to take the statue in his arms again and protect it. He would have to buy it, whatever the cost.

While Benedict Cavalier's friends dined in a relaxed fashion at Brown's, Bernard repaired to a public house and planned his strategy. It would take courage: Dutch courage. He bought three pints of ale and slowly downed them. During the first pint, he planned exactly how he would behave before *Untitled* was on the podium; during the second, he decided how much he would be prepared to bid for it; during the third, he put the whole thing out of his mind and just drank his ale. At five minutes to three he returned to Christie's and joined the throng of people in the auction room.

Bidding was enthusiastic and most items went for a good price. There was one serious collector there: a tall American in a long coat and large hat. He bought two statuettes and bid for several others, raising the prices and giving the occasion a feeling of real excitement. Finally, *Untitled* was on the block.

'What am I offered for this beautiful bronze,' began the auctioneer. 'I should point out that the seller has put a reserve of one hundred pounds on this final lot.'

'Two hundred pounds,' called Bernard, bravely. If he started the bids high, then it might dissuade others.

'Three hundred,' drawled the American at the front.

His confident response to Bernard's bid seemed to wake everyone else up, as if they realised this was the last chance to purchase a Benedict Cavalier. There was a flurry of bids, creeping up towards the three hundred and fifty mark.

'Four hundred!' shouted Bernard.

The room fell briefly silent. This was the highest bid that had been made all day.

Then someone at the back, perhaps a journalist, cried: 'It's the girl in the bath!'

Bidding became frantic. People waved their handkerchiefs and waved their arms and the auctioneer struggled to keep up. The price shot up past six hundred pounds and was nearing seven hundred. Suddenly, there was a call from the front, loud and clear. Bernard recognised Toby's voice: 'One thousand pounds!'

A hush fell over the whole room.

The auctioneer raised his hammer. 'Going, going,' he started.

Bernard couldn't believe it. Toby, his trusted friend was trying to buy the statuette. He must have realised it was Evie and yet he was trying to grab her for himself. Bernard saw the statue disappearing from sight, snatched from his grasp by a man he used to like. A moment of madness descended and he raised his hand.

'Two thousand pounds!' he yelled, just before the hammer hit the block.

'Gone to Bernard Cavalier for two thousand pounds!' cried the auctioneer.

A photographer turned and flashed his camera in Bernard's face. Toby turned and gave him a sad, disappointed look and then Bernard was surrounded by employees from Christie's.

'It is indeed a record price for a Benedict Cavalier,' he heard the auctioneer say to the journalist as he was led away to settle his bill.

The room emptied slowly; everyone was talking, no one wanted to leave the scene of so much drama and excitement. Meanwhile, deep in the bowels of the auction house, Bernard smiled uneasily at his captors.

'So, how are you planning to pay?' asked the smart-suited manager. 'Cash or cheque?'

When Bernard finally emerged from Christie's, he was a much poorer man. He'd surrendered a savings account he'd opened after selling *Girl in a Bath* to the Tate and he'd agreed to hand over his Degas and Rodin statuettes. He'd also signed up to paying Christie's one hundred pounds a month for six months in order to clear the remaining debt. He would have to give in his notice on the mews flat in Warwick Mews and move back to the studio; he would also have to paint like billy-o. The wheel had come full circle. No home, no wife, not even a girlfriend. He was back to where he had been two years earlier. All he had was a bronze statuette of a woman he would probably never see again and the rumour of a baby he would probably never meet. He staggered out into the evening and there was Toby waiting for him, leaning on Daisy's car.

'I was only trying to help,' Toby began, half apologetic; half belligerent.

'It was a huge help, thank you,' retorted Bernard, sarcastically.

'Well, that's nice you're finally thanking me for something,' said Toby, his voice acid. 'Because I didn't hear you thanking me for nursing you back to health; or paying your doctor's bill.'

'You and Daisy tricked me—' began Bernard, glad to feel the heat of anger replace his terrible feeling of despondency.

'Daisy and I have wasted far too much time on you,' interrupted Toby. 'I'm not as nice as you think and certainly not as nice as my wife. I'm a fair-weather friend, Bernard. I like happy endings. I'm not going to hang around and watch you destroy yourself.'

'You tried to buy Evie!' cried Bernard.

'Yes, I did,' said Toby, quietly. 'I tried to buy her for you, Bernard, but you put a stop to it.' Toby sighed, shook his head, got into Daisy's six-cylinder Bentley and drove slowly away.

A View of St Luke's

It was an interesting picture: a church, painted with a two-dimensional naivety; a few figures emerging from it into a snowy landscape; snow-capped gravestones standing in silent contemplation. If you looked closely, the figures were almost recognisable. There was a woman on her own, dressed in black lace. Her expression was one of total disappointment, but it looked as if she might have been like that for a while, not just on this particular occasion. There were two men walking together, one with a bald patch and smart overcoat who looked like a servant, the other older, greyer and with a furtiveness about him. There was a couple, holding hands: he, young and foppish, with floppy hair; she serene and attractive, with a dark bob and sharp green eyes. Finally, there was a tall, broad, flame-haired character, slightly bent, weighed down by something. He was looking towards a gravestone with an air of complete bewilderment as if a ghost was about to appear from behind it.

But the painting wasn't finished. Bernard picked up his brush and started up in the left-hand side of the pale wintry sky. He painted a long white dress covered with flowers. The dress floated right across the top of the picture, but it dipped down in places so it almost touched the figures and the gravestones. Then he painted the girl who was wearing the dress, a blonde-haired girl. She was facing away from the church, looking upwards with a thoughtful expression on her face. He worked on the face for a long time, in fact he nearly overworked it, but at the last minute he managed to pull his brush away.

Bernard sat on the floor of his studio, lit his pipe and studied his painting. Like a child who is trying to understand a strange concept from the grown-up world, his eyes moved from one face to another, studying the expressions over and over. The floating bride was always the last face he came to.

Once the painting was completely dry, he lifted it off the easel and started carefully wrapping it up in brown paper – layer after layer, to shield it from any knocks, as if it was his heart that he was sending out into the world and he wanted to protect it. Layer upon layer, like successive falls of snow, creating a blanket of protection. Then he wrote in big letters: Evie Cavalier, North Lodge, Key Lane, Colyton, Devon. And underneath: Please Forward if necessary. Finally, he wrapped the parcel round and round with string, making a secure pattern of knotted squares. Then he heaved the package up and under his arm and set off for the post office.

Distractions

Evie stopped for a rest. The parcel had been heavy to carry upstairs and she decided to push it along the landing towards her room, dragging it with her fingers and thumbs, shoving it along the carpet. Then she opened her door, pulled the parcel inside and leaned it up against the bed. Some of the brown paper had ripped away, revealing a glimpse of canvas at the bottom right-hand corner. No, she wouldn't look at it. Not now; she had to get her chapter finished. Turning her back on the picture, Evie returned to the desk and sat down in front of her typewriter. Right, where was she?

Born in 1759, Mary Wollstonecraft was a writer and philosopher. She held the 'shocking' belief that men and women should have equal opportunities. Her treatise, 'A Vindication of the Rights of Woman', was revolutionary in its thinking. She was radical and forward-looking – a real comet, crashing into the male-dominated atmosphere of the late eighteenth century. Her ideas were ahead not just of her own time, but of our own!

And Wollstonecraft did not just have wild and dangerous ideas; she also lived a wild and dangerous life. Having written her manifesto for women, she went to Paris in December 1792, arriving in the middle of the French Revolution!

It was just one month before Louis XVI was executed at the guillotine. France was in chaos but Wollstonecraft saw it as an opportunity for change. She was optimistic that a better future would emerge out of the turmoil and wanted to be there to celebrate it.

It is wonderful to imagine a young woman embarking on such a trip at a perilous moment in history. Wollstonecraft was attracted by the power vacuum and confident that something exciting would arise, like a phoenix, from the ashes of the French monarchy. The political upheaval in France gave her confidence that social upheaval would follow. She wrote: 'The divine right of husbands, like the divine right of kings, may, it is hoped, in this enlightened age, be contested without danger.'

Evie paused and pushed the carriage return lever on the typewriter. Then she stopped and glanced over at the picture before continuing.

One hundred and thirty years ago, Wollstonecraft argued for equal educational opportunities as a right. How far have we actually come since she begged us to 'strengthen the female mind by enlarging it'? What, one wonders, would she have made of the current situation in one British university where women are still not awarded a real degree even after they have studied long and hard for it and passed the exams. So-called 'Titular degrees' would have incensed Mary Wollstonecraft and

Evie jumped up and returned to the picture. She unwrapped it hurriedly, ignoring the string, tearing the brown paper underneath it away, so that when the painting was exposed, it looked as if it had been caught in a fishing net. She stared at it for a long time, then she went back to her desk, lay her head on *Stars, Comets and Disobedient Women*, stacked neatly in a pile two hundred pages high beside her typewriter, and silently wept.

Broke and Broken

Mr James frequently worked late. He was often to be found in his office long after his secretary had gone home and long after the doorman had retired for the night. Mr James had a key for these sort of evenings, and he used it to let himself out of the back door of the Inns of Court into an overgrown garden. The garden was so unkempt that he sometimes felt he was leaving the safety of his office to step into a jungle. Mr James didn't like jungles; he liked law and order. He felt there was something overblown and out of control about the gnarled apple trees and giant rhubarb leaves, silhouetted against the wall of the chambers by a lamp on the main road.

Mr James always hurried through the garden as quickly as possible and tonight was no exception. But halfway across, as he fumbled past a particularly large apple tree, the lawyer found himself to be the victim of some sort of attack. A man stepped out from behind the rhubarb and quickly and quietly put one hand around his neck – right around, and the other over his mouth. Was it a mugger? A highwayman? No, worse than that, it was the son of his late client, Benedict Cavalier. Mr James tried to make signs with his eyes, complicated signs which meant *I know who you are, please let go of me, I will come quietly.* The son seemed to understand for he took away the hand covering the lawyer's mouth, although he tightened the grip around his neck.

'I'm sorry to bother you so late,' said the son, 'but I need to speak to you quietly and confidentially about something.'

'Be my guest,' said the lawyer, as politely and pragmatically as he could under the circumstances.

The son released the lawyer's neck but quickly gripped both of his arms, pinning him up against the apple tree.

'I'm going to contest the will,' he hissed, 'I'm going to sue my father's estate and claim what I'm due.'

'But you don't even know who you're suing,' exclaimed the lawyer, 'and until probate is granted—'

Mr James was not a small man, it was just that Benedict's son was as tall as a giant and he picked the lawyer up and carried him gently but firmly over to a wall that separated this particular Inn of Court from the other ones. Then he placed him carefully on top of it. The wall was low on the garden side, but it plunged down much further into the next courtyard.

'I want to know who I'll be suing. And I won't let you down till you tell me.'

Mr James mulled over his options. It would be a long night, on a wall that was already wearing a hole in the seat of his trousers. And when probate was granted, Bernard would know the name of the beneficiary anyway.

'I can give you their first name and their first name only,' he said. 'When I am safely back on the ground,' he added.

The gigantic son put his hands under the lawyer's armpits and lifted him down again.

'Her name is Sophia,' said the lawyer, as he brushed down his trousers.

Even a man with as much professional experience as Mr James could not have known the effect this small word would have. The name *Sophia* seemed to hit the son between the eyes and he reeled backwards. He looked so devastated and flabbergasted that the lawyer felt almost sorry for him. He rubbed his hands nervously together and watched while Bernard's legs buckled under him, forcing him to the ground.

'Will you still be suing?' the lawyer anxiously enquired.

'No,' gasped Bernard, lying on the ground, his face buried in the cold, damp grass.

'Well then,' smiled the lawyer, suddenly realising that this incident in the garden, terrifying though it was initially, might have saved him hours of paperwork, 'I'll be off home, unless I can be of any further assistance?'

Bernard shook his head and Mr James tip-toed quietly away.

After the lawyer disappeared, the garden went strangely quiet, just the rustle of the rhubarb leaves, swaying in the evening breeze, and the gentle tapping of a branch on a window. Bernard lay where he had fallen, like an enormous tree felled with a single blow. Well, at least he knew now. The beneficiary of his father's estate was his mother. Benedict had left all his money and all his property to a woman who he hadn't laid eyes on since the moment of his conception.

The whole situation was a nightmare triangle. His mother had abandoned him; his father had brought him up but refused, until very recently, to acknowledge he was his real father. Benedict had made no attempt to find the mother when Bernard was a child. Now, out of the blue, he had left her everything. He must have traced her in the end, when it was too late for Bernard; when he had nothing to gain and everything to lose from a reunion between his parents. Stitched up. That was the only word for it. And how could he possibly sue Sophia, a woman who he didn't even remember? No, he couldn't bear to sue her; he couldn't bear to even see her. He could never face her in a court of law – the very thought of it was intolerable. Let her have the house and good luck to her.

Bernard got up, returned to the garden wall and swung himself up onto it. He walked a few steps along to where it intersected a second wall, and jumped back down into Gray's Inn Road. The last time he'd found himself alone on this road was just after the funeral, when he'd heard he wasn't Benedict's beneficiary. At the time, he'd thought that nothing could be more hurtful than being disinherited. It turned out that Benedict could and had hurt him even more. Leaving everything to Sophia was the final straw and Bernard felt well and truly broken.

It was quiet on the street. Just two other people out walking. He passed a street hawker, still carrying his box of wares around his neck: pipe cleaners, matches, bootlaces. And a porter from Covent Garden, with a pile of baskets on his head. Both heading home.

Bernard wanted to run away, far away from everything, but he couldn't seem to keep away from Chelsea. He found himself wandering down King's Road and gazing up at his father's house. By chance, Jones was bringing something up from the studio and noticed Bernard walking slowly past.

'Mr Bernard.'

'Jones.' Bernard couldn't think of anything else to say.

'I'm so sorry about everything, Mr Bernard.'

'Did you know?'

'Only that it wasn't you, I had no idea who the beneficiary was, still don't.'

'You *don't*?'

'No, I get all my instructions from Mr James. I'm to shut up the house, mothball everything and then wait.'

'For what?'

'No idea. I'm to be kept on some sort of retainer so perhaps I'll be reemployed again eventually.'

'I'm sorry, Jones.'

'No, *I'm* sorry, Mr Bernard.'

'It's Sophia,' Bernard whispered.

'What?' Jones looked absolutely amazed, but also very pleased, as if having Sophia for an employer was the best possible outcome. 'Well, I must get on. Good luck, Mr Bernard.' And the butler shook hands, warmly and firmly, as if Bernard was about to undergo a difficult task and he wasn't allowed to help him in any way. Then he disappeared quickly inside the house and shut the door, leaving Bernard on his own.

The Baby Snatcher

The following Sunday, having packed Toby off to church with his mother, Daisy sat back down at the breakfast table with the latest edition of *The Views of the World*. She opened the paper less enthusiastically these days, more suspiciously. But she couldn't stop buying it; it was compulsive reading. As she expected, there was a huge picture of Bernard on page two, blinking into a flashlight with a look of dismay on his face. 'ARTIST PAYS RECORD SUM FOR NUDE OF ESTRANGED WIFE,' read the headline. She sighed and was about to begin reading the article when she noticed a strange figure in the square opposite their house.

It was a man, raggedly dressed, walking along like an old crow; his head bent forward and his arms bent back behind him like wings. The figure hobbled over to a perambulator parked beside a bench. A nanny, dressed from head to toe in black, was sitting beside it reading a newspaper. While she was engrossed in reading, the crow took the opportunity to peer into the pram, pulling the baby's blanket down slightly, so it could have a good look at whoever was inside. The nanny suddenly noticed and, flinging her paper to one side, starting waving her arms around like a scarecrow, sending the large bird flapping away to another bench and another perambulator. As it moved off, it turned slightly to glance towards the house and Daisy caught sight of Bernard's tragic face. She stuffed the newspaper under the sofa and rushed to the front door.

'Bernard!'

He looked over with a bemused expression on his face, saw her and looked away again.

'Bernard!' Daisy trotted across the road and into the square. 'Come on, Bernard. Come and have a coffee, Toby's been missing you. He'll be back from church soon.'

Bernard looked at her and appeared to swither. He glanced at the next pram along, then he turned and took a step towards Daisy.

'That would be nice,' he said, so simply and sweetly that she could have wept. She led him into the breakfast room, rang the bell for the maid and ordered fresh coffee and toast.

'Where've you been, Bernard?'

'Keeping away from your husband,' he said gloomily.

'Well, it's time the two of you made up.'

In the warmth of the house, a strange aroma was coming off him: a mix of bonfire and something more unsavoury. Daisy wrinkled her nose.

'I've been letting things slide,' he muttered by way of explanation, as though he could smell it too. He slurped his coffee and gobbled his toast and then Toby burst in.

'Bernard!' he cried, as if they hadn't seen each other for years.

'Toby!' Bernard jumped up, beaming.

'Great to see you, old man!' exclaimed Toby. 'I would hug you but...' his voice trailed off.

The two men slapped each other boisterously on the back.

'I love her,' said Bernard, as if it explained everything.

'I know, I know,' said Toby, continuing to slap Bernard on the back as if he was a child who had choked on a sweet, 'you need to persuade her to see you.'

'Well, first I need to find her.'

'The last letter Daisy got was postmarked Devon.'

'What, not Constantinople?' said Bernard, before he could stop himself.

'We thought you weren't ready,' said Toby. 'We thought you'd mess up again.'

'It's all right.' Bernard waved the explanation away.

'Anyway, things have moved on since then,' said Toby. 'When we planted the Constantinople postcard you were squandering your time and money at the Embassy. Now, well now you're much poorer, I imagine?'

'I'm not quite the catch I once was,' Bernard said, ironically. 'No home, no savings. Although I do have a son.'

'The future doesn't look bright,' agreed Toby, 'but I think the exorbitant amount you paid for a statuette of your wife would have melted the hearts of even the cruellest of the Fates. It feels like you've passed a test, somehow.'

'Yes, the poverty test,' muttered Bernard.

'But you squandered your money for her,' said Toby, 'in a way,' he added doubtfully.

'You must try to get in touch,' said Daisy. 'My hunch is Devon, I bet she's with her parents. I mean, where else would she go?'

'Where else,' agreed Bernard. 'But right now, Constantinople sounds more attractive.'

The Statuette

She was waiting for him, just like she was every night, sitting on the Georgian windowsill, gleaming in the glow of the gaslight shining in from the street.

'I'm home, darling,' he said.

But she didn't look pleased.

He dropped his coat on the floor and came over to her. 'I haven't had a drop to drink. Even though I'm miserable as sin.'

But she didn't look impressed.

'And Carruthers has sold another picture. So I've covered next month's payment to Christie's.'

But she didn't look interested.

'You're not cheap to keep!'

But she didn't appreciate the joke. She was lost in her own world, oblivious to the trouble she'd caused. He'd given up his mews for her, his social life, his savings. But she didn't care. Suddenly he wondered if the statuette was proving to be, not only a curse to buy, but also a curse to keep. For the perfect bronze reminded him continually of what he'd forfeited; not just his home and money, but also the woman she was imitating. After all she wasn't Evie. Just a likeness. He had a copy of Evie, but that was a million miles away from the real thing. It was the difference between visiting the moon and gazing at it through a telescope. Like the moon, the real Evie was far, far away. The cold statuette seemed to emphasise the distance, and looking at it doubled his longing for his wife.

He had bought the bronze at great cost, but he was beginning to realise that he couldn't keep it. That was the final irony. He had thrown Evie away. He had thrown everything else away trying to retain a memory of her and now he was finding the memory unbearable. But he wouldn't throw the memory away; he would give it to Evie. He would write to Mrs Brunton and he would beg her to see him and he would take the statuette down to Devon and ask her to pass it on. Evie's father hadn't replied – but her mother might. He could only try.

Letter to Mrs Brunton

3, Warwick Mews, Pimlico, London, SW.
Friday 17ᵗʰ March 1922

My Dear Mrs Brunton,

I desperately hoped that I would never have to write this letter to you. I didn't want to admit that I have hurt Evie so much that she has probably left me for ever. She has disappeared without a trace: without a phone number or an address. I have been trying to get hold of her for months. I have no idea where she is and can only assume that she doesn't want me to find her. I wanted to spare you from my frantic search. I even wrote to your husband a few weeks ago, but have had no reply.

Mrs Brunton, I am a broken man, but not a stupid one – I realise that I have little chance of ever seeing Evie again. But I am desperate for news of her. I must know that she is all right. I also need to know what she wants to do next. I have hurt her past forgiveness, not once, not twice, but three times. My third enormous and selfish blunder is unforgivable and inescapable. If you read the gossip columns of any London newspaper you will almost certainly know what it is and why it will prevent us ever being together again. I have ruined my life. I had everything and now I have nothing. That everything was your daughter. I am nothing without her.

I am writing to ask if I could possibly come down to Devon to see you. It would help me enormously just to talk to you. I am dying to see Evie, but I realise that she may not be with you and, even if she is, she may not want to see me. But I have something for her, something precious, and I thought I could perhaps leave it with you for safe keeping. I implore you to allow me to come and visit, even just for a few minutes.

Please forgive me, even though I cannot begin to forgive myself.

Bernard

Mrs Brunton prepared all Mr Brunton's favourite things for their cosy fireside supper: cold pork sandwiches in soft brown bread and apricot tart and custard. She waited until he had finished his second helping of pudding before she ventured: 'I have written to Bernard.'

'You've what?'

'We can't go on avoiding him. Sooner or later we will have to see him.'

'What on earth possessed you?'

'He wrote to me – and I know he wrote to you too.'

'But Evie asked us to ignore any communication from him.'

'This wasn't any communication, this was a heart-wrenching letter. Bernard is a broken man.'

'You're too soft—'

'And you're too hard.' Mrs Brunton spoke boldly, but her eyes were full of worry. 'We can't put it off any longer. You and I will have to face him eventually. We don't want him lurking around town, spying on us. I would rather know when he is visiting Colyton. By inviting him we can remain in control.'

'And what will we say?'

'That we don't know where Evie is.'

'And you think he'll swallow that?'

'If he hears it from us in person, he'll have to.'

'Well, he'll hear it from you, I won't go near him.' Mr Brunton humphed with annoyance. 'I don't know what Evie will say,' was his parting shot, as he took off his napkin and headed up to his study.

'Neither do I,' thought Mrs Brunton, as she put the remains of supper back on the trolley, her anxious eyes staring back at her in the glass pudding bowls.

Waterloo

'I'd like a ticket to Colyton.'

'Single or return?'

Bernard stared at the man behind the glass of the ticket office. He'd been so busy trying to negotiate a visit to Devon, he hadn't given any thought to what he would do when it was over.

'Er,'

'Single or return?' repeated the man.

'Return,' said Bernard.

'Day return?'

He had no idea. Even if Evie wasn't at home, there was always the faintest chance that her parents would ask him to stay for supper.

'Um...'

Someone in the queue behind him tutted.

'Return. Normal return.'

But there was nothing normal about his trip to Colyton, the aim of it being to try to find his wife. And he had no idea if she was even there. He had no idea where she was. *My hunch is Devon.* That's what Daisy had said. He paced up and down the platform waiting for his train. It reminded him of all his visits to Waterloo station when Evie first disappeared. He had come here every day to meet the afternoon and then the evening train. What had he been playing at? Why hadn't he just gone to find her? So much time wasted and all the while she had slipped further away from him, first to Paris, then Nice, then Florence and now, heaven knew where. But surely Mrs Brunton would take pity on him, give him some clues, reveal her hiding place? Anyway, whatever happened, he could deliver the statuette. It would be a relief to be rid of it; it was weighing him down in more ways than one. He could feel it now, a heavy weight in his rucksack, pulling on his neck.

The Devon train came steaming into the platform. A squeal of brakes, a banging of doors and then a stream of passengers alighted from the train. He stood and waited for everyone to get off, just in case. No sign of her. He jumped aboard.

The carriage he got into was empty, apart from an old lady who sat reading, in an enormous hat. He plonked himself on a seat by the window, took off his rucksack and placed it on the seat beside him. The old lady gave him a suspicious look as if she knew him from somewhere, then returned to her book. The train set off and Bernard looked out of the window. *My only hope, my only hope,* rattled the wheels.

At Salisbury, two girls got on, with several hat boxes.

The old lady lowered her book and glared at him.

'You may have to move your sack,' she said.

'Rucksack,' countered Bernard.

'Rucksack. These young ladies have hats which are almost certainly too fragile to risk the luggage rack.'

There was a time, he thought, when he would have made a performance out of the situation. He would have revealed the nude, like a magician pulling a rabbit out of a hat and explained to the shocked octogenarian that art was more important than fashion; and besides, as the bronze was of a lady, she was entitled to a seat. But not today. Today he obediently picked up the rucksack containing the priceless statuette and placed it in the overhead luggage rack. Then he sat down again and carried on looking out of the window.

Just how much had it cost him? A Degas, a Rodin, a flat, even a friend – for a bit. And it was still costing, even now.

He started writing on the window, calculating how much more there was still to pay. The two girls watched him, nudging each other and giggling. *My only hope, my only hope.* It was impossible to concentrate, so he rubbed out the sums with his sleeve, blew on the glass and instead wrote *Evie* over and over. The two girls looked away.

The Lawnmower

One of the things Mr Brunton was most proud of was his Ransome lawnmower. He had bought it as a present to himself on the eve of his retirement when he'd slipped seamlessly from solicitor to gardener. He spent hours cleaning the iron blades and smearing them with grease. He loved everything about the lawnmower: its shape, its green colour and its energetic purring noise. For Mr Brunton's Ransome was extremely noisy and this made it the perfect weapon against his son-in-law.

As soon as Bernard opened the garden gate that led up to the front door of North Lodge, Mr Brunton started pushing his trusty Ransome up and down the back garden with such force that the sound of chopping blades drove the birds off the lawn and up into the trees. Bernard, already nervous, gave a start and his hand stumbled at the bell, so he couldn't tell if he'd pressed it too hard or not pressed it at all. Evidently, he had pressed it, for Mrs Brunton appeared. With the faint, regal smile used by Queen Victoria and other elderly monarchs, she motioned Bernard into the parlour.

A glance around told the visitor he wouldn't be staying long. There were no teacups winking on the coffee table, no welcoming fire in the grate and not even the faintest whiff of a scone. Bernard could feel the sands of time slipping through his fingers, as if someone had turned an egg-timer over in a parlour game and he had less than four minutes to work out what on earth had happened to his wife.

'Mrs Brunton,' he began.

At that moment, the lawnmower started coming slowly but steadily around the house into the front garden. As it grew nearer, its sound increased: an annoying hum became an angry buzzing and then a raucous screech like an aviary of birds or perhaps a cage of monkeys. By the time it reached the front garden, Bernard could hardly hear himself think. But it wasn't just the sound that was off-putting. The lawnmower's operator had decided to concentrate on the patch of grass nearest the parlour window and he marched backwards and forwards, to and fro, staring defiantly in front of him.

'Mrs Brunton,' Bernard began again, 'I am desperately trying to find your daughter.'

'I can't help.' Mrs Brunton's regal smile disappeared and her mouth set itself in a determined line which made her look suddenly older.

'But you must know where she is.'

Silence.

'If you could just give me a clue,' he begged, knowing the clock was ticking on this nightmare game of charades.

'No.'

'So you don't know where Evie is?'

'Did you come down for the day?'

And that was it. His turn was finished. He gestured helplessly with his hands, like a drowning man. 'Please help me.'

'I will tell Evie you called to see us and asked for news.'

'But you haven't given me any.'

'Evie is well. Very well.'

'And that's news?'

'Mr Cavalier, if Evie wanted you to have news, she would have contacted you herself.'

Bernard reeled, both from her formal use of his surname and from the truth in her words. It was up to Evie. And Evie didn't want him to know either where she was or how she was. And he would have to accept it.

Unexpected

After being politely shown off the premises, Bernard went straight to The Bear Inn. He'd never needed a drink so badly. He went up to the bar to order, tossing his rucksack on the floor in a gesture of despair. The canvas bag hit the ground with a clunk; Bernard gave a start. Oh no, the statuette! He hastily bent down and took out the mini Evie. How could he have forgotten?

He lifted the bronze up onto the bar and stared at it. He couldn't face taking it back to Evie's parents, but he couldn't face taking it back to London either. Perhaps he could just leave it in the pub and sidle off, back to the station. But no. He'd had enough of being a coward. He would go back and see Mrs Brunton *again*. Bernard sighed, stood up and heaved the rucksack onto his shoulders. Then he wearily walked the few yards back to North Lodge.

As he came around the corner, he spied Mr Brunton cycling out of the back gate. The grass-cutting was obviously over. Well, at least he wouldn't have to see *him* again. Bernard trotted up the path, keen to hand over the bronze before Evie's father got back. He rang the doorbell and waited. No one came. He rang again. Still no one. He was just about to push the door open and leave the statuette inside, when Mrs Brunton appeared. She looked flushed and extremely nervous. There was a smell of washing soda and a sound of boiling from the kitchen.

'Bernard!'

He was relieved to hear her use his first name. This was a different woman from just a few moments ago. He had taken her by surprise and her guard was down. Perhaps he would get more information from her now her reactions were unrehearsed.

'I'm so sorry to bother you again,' Bernard said, stepping inside, 'but I forgot to give you this.' He reached inside the rucksack and held out the statuette. The bronze glimmered eerily in the dark hallway.

'Oh!' Mrs Brunton seemed unsure how to react. 'Is it Evie?' she asked, glancing at the figurine.

'Yes. My father sculpted it. I bought it.' The words sounded so simple and straightforward. There was no point adding *it ruined me*. 'Could you give it to Evie, when you next see her?'

'Of course. Thank you for bringing it down.' Mrs Brunton tried to revert to the regal approach that had worked so well earlier, but beneath the firmly set jaw, waves of anxiety were welling, just under her skin, so her whole face seemed to be fluttering.

'Well…' Bernard glanced around the hall. Still no clues. Nothing different from his last visit apart from the smell of washing, rather a lot of washing judging by the steam. Mrs Brunton was much more nervous, probably because Mr Brunton wasn't there, but he hadn't managed to wrong-foot her and now his time was running out again.

'Well, if you could just tell Evie it's from me.' He put the statuette down on the hall table and turned for the door.

'Goodbye,' Mrs Brunton said. He could hear a quiver in her voice.

'Goodbye.'

He glanced back with a half-smile and then, when his right foot was already back in the front garden, he heard it: a small wavering cry from an upstairs bedroom – a baby. The front door was closing quickly behind him, but he stuck his left foot out to jam it, then forced it open again with his fingers.

He was back in the dark hallway and Mrs Brunton was blinking at him like a trapped mole. There was another sob, soft and gentle. Bernard raced past her and up the stairs. Four doors faced him along the landing. He listened, but he could only hear Mrs Brunton pattering up behind him. Then, from the door on the far right, came a gurgle. He bounded across the landing and burst into the bedroom.

Evie was sitting on a bed, long hair gleaming in the bright sun streaming in at the window. On the walls were three paintings: one of the Cam, one of the Thames and one of a churchyard in Chelsea. On the floor, the windowsill and the chest of drawers, sat bundles of papers, stacked neatly into what looked like chapters. On the desk, a typewriter. And in her arms, was the most beautiful creature Bernard had ever seen: a gorgeous baby, with fluffy auburn hair, rosy cheeks and enormous blue eyes. The baby was sucking on its mother's finger but, when it saw Bernard, it pushed the finger away and held its little hands out.

'Evie!'

'Bernard.' She gave him a quick glare and then stared out of the window.

'I found you!'

'So it seems.'

She carried on staring out of the window and he took the opportunity to gaze at her. She was even more beautiful than he remembered. Her skin was glowing and, although she was tired under the eyes, she looked absolutely lovely. There was an energy and a fragility he hadn't seen before. He wanted to touch her, to hold her, and to paint her. But her face was constantly changing, different emotions flickering across it, like light changing the hues on a hillside, and he wondered if he would ever be able to capture it again. She seemed so different and so familiar; it was like coming home, and yet everything had changed.

'Evie, you've had a baby!'

She looked at him suspiciously, 'Yes.'

'How old?'

'Five months.'

'And is it mine?' The question was out before he could stop himself.

She hesitated, 'I'm afraid so.'

'Oh Evie!' He knelt down on the floor, hugged her knees and wept profusely into her black and white tweed skirt. The baby leaned over to have a better look. Then it threw back its head and started chortling.

'Could I?' he asked, letting go of the skirt and holding his arms out.

'You must be very careful,' said Evie doubtfully, but she handed the baby over to its father.

'Hello,' said Bernard, looking into the tiny face, 'hello, little one.' His voice broke and more tears started streaming down his cheeks. 'I've been looking for you all over London!' he wailed.

The baby chortled again, beaming at its father and Bernard beamed back, but his eyes were drawn again and again to the baby's mother.

'I just want to hold you for ever,' he said. He glanced at Evie, but she was keeping her gaze on the baby. 'Why didn't you tell me?'

She hesitated, 'I did come up to London once. I thought I should see you, but then I caught sight of Benedict in Fortnum's and I realised I couldn't face either of you. I just wasn't ready. And then, shortly after that, I heard rumours that you'd fathered a son. It was, well, very off-putting.'

She stared down at the carpet, but he could read her expression. She was angry, but also hurt. The bit that still hurt was the chink in her amour. If he could find a way in, through the chink, there was a chance.

'Does anyone else know?'

'I only told Phoebe. I couldn't risk telling anybody else, not even Daisy. Then Benedict found us.'

'He *found* you?'

'Actually Jones found us, just before Benedict died.'

Dear God. Then Benedict knew. And Jones knew as well. He thought back to their last meeting, remembering the butler's hopeful, 'Good luck, Mr Bernard.'

'So, this is the baby!' he exclaimed.

Evie bristled, but the baby grinned from ear to ear, clearly as relieved as Bernard that it was the only heir.

'I've let you both down,' he said, looking only at the baby.

The baby stopped smiling and looked back with an unflinching gaze as if considering his words.

'I behaved unforgivably,' Bernard added. 'But I've never stopped thinking...' he could feel his voice breaking again and struggled to contain it. 'And now I've found you both,' he gulped, 'perhaps I could be involved in some way...' his voice trailed off.

'You mean financially?' said Evie, dryly.

Bernard swallowed, 'Eventually.'

He glanced over at her again. She'd gone back to studying the carpet, but the tiniest of smiles played around her lips. It gave him tremendous courage.

'I still love you, Evie.'

The smile disappeared, but the baby seemed to approve of the declaration, suddenly babbling away, as if it had a lot to tell this new father.

Bernard immediately started swinging his precious bundle up and down and the baby didn't stop babbling and didn't take its eyes off his face. The swinging created quite a breeze in the room and some of the papers twitched.

'You've been busy,' he observed, as he twirled around.

'Yes,' said Evie, defiantly.

'A novel?'

'A book.'

'You're so clever. I don't know how you've done it, having a baby and writing a book...'

She didn't respond so he addressed the baby, 'Your mummy's a writer now!'

The baby gave a huge smile and Bernard began to swing it more vigorously, like a fairground ride, first up, up, up, perilously close to the ceiling and then down, down, down, right down to the carpet. The baby gurgled with delight.

'Be careful!' cried Evie.

'Don't worry, men can cope with rough and tumble, even little men.'

'Men?'

He glanced over at her. She was frowning the old frown, the one he used to tease her about. He wanted to smooth away the lines with his fingers: all the worries he'd given her, all the disappointments.

'I mean my boy, Evie, my wonderful, wonderful boy.'

'Boy?' Evie gave a little laugh, the first of the day. 'Trust you to presume it's a boy. This is your daughter – Sophia.'

What Would You do?

North Lodge, Key Lane, Colyton, Devon
Thursday March 23rd 1922

Dear Phoebe,

Well, he found me – and you were right. He was contrite, guilty, all the things you said he would be. And he is obviously crazy about his daughter. He can't stop holding her. I barely get a look in now – still at least I can get on with my writing. And she loves him, I mean she took to him straight away. You wouldn't believe it – they play the piano together and she hums along loudly when he sings! He's sleeping in the piano room, well I mean, there's no room in with me, especially with the baby. Besides, I'm not ready yet. He plays the piano all the time and Sophia coos along.

Mummy loves it. She's always hovering outside and peeping in and smiling. (My father barely goes near, he's more or less living in the potting shed.) And when Bernard's not singing to her, he's drawing her, and when he's finished, he puts the pencil in her fingers and helps her make marks in his sketch book. She'll be painting next!

So he's back, for now anyway. And if Sophia gets any fonder of him, I won't be able to put him out. It's lovely being at home but my father will eventually reach the end of his tether and, when that happens, I expect we'll go back to London and live in Chelsea. I didn't want to rattle round that big house with a baby on my own, but I suppose three of us is a family. I mean, what would you do if you were me?

Your loving friend,

Evie

Nearly the End

The Times Thursday 28th December 1922

BOOK REVIEW:
STARS, COMETS AND DISOBEDIENT WOMEN

By Evie Brunton-Cavalier

Evie Brunton-Cavalier's first book has created something of a stir. It traces the rise and fall of famous British women from ancient history up to the present day; from Boadicea to Emmeline Pankhurst. While there is an obvious lack of academic research, some of the connections the author makes are illuminating. Like a fierce comet, Brunton-Cavalier blazes a new trail with her perceptive appraisals and offers a surprising insight into why so many important female figures have been rather overlooked. Definitely a book for the fairer sex, but Mrs Brunton-Cavalier is one to watch.

By Miss Edna Michaels

BIRTHS

CAVALIER On 24th December 1922 to Evie, (neé Brunton) and Bernard, a son, Tobias Horatio, brother to Sophia.
HAZLITT On 25th December 1922 to Phoebe, (neé Carson) and Robert, a daughter, Jemima.

FORTHCOMING MARRIAGES

**Conte G. di Caldonazzo
and Miss C. Richardson**

The engagement is announced between Conte Giacomo di Caldonazzo, decorated veteran of the Third Italian War of Independence and Miss Cassie Richardson, daughter of Lord and Lady Richardson of Kensington. The wedding will take place in Padua.

About the Author

Liz Treacher is also the author of *The Wrong Envelope*, the story of how Bernard and Evie first meet. Liz is also an art photographer and a love of images influences her writing. She is married with two children and lives in the Scottish Highlands, by the sea.

www.liztreacher.com